Re-disco\
kind (

FOUNTAIN INN

Victor Canning

This edition published in 2019 by Farrago,
an imprint of Duckworth Books Ltd
13 Carrington Road, Richmond, TW10 5AA, United Kingdom

www.farragobooks.com

By arrangement with the Beneficiaries of the Literary
Estate of Victor Canning

First published by Hodder and Stoughton in 1939

Ebook ISBN: 9781788421751
Print ISBN: 9781788421799

With grateful acknowledgment to John Higgins

Have you read them all?

Treat yourself again to the first Victor Canning novels—

Mr Finchley Discovers His England
A middle-aged solicitor's clerk takes a holiday for the first time and meets unexpected adventure.

Polycarp's Progress
Just turned 21, an office worker spreads his wings—an exuberant, life-affirming novel of taking your chances.

Fly Away Paul
How far could you go living in another's shoes?— an action-packed comic caper and love story.

Turn to the end of this book for a full list of Victor Canning's early works, plus—on the last page—the chance to receive **further background material.**

Contents

Chapter One

Quarter past eight. Grace Kirkstall's wristwatch showed twenty-past, but it was really quarter-past. Her watch was always five minutes fast. It was a watch of individuality. It defied every manoeuvre of watchmakers and Grace to control it. She would regulate it, correct it by the city clocks twice a day, yet always it spurted five minutes ahead of Greenwich and then, content with its brief lead on the crowd, it settled down to maintain its advantage steadily. Grace understood it and automatically amended its reading, so that now as the hands pointed to twenty-past she murmured "quarter-past" to herself. It was a neat watch, hardly bigger than a postage stamp, its face elongated and marked with black lines which gave it a severity that might have been expressive of a purposeful disapproval of time and its own duty of recording what was at once the insubstantial and the imperative. Its spirit and small heart might have been happier could they have been transferred to some enormous tower or façade where they could have forgotten their bondage in the delights of setting off bell mechanism, rousing the air with noisy carillons, and turning the eyes of pedestrians to the stilted movements of jousting knights brought alive by the fall of hourly trips and catches. It was a watch which craved more vigorous employment than it found on Grace's wrist.

Grace never suspected that her watch had a soul. She was romantic, but confined her imagination to people. If she daydreamed it was in terms of everyday events and possibilities, like fortunes and winning sweepstake prizes. She was sure, for instance, that gallant princes never did come these days to woo woodcutters' daughters, but she reserved her feminine right to show no surprise if a handsome stranger did get aboard the eight-thirty to Cannon Street and, dazzled by her charm, involve her in a series of romantic adventures culminating, of course, in a brilliant marriage.

But quarter-past eight in the morning, even for Grace, was no time for romantic thoughts. She put her handbag and the *Daily Sketch* on the hallstand while she adjusted her hat in the glass, calling over one shoulder to her mother in the kitchen:

"Goodbye, Mother! Shan't be late tonight, and don't you keep me waiting when I come in. You know what it's like trying to get into the Granada on a Friday night, and I do want to see the programme. Paul Muni. You know what he means to me. Cheerio ..."

She sailed out of the house on the breath of her talk and left Mrs. Kirkstall replying absently from the kitchen where she was pottering, vaguely undecided between preparing herself some breakfast or going without it.

As she went down Fisher Road, Grace noted with gladness that the sun was shining. It was right that it should shine today. For this was Friday, the ending of the week, and pay-day. There was something about Friday morning, she felt, different from any other morning of the week. It was exciting to have her money and come home, eager to be out again on the weekly treat which she and her mother shared; a show at the Granada, or a variety hall or sometimes a theatre, and then the bus ride home, nursing on her lap the delicacy she had bought and hugged through the film, an expensive delicacy to be eaten for supper, a gesture to give appropriate finality to the day.

She passed the United Dairies man, his shiny cap pushed back against the June heat, his blue-and-white striped apron flapping in the breeze against his knees as he ran his trolley along the gutter.

"Nice day, miss. Beginning of a heat wave, maybe," he observed as she passed.

Grace gave him a smile. He was a friendly but polite man. She liked milkmen to be polite. She turned out of Fisher Road into the main thoroughfare. There were other people on the way to the station. She knew a great many of them by sight. There was the man with the yellow pigskin brief case embossed with the initials B.A.T. Many a time Grace had wondered what those initials stood for but she had never worked out a harmonious sequence and now she referred to him in her private thoughts as Mr. Bat, and he did look a little bit like a bat; his ears were large, his shoulders humped and his face long drawn with round eyes. There were typists like herself, young clerks in sober office dress and elderly men who greeted one another with little cries about the weather. They all streamed down the road towards the station, where, in the vestibule and along number four platform, the sound of their voices, collected together, rose up in a thick, swaying murmur, a contented bumble of sound like a hive of sleepy bees waking to work.

Grace stood on the platform amongst them. Some of them walked up and down, and as they passed she could catch snatches of their talk: "It's always the same with me. I can't stand it ..." "Gloire de Dijon! He began to tell me about roses. Me! What do you think I said? I just gave him ..." "No thanks, old man, I'd rather you did that." These tantalising scraps floated by leaving Grace wondering.

And then from up the line came a different sound, the swelling clack, clack of the train until it came into sight under the railway arch, the front coach lurching and tugging persistently at the rails around the bend, the wheels beating out their peculiar rhythm, which died slowly as the train was braked, and then the noise of compartment doors being opened and people scrambling for places filled the morning.

Grace got a place in the corner on the far side of the carriage and opened her paper. The carriage filled up with men until there was only one vacant seat, in the middle of the row opposite to Grace. The train moved off and she settled down to her paper, shaking the pages out dexterously as she skipped from one feature to another. Around her other papers were shaken and patted and thick bands of tobacco smoke rose above each white folio like the gentle expiration of a sleepy volcano.

After a time the train began to slow for the next station and as it drew alongside the platform Grace lowered her paper a little and looked out at the row of faces that flickered by the window. As she looked at them she was hoping, without any great faith, that one of them might belong to George Crane, and that he would find his way to the empty seat near her. This miracle happened about once a month, and, because it was Friday and Grace was feeling happy, she hoped it would happen today.

The moment the train stopped a man flung himself towards the door and grasped the handle. He was a fat man, his head not much higher than the sill of the window and as he wrestled with the catch he looked in and saw at once the empty seat and the frown which Grace was directing towards him. Grace was sure it was her frown which made him turn away suddenly and seek another compartment, but more likely it was the sight of the seat which was narrow and unsuited to such a big body. He went away and immediately his place was taken by a young, sturdily built man who jerked the handle back adroitly and stepped into the carriage. At the sight of him Grace gave a little gasp and hid quickly behind her paper. The miracle had happened. Out of so many carriages and from so many people George Crane had found his way to the seat. He sat down and began to unfold his paper and as he did so Grace gently lowered her shield and smiled at him over the edge. George saw her at once and for a brief, negligible second the lines of his face contracted to a frown and then he smiled and nodded to her politely.

Grace did not notice the fleeting dark look. She saw only his smile and she sat watching him, waiting for him to speak to her, and George, aware that she intended to talk, hesitated to raise his paper rudely. For a moment they eyed one another.

Grace looked at George and George looked at Grace and through their minds sped an array of thought and comment private to each and safer unpronounced.

We are each familiar with our own figure and face thrown back to us from our glass. We know ourselves and have a comfortable, general idea of what we look like. But it is never the appearance we imagine ourselves to present that matters. The important aspect is that which we present to other people, and this hardly ever tallies with the reflection from our glass. One person may present fifty different pictures to as many people. So it was with Grace and George. Grace knew what she looked like to herself, but she didn't know what she looked like to George, and George had an impression of himself quite different from the image which was mirrored in Grace's thoughts.

George looked at Grace as the train pulled out of the station and he saw a young woman, not more than twenty-two, he was sure, of by no means a striking appearance. Her skin was sallow, her face thin, her eyes large and dark and her mouth small—a tight, vigorous mouth. She was neither tall nor short, her clothes were undistinguished and her choice of colours was odd. George had decided that she was one of those girls who, being neither ill-looking nor yet good-looking, wander dowdily in the borderland. Also she was really a bit of a nuisance and more than once he had regretted the momentary lapse into friendliness which had given her the right to badger him with her company. As a casual acquaintance, a girl who happened to work in the same office building as himself, who demanded no more than a nod and then could be forgotten, he offered no resistance, but after the first two or three nods he had been made aware of a remarkable tenacity in Grace's character.

For Grace, where she had assumed friendship there was an automatic loyalty which debarred her from criticism. She saw George more clearly perhaps than he saw her and if there were exaggerations in her picture of him they were on the side of kindness. For her he was a manly, solid figure. What she liked about him was his steadiness, the impression of strength and courage he gave her, and his actual physical appearance was well suited, she thought, to the qualities which marked his character. His fair hair, the broad, frank-featured face and the well-set body all indicated his nature. He was Scottish, of course; a lowland Scot. His voice, after many years in London, still retained that echo of his homeland which made ordinary English words seem strange and fresh when he spoke them. And he was twenty-seven. She had ascertained that, by various bits of detective work, from his own conversation and from other sources. He was also an architect, a profession which, in George's hands, took on an added mystery and wonder.

"Isn't it a nice morning?" Grace leaned forward slightly to put her question.

George nodded and replied slowly, "It is."

That was all Grace wanted, leave to talk. If George had indicated firmly that he wished to be left alone to his paper she would have obeyed, realising that a man and his paper are not to be separated in the morning ride to Town, but George had made no sign that he did not want to talk.

"Yes, it's a lovely morning. Makes you wish the train was going the other way, out into the country instead of taking you to the office. Still—" she gave him a gay, comforting smile "—still, we mustn't grumble. Anyway, tomorrow's Saturday and there's the weekend to look forward to. I always think that people of leisure—you know, the ones that don't have to go to work, can't really enjoy the weekends. Not properly ..."

The man on Grace's right fidgeted and shook his paper as she went on talking, but she took no notice of him. Other men grunted behind their barrages of news and wished that some people would not disturb the early morning with their chatter. George caught up in Grace's flow of words could do no more than murmur an occasional "Yes" or "No" to her and finger his newspaper longingly.

There was no escape for George. When they left the train, Grace was with him and they walked along Holborn together.

"You know, you're very silent this morning," said Grace. "Why, you've hardly had anything to say at all. Is something worrying you?" She secretly hoped that something would be worrying him and that she might be able to help him.

George breathed deeply and said slowly, "You know, Miss Kirkstall—" the way he pronounced her name thrilled her, he made it sound so Scotch "—that I am not what is known as a good conversationalist at any time. But, if I seem less attentive this morning, perhaps it is because my mind is occupied with the thoughts of my work. I take my work seriously, Miss Kirkstall, and there are several problems I shall have to face this morning which need a deal of reflection and consideration."

"Oh, Mr. Crane—why ever didn't you say so before? You shouldn't have let me go on chattering away like I did. I should have quite understood. All those plans and things you have to draw—goodness knows how you do it! It's very clever. Now, I won't say another word and you can forget I'm here. I hope you're not annoyed with me for being so inconsiderate?"

For a moment George was tempted to chuckle. The girl had an absurd innocence at times that made him quite like her, and her awe of the intricacies of architecture was definitely flattering.

"If I were annoyed with you, Miss Kirkstall, I hope I should never be rude enough to show it. There are times, of course, when I think you talk too much. However, that is a failing of all your sex, so I should not grumble at that."

"Now you're laughing at me." Grace chuckled delightedly. "But I don't mind. I like a man to have a sense of humour, especially when he has a Scottish accent to go with it."

"I have never obsairved anything humorous about my speech," said George a little stiffly, his accent strengthening, as it always did when anyone commented on his voice.

"Of course not," said Grace timorously, and she said no more.

They walked, two silent figures, up the wide pavement of Holborn towards their work, and with them walked hundreds of others on their way to office and shop. The pavements were crowded, the buses were crammed full and from the underground exits came a steady outpouring of passengers. Everywhere was the morning movement of London settling down to work after the respite of the night. Men and women were returning to their places at desks and counters, and the noise they made as they came back was like the noise of a great sea sweeping in over the rocks and sands of a dry shore, overflowing the pools and gurgling into crevices and dark canyons. And as the tide swept along, men and women turned aside from the main street into warehouses, factories, office blocks, into the towering, palatial buildings of stores and down narrow, brown-shadowed streets.

When Grace and George were not far beyond Holborn Circus they turned aside to find their work. Together they passed under the wide archway that led to Fountain Inn.

*   *   *   *   *

George was not a fanciful person. He had been born near Kirkcudbright, which is a plain little town close to the shores of the Solway Firth and unlikely to spur the imagination. George was a Scot and distrusted emotions which made men sentimental and set them walking on clouds. He was an architect, an acolyte in an exacting order of men who put their trust in buttresses rather than poetry; who saw, not castles in the air, but elevations and ground plans for every edifice. George was always openly irritated when popular magazines talked in a visionary way of the future of building and allowed themselves the necessary indulgence of poetic speculation.

"Common sense," George would say to himself, "that's architecture." And aloud, if he were alone "Lavatories and kitchens." It was a way of affirming to himself that architecture had no business dallying over long with the future. Its job was to interpret and answer the needs of the present. But for all this, George was, at heart, a sentimentalist. He was intolerant of the tinselled future, perhaps, but he loved and dwelt fondly on the past.

He loved Fountain Inn, not because it was the place where he worked happily, but because it was part of the past, the substantial, architectural past. Grace would have been surprised at the depth of his affection for the place, but he was careful never to give himself away. The moment of turning under the archway and coming out into the open Inn court was always a pleasure to him. This morning, with the grey stone of the surrounding chambers touched by the June sun, his eyes moved around the great yard, welcoming each angle, greeting each familiar aspect.

The middle of the Inn was taken up by a rectangular lawn, surrounded by polled limes, and a spare, London plane tree stood in its exact geometric centre. Around the tree, whose bark had peeled to show ugly yellow patches, were groups of shrubs, forsythia, laurels and viburnum, crowding close to the plane, as though they would from kindness hide its scrofula. As George and Grace came out into the sunlight from the arch, they could see old Hindle's cat playing with her kittens on the lawn. Hindle was the caretaker and lived with his family in a little pent-roofed house tucked under the left wing of the archway. One of the castellated turrets flanking the arch was no more than a mask to hide the chimney-pot of the house. You could see it smoking away mysteriously all day long. Running at right-angles from Hindle's house until it met the opposite line of chambers that housed the offices of solicitors, accountants and other business folk was the steep side, blank and discoloured by London dirt and weather, of Bruce Brothers' Store. The original line of chambers on that side of the Inn had disappeared when the great store was built. George always tried not to see the cliff-like wall. It offended his sense of proportion and made him feel angry that men had been stupid enough so to despoil one of the few remaining Inns of Chancery. From the right of the archway the Inn ran unbroken to form the other two sides of the quadrangle until it reached the far corner of the court where it ended, giving room to a tiny garden, bright now with lupins and antirrhinums, that held, cupped in a tiny, seat-lined hollow, a fountain. From the garden a wide flight of steps ran up and gave access through an ornamental gate to Chain Walk.

Grace and George turned along the wide gravelled stretch that ran around the lawn and entered the first doorway. Over its lintel was painted the figure 1. Similar doors, each numbered, marked the other stairways that served the Inn.

The doorway led to a small hall from which rose a wide oak stairway that twisted angularly from floor to floor. To help strangers, there was in the hall a black board into which had been slotted the names of the firms and occupants of the various floors. It read

Ground Floor	Granada Finance Corporation.
First Floor	Craddock and Couch, Ltd. Architects.
Second Floor	Eastern Imports, Ltd.
Second Floor	Society for Progressive Rehabilitation.
Third Floor	W. Rage. Investment Specialist.
Third Floor	General Factotums.

George left Grace at the first floor and he turned into the offices of Craddock and Couch, where he worked. Grace climbed on to the top floor and with her own key let herself into the small office which served Mr. W. Rage. Mr. Rage was not there yet, but that did not surprise her.

* * * * *

Not long after George and Grace had passed through the archway of Fountain Inn a man entered the court through the iron gates from Chain Walk. Instead of walking around the gravel sweep, he headed in a straight line across the lawn towards door number one. He was a tall man, in his middle thirties, dressed in a grey suit with a dark line in it and he carried in one hand a malacca stick and in the other a light trilby. In his walk there was a certain gay spring that was in keeping with the fresh morning, yet a little out of place in the quiet quadrangle of the Inn. His bare head showed his smooth, well-brushed dark hair and, freeing his face from shadows, revealed an expression of intelligence. His mouth dropped a little at one corner to give him a gentle smirk, a faint malicious suggestion that was at variance with the open, frankly happy mood of his eyes.

Half-way across the lawn he came upon the cat and her family.

"Good morning, Elizabeth. How's the family?" He squatted beside the tabby and began to scratch her behind the ears. The family, who were at the stage when they were discovering that by a synchronised movement of the legs they could propel themselves from one desirable place to another, immediately accepted the challenge of his trousers to take their first lesson in mountaineering. He suffered this assault pleasantly and even put out a hand and helped the most enterprising kitten to establish itself on his knee. Elizabeth purred happily at this interest in her family and rolled over on her back, presenting her belly for scratching.

"You're taking advantage of my good nature," he complained. "Still," he began to scratch her obediently. Her purring swelled to a fuller, louder note.

Suddenly from across the lawn came the sound of a window being pushed up, then the air sung as it was whipped by the passage of a projectile and the man jumped hurriedly to his feet, his hand going to the back of his neck which showed a dull red mark. A broad-bean seed with a grey, wrinkled skin dropped to the grass among the kittens.

"I must leave you, Elizabeth," he said and he started away, leaving the kittens to play with the bean. He gave no look towards the window which had been opened, but entered the doorway and climbed the stairs to the top floor.

The top landing was marked with two doors. The one which Grace had entered and another on which was painted the inscription, *General Factotums: Enquire Within.* This door the man pushed open and he entered a small, rather long room whose window looked over Holborn. It was furnished with a green, steel filing-cabinet, a yellow wood typing chair and table that held a typewriter and telephone, and a bookcase that was full of reference books and directories. From this room a half-open door led to another and larger room that overlooked the

Inn. This room was furnished with scarcely more pretence of comfort. A long table faced the open window, a mahogany desk with a leather inset stood near the empty fireplace, and two armchairs stood about the carpet as though they were uncertain of their places.

At the desk sat a fair-haired, good-looking woman. She had a well-marked face of the kind which is capable of swift transition from severity to smiles. Looking at her, it was easy to speculate about her character. Her looks, her obvious smartness of dress, spoke of one impatient of carelessness and untidy ends. She was a logical capable creature, intolerant of humbug, and yet there moved in her eyes and the momentary play of her lips as she looked up a mocking, good-natured indication of humour that spoke of a love of laughter when it arose from pleasant premises.

She greeted the man with the one word: "Loiterer!"

"Maybe," was the reply; "but loitering is an art. It's not a question of having time to stand and stare—staring's rude—but of having the gift of letting time flow by you as though you were a rock in mid—"

"Give me the paste you've bought," she interrupted him.

He took a small pot of paste from his pocket and handed it to her and then went to the window and sat down at the long table. There was a catapult and a bag of beans lying on it. Yesterday, he thought, he had made the catapult and bought the beans to relieve his own boredom; today they had been used against him as he had used them against the sparrows on the roof. He took up the catapult, sighted Elizabeth on the lawn and then, thinking better of it, put down the weapon and turned to his wife.

"Helen," he spoke seriously; "The time has come for us to acknowledge that this business is a failure."

"Last month," said Helen, "we made seven pounds, sixteen shillings and fourpence profit. It would have been eight pounds and tuppence had it not been for the repair bill for the office chair which you broke by continually tipping it backwards." She grinned as he dropped his chair on to its four legs quickly. She went on sticking the fragments of a torn letter before her on to a sheet of white paper.

"That's not the point. General Factotums is a monstrous disappointment to me. You don't measure disappointment by money always. In my time I have been many things—"

"Don't let's go into that."

"I'm not ashamed of my past!"

"Obviously, my dear Benjamin, otherwise you wouldn't talk about it so much."

"And don't call me Benjamin."

"Yes, darling."

"As I was saying, General Factotums is a disappointment, a failure. When we started it four months ago, do you know what we imagined it would be?"

"I ought to, I drafted the prospectus. I can even repeat it by heart." Without interrupting her work, she recited in a level voice: "'General Factotums exists to serve others. We are a concern that specialises in the execution of all those odd jobs and awkward commissions which, for one reason or another, you find yourself unable to do. If you want your child met at Paddington and safely conducted to her aunt in Plumstead—we will do it for you. If you have a dog and no time to exercise it—we will find someone to take it out. If you want an accommodation address—use ours. If you live in the country and want a material matched at Liberty's— send us the material and we will do it. If you want a friend to share a holiday we will find one. In fact we will do anything which does not involve illegality. We have a numerous and competent staff of courteous, intelligent men and women who are ready to serve you, to help you in your difficulties and to give you advice and assistance in any problem...' Need I go on?"

Ben waved her down. "And what happened? I'll admit, I thought the idea was a good one, but I expected that we should tap at once that vast, mysterious, romantic sea of troubles which surrounds humanity. I saw myself playing knight to maidens in distress, acting as emissary between men of strange destiny. I knew, of course, that there would be the odd, humdrum little jobs like escorting and chaperoning folk, and matching ribbons—but those were your responsibility, my talents were reserved for the more important affairs. Well—there just isn't any vast, mysterious, romantic sea of human trouble. It's a dead sea, a tideless, stagnant sea. What are the most interesting jobs we've had? I'll tell you. The first was that Lord Somebody's son who goes screwy at times and tries to work the confidence trick on people. The last time he escaped from his keepers at Selfacre Hall and shot off to Paris I had to go over there and let him work the trick on me. Then he went home happily with the two hundred pounds of his father's money that he'd taken from me. He didn't even work the trick convincingly. And the only other thing is the letter we got today which you're working on now. Some old lady from Hastings sends us the torn scraps of a letter and wants them pieced together because she must know what is written there. Well—could any writer of fiction resist a gambit like that ? No, sir, and very sensibly—it cries out for excitement. But I know now what kind of dull coil life shuffles off on one. I'll bet that letter is about the most pedestrian, uninteresting piece of pedagogics that any nephew ever wrote to his aunt. These are the two most interesting commissions that have come to us— the rest have been flat, routine affairs. Against all that I protest. And while I'm airing grievances I'd like to mention that I object to being catapulted at with broad beans while I'm talking to a lady friend. At times you presume too much upon your position as my wife. Now I'll go and join the Foreign Legion before you send me on another prosaic errand."

"You talk too much, Ben," was Helen's only comment as she stuck the last piece of the torn letter in place.

"I talk because action is denied me. I'm a vital, intricate piece of machinery—if I'm not used I go rusty, but you wouldn't appreciate that. When I was very innocent I thought that married life gave a man the opportunity and right to share his troubles, now I know that it merely limits his rights and cripples his opportunities—"

"Do you want me to read the letter to you? I've got it together—"

"Rather!" Ben leaped hopefully to his feet and went to the desk. Perhaps, after all, he had maligned life's sense of the mysterious; perhaps this very letter which he had castigated would take him through the looking-glass into a world of substantial excitement.

"Here it is then." Helen began to read with deliberate and maddening punctiliousness, first the address, then the date and finally the body of the letter. It went:

17 HARPTREE ROAD,
TAUNTON.
May 28th.

DEAR MISS HARRINGTON,

This is to tell you that I am having a good time with my brother and his wife and hope that I shall soon be well enough to come back to work for you. The doctor here is a fat man and sniffs a lot, not like Doctor Halthorpe at all. My brother has a little house and he is building a pool of concrete in the garden which is clever as he is really a insurance agent in real life. My brother says from what I tell him of Peter that he must be a very clever bird and worth at least fifteen pounds as he talks so well. He is fond of birds hisself but would go in for love-birds instead of parrots because he likes to see them nesting and having young and he is aginst parrots because he says they only lay an egg once every ten years and that is usually addled on account of the cold climate.

The doctor says I shall be well enough to come back by the end of next month.

Yours respectfully, IDA MINGELS

"Our last hope gone," groaned Ben. "Parrots, lovebirds! Why on earth did the old lady send that to us?"

"It's fairly obvious, I should think. She must have torn the letter up by mistake before reading it and, her eyes probably not being good enough for her to fix it together, she sends it to General Factotums. Cheer up, Ben—"

"I refuse to be cheered up. It's too easy a way out of disappointment. I'm going out and I'm staying."

Helen watched him go. After four years of married life, she knew when to be really worried about him and she knew now that she could discount his present tirade against General Factotums. It was a natural mood that would pass, for they both enjoyed the business which they had started and which was growing, if slowly, at least steadily. But as she slipped the pasted letter into an envelope to send it back to Hastings she caught herself half-wishing that it might have proven more exciting. There were odd, queer things in life—they filled the newspapers each day, and yet they never seemed to come out of the sanctuary of print and actually touch one's own life. It would be nice for Ben—and for her, too—if something did come along which was exciting and mildly—she insisted upon the qualification—dangerous.

*　*　*　*　*

And as Helen sat staring out of her window at the cool, green tops of the limes, thinking of Ben, down below her on the ground floor in his private office, Sir Athelstan Lee, managing director of the Granada Finance Corporation, sat staring through the halfgauze of his window at the trunks of the limes and the shrubs on the lawn.

Sir Athelstan was a fussy, bald-headed little man who had made and was still making his money from the financing of hire purchase schemes. The life blood of the Granada Finance Corporation came from thousands of homes all over the country; from cottagers who paid their shilling-a-week instalment on gramophones and radio sets, from housewives who coveted vacuum sweepers, and from lovers who feathered their nests with credit. He was proud of his business. Had it not been for a curious sentiment, he would have transferred it from Fountain Inn long ago. The business had begun and grown there until now it occupied the whole of the ground floor of number one stairway and most of the floors on the wing which faced Chain Walk. Sometimes he converted his sentiment into materialism by privately deciding that he would stay in Fountain Inn until the firm was so big that there would be room for no one else and then Fountain Inn would be his.

He sat for a while listening. Through the thick panels of the room came the faint, irregular, but insistent sound of typewriters tapping away like the noise made in an incubator when a hundred chicks begin to peck their way to dubious freedom. In the main office there were nearly a hundred girls clacking away on their typewriters, working for him, moving and trembling at his bidding. It was a pleasant feeling. Sir Athelstan revelled in power. That morning he had made his chief clerk, Adler, shiver in his shoes over a quite venial error in one of his accounts. It would have to be something very grave for him to sack Adler, but Adler did not know that and Sir Athelstan got a lot of amusement from the man. And he had been angry with Hindle, too, about the disappearance of his paper clips. Hindle had not shivered in his shoes, although he had been sufficiently obsequious. Paper clips and odd stationery were always disappearing and Sir Athelstan suspected someone outside his own staff; if not Hindle, then some of the women cleaners.

He leaned back shaking his head at the failings of mankind. Hard work had brought him where he was. It was a pity other men had not found the virtue he had in work. He pulled out his cigar case and prepared to smoke. Hard work gave you the privilege of being the only person allowed to smoke in an office of over a hundred and twenty people. Life was good.

And on the floor above Sir Athelstan Lee, George sat in the drawing office of Messrs. Craddock and Couch and watched, with unconcealed disapproval on his face, the antics of his two fellow architects, Smith and Hines, as they played office cricket, Hines wielding a T-square for bat and Smith bowling with a large red piece of indiarubber. They always celebrated the absence of the partners from the office with this ceremony. George would not have been so openly disapproving if the ceremony had not a tendency to last the better part of a morning and interrupt his work.

"The Scotch," said Hines meaningly and trying to hit the rubber towards George, "have no love of cricket. It is a foreign game to them."

"That's true," said Smith. "Since cattle-raiding went out they have no sport left to them. Their only relaxation is work."

George smiled good-naturedly. He liked them both, but he could not pretend to condone their frivolity. He was the senior assistant and the only way he felt he could reasonably impose his authority was by the force of his example. It was a pity that Hines and Smith loved office cricket more than a good example of diligence.

And while Hines and Smith continued their play, in the office of Eastern Imports Ltd., which was directly above them, Mr. Parcross, the London representative of Eastern Imports Ltd., and in himself the sole office staff, sat at his desk with the drawers pulled wide on either side of him, examining their contents.

The office consisted of one large room overlooking the street at one end and the Inn at the other. It was dark and crowded with files and an accumulation of office litter that had been amassed through long years. The office smelt, too, in the way of an office which has known only one tenant for a long time and that tenant a person of settled but not vigorous habits.

Mr. Parcross was an old man. One of those men who seem to have easily conspired with the mounting years to present age as a pleasant spectacle. He had soft white hair that was thin but carefully brushed to camouflage his baldness. The skin of his face was clear, but drawn over the bones and falling into hollows that gave his face a lean, unaccountably wise cast. He wore a black stock with a pin, black coat and pin-striped trousers. His body bent forward a little over one of the drawers in a stooping movement that had the perky, uncertain yet innocent suggestion of a jackdaw examining a coloured stone. His right hand fluttered over the drawer, touching its contents occasionally.

The drawer was filled with a neatly arranged collection of drawing-pins, paper clips, pencils, pen-holders, rubber bands, envelopes, ink bottles and other stationery. The two drawers of his desk held a collection catholic and curiously over adequate for a one-man office. It was a store that would have sufficed for more than a year of Mr. Parcross's normal demands, and over this store Mr. Parcross let his eyes wander with satisfaction.

After a time he locked the drawers and went to the window, looking out over the Inn and to the far line of chambers with a bold affection in his eyes. His shoulders lost some of their curve and he was filled with the brief vigour of a man who surveys a pleasant past and fills himself with bright memories.

And as Mr. Parcross stood at his window, across the landing from him, in his private office overlooking the Inn, Mr. Tomms of the Society for Progressive Rehabilitation stood at his window, his eyes not on the far line of the Inn, but, half-veiled, on the sun which hung above the jagged London roof line.

Mr. Alastair Tomms, founder and president of the Society for Progressive Rehabilitation, was doing his exercises. These exercises he had performed regularly each morning for the last five years. If they had been designed to produce an improvement on the body alone Mr. Tomms would have had reason to doubt their excellence. But they were not. The exercises were largely for the good of the soul.

Mr. Tomms was a short man, built loosely and broadly, and somehow he conveyed the suggestion that all his muscles and joints had been pulled and strained so that his arms and legs seemed only on distant terms with his body and ready to drop away from him if anyone happened to shake him violently. His age was indeterminate and appeared to be advanced, and he wore his hair white and long so that he looked rather like Lloyd George. There was about his face a faint leonine stamp and in his eyes a blue twinkle that spoke of a spirit which found living to be good.

He had his jacket off, his shirt sleeves flapping loosely, and he stood facing the sun which shone directly into his window. His eyes were half-closed and he was swaying his body with a regular movement from one side to the other and, as he swayed, he conveyed a faint circular action to his body so that his head, instead of moving through the straight line of a definite pendulum swing, traced a rather unsteady circle. He did this for five minutes, letting the sun beat against his half-closed eyes. He stopped, rocking gently to rest, smiled with evident satisfaction, and then put on his jacket.

He sat down at his desk and with his eyes fixed steadily on the opposite wall he declaimed loudly:

"Man is a Flux. The Body is the Spirit's Habitation. The Spirit is Man's link with the Great Mystery." His voice was the kind which could impart capital letters to words and leave no doubt about it. With him some nouns became personalities of impressive importance.

This done he rang the bell for his secretary and began to pick his teeth with a match-stick, his eyes going around his room.

It was a neat, comfortably furnished room. The furniture was good, the carpet on the floor substantial and tastefully coloured and the bookshelves had that subdued, prosperous look that seldom comes from a collection of works of fiction. On the walls were two Medici reproductions, and a series of charts, hanging like schoolroom atlases, two showing a series of exercises and two others given over to diagrams that were concerned with the sun's planets and their movements. Over the doorway leading into the outer office was a long white streamer with the inscription LIGHT→SIGHT→RIGHT→MIGHT.

It was through this doorway that his secretary now entered. She was a middle-aged woman with thick-lensed glasses and a hatchet-shaped face.

"I want this circular stencilled and distributed to all our branches," said Mr. Tomms.

She took the paper he handed her, and he went on "Has Rab El Tingra called this morning?" "He has not," was the answer.

"Show him in when he comes. His influence in India may be useful if we do start over there."

When she was gone Mr. Tomms took up his paper. He skipped through the news pages quickly and began to read the financial columns with a great deal of interest. He read for a long time, occasionally putting down the sheet to make rapid calculations with a little silver pencil in the margin.

And as Mr. Tomms figured in the margin, Grace sat above him in Mr. Rage's office wondering why her employer was so late.

Chapter Two

At twelve o'clock Grace Kirkstall was still wondering why Mr. Rage had not appeared. It was unlike him to be so late. Mr. William Rage was a neat, dapper man with well-manicured hands and a habit of stroking his blunt chin as though he believed that by continual massage he could mould it into a pointed, more emphatic shape. He came into the office most mornings regularly at ten-thirty, opened his post and dictated letters to Grace. He left at twelve-thirty and stayed away until five, when he returned to sign his letters. Grace was fairly busy filing letters until he came in the morning and was adequately pressed to finish her typing in time for him to sign his correspondence in the evening.

There was not a great deal that Grace knew about Mr. Rage. She liked him because he had nice manners and never adopted any other attitude towards her than that of employer. His business, she knew from her work, was largely concerned with advising people in the investment of their money. He held long telephone conversations with acquaintances variously hailed as "Bill," "Simmy, old man," "Reg" and others about these investments. Sometimes, but not often, he interviewed people in the office about these same investments. She did not know his home address, whether he was married or where he went for his holidays. She had worked for him for a year and every Friday morning regularly he had paid her three pounds five shillings as wages and she had accepted this and kept her natural curiosity about him to herself as became a good typist.

At twelve-thirty Grace's wonder had changed to anxiety. It was the first time Mr. Rage had missed coming to the office without telephoning or writing to her. She was sure something terrible had happened to him and she began to accuse herself vigorously of negligence because she had never insisted upon knowing his home address.

She was so worried that she went into the inner room which had served Mr. Rage as a private office and searched his desk in the hope that she might find his address. The only papers in his desk and files were mostly printed prospectuses, lists of names and addresses which she had herself typed for him, and a collection of theatre programmes that suddenly gave her a new light on Mr. Rage. He had never mentioned any liking for the theatre to her, nor even discussed any plays or films.

While she was doing this there came a knock at the door. She went, rather guiltily, back to her typewriter and called "Come in!"

The door opened and Mr. Hindle entered. Thomas Hindle was the Inn caretaker. He looked like a caretaker, but he had the soul of an actor, a grand, end-of-the-century actor, an Irving, a Tree. He saw the world as a magnificent backcloth for man, a setting for his actions, and he was convinced that each disappointment, every joy, all tragedy and, without doubt, any misfortune was no more than a part to be played with a fine regard for exits and entrances. This abnormal attitude sprung from a youthful period when he had worked as a scene-shifter at the old Oxford. There was no doubt that almost each moment of his existence was lived with a strict regard for effect and a nice selection of background. He stood now in the doorway, his fat arms abreast his green baize apron, his plump chin sunken so low that it hid alike his neck and collar, while his small eyes regarded Grace over the brink of steel spectacles, mended on one side by tightly wound cotton, from a chubby, coruscated face. His legs were straddled firmly apart to support his weight and he faced Grace as though beyond her waited an audience of a thousand, eager for his words, dreading the news he brought.

"Good morning, Miss Kirkstall. Mr. Rage, I suppose, has not come yet?" His voice had a booming, deep quality.

"Good morning, Hindle. No. I can't understand it. If he's not coming to the office he usually telephones me. It's very worrying. I can't help thinking that something has happened to him."

Hindle's eyes widened as Grace gave him his cue. He paused, then said:

"Something has happened, Miss Kirkstall." And then, after another pause to add solemnity to his words: "Something has indeed happened."

"Hindle—what's happened?" Grace looked at him sharply, her mind full of a medley of images. Poor Mr. Rage, run over …

"Ha!" Hindle sighed long and loudly. "Don't you upset yourself on his account, Miss Kirkstall. He's gone, like all his kind. I've seen it happen before. Seen it happen from these very rooms where we are now. It's an old, old story, and it happens again and again."

"What do you mean? You sound so serious. I'm very worried about him."

"And I am, Miss Kirkstall. Serious it is! You want the truth; you shall have it." He paused. This was a moment that held the crowd. He secretly wished his family could have seen him. Young Bert that was touring as an attendant with Marley's Midgets—it would have been a lesson for him, a valuable lesson. "Your Mr. Rage was no good. This business of his—you may not have spotted it—was dishonest. And now he's gone. He's flitted. Things began to get too hot for him, I'll bet. I know. I've just come

34

across from Mr. Walter's office." Mr. Walter was an accountant who had offices in the Inn and looked after the collection of rents from the various tenants. "He's had a letter this morning from Mr. Rage—no address given—saying as how he must give up the offices as he's got to leave England unexpectedly—and regretting that he can't see his way clear to make up the month's rent which is due."

"It can't be true!" Even as Grace denied it, she felt that she was merely saying so because she had liked Mr. Rage personally.

"You must face the facts, Miss Kirkstall. I've seen it happen often in my thirty years here. I know exactly how it'll be. He's gone, and you won't find a scrap of paper or letter in his drawers that'll help you to trace him. The furniture is always hired, and always there's some unlucky young lady, like yourself, that's left behind to find herself out of a job and done in for her week's wages. Sometimes they're gentlemen enough to send along the wages, but I doubt whether Mr. Rage will do that. Ha, well! It's hard, but it's life and we must grin and bear it." He turned away sadly and added over his shoulder, "I shall have to lock the place up after lunch, so you got plenty of time to pack up your things. I'm very sorry, Miss Kirkstall."

He went out and down the stairs, leaving Grace sitting before her typewriter trying to accommodate herself to his news. At the foot of the stairs, Hindle stopped before the notice board, eyed it for a moment as though it were the villain in a piece, taunting him to action, and then, regretting that there was no one on the stairs to see his response, he swept up a plump arm and with a grunt jerked out the sliding board with W. Rage—Investment Specialist on it and turned away. Behind him the board showed a black space with the awful word—Vacant—already printed on it, a word which lurked at the back of each notice, waiting.

For a time Grace stared at her typewriter, uncertain what to do or think. Then gradually her mind began to put order into her thoughts. Mr. Rage had deserted her without a word, and, what was worst, he had somehow got her to help him in his dishonest business. Little incidents and scraps of conversation came back to her now and made clear Mr. Rage's position. Then suddenly she forgot Mr. Rage as she remembered that she was out of a job. The thought set her moving. She got up from her typewriter and began to clear her table drawer of her possessions, dropping them into a carrier bag. Hopefully, she had another hunt around Mr. Rage's desk, but she found nothing fresh to help her.

She went out, locking the office door behind her. She left her carrier bag in Hindle's office and then walked briskly up to an employment agency she knew in Southampton Row, the agency which had sent her to Mr. Rage, and had her name put on their books again. There was nothing at that time of day. Things were very slow, the manageress said, but as soon as they had something they would let her know. Grace came away with a gathering sense of depression. She cheered up a little during the walk back to the Inn. She did not feel like lunch, so she bought herself a threepenny ice-cream block and, retrieving her bag from Hindle, walked across the lawn to the fountain to find a seat where she could eat her ice in peace.

The fountain and its garden was a pleasant little oasis and it was seldom that any of the seats around the circular basin were empty during a lunch-hour on a fine day. Grace was lucky. It was now nearly three o'clock and the seats were deserted.

The fountain and its basin were sunken low in the garden and the curved seats were set into dwarf retaining walls of Cotswold stone where aubretia and other rockery plants bloomed in the spring. When you sat on a seat facing the fountain, the back of your head was on nodding acquaintance with formal beds of lobelia and roses. The fountain itself was a curious fabrication. There had always been a fountain at the Inn and always on the site in the small garden, but from time to time different architects and different ages had re-designed the fountain and pool, replacing and renovating until now it was a curious hotch-potch which held no trace of the original structure. A low, circular basin of grey freestone, worked along the edge with a moulding more fitted for a tomb-rail, held the excess water of the fountain. In this water, in spite of Hindle's clearings once a month, accumulated an odd drift of matches, paper, buttons and other small objects which Londoners are prompted to toss into a pool when they sit near one. There was a story, almost a legend, that once the pool had held fish and that the quiet beauty of the Inn had known the exotic flash of kingfisher colours, a depredatory invasion that made the keeping of fish impossible. But it was more likely that cigarette-ends and not kingfishers made conditions intolerable for fish. The fountain itself was fashioned of a cairn of mossy stones rising to a point from the water and crowned with a leaden figure of Father Neptune, a Neptune with trident and curled fish-tail who faced towards the blank wall of Messrs. Bruce Brothers and with an incomparable solemnness of expression spurted a fine, four-pointed jet of water through the top of his head. He had dignity, this Neptune and, despite his trepanning, managed to make it seem perfectly natural that he should sit upon his cairn and spout water through the top of his head. There was even a faint suspicion of pique on his face at those times when the water authorities, harassed by drought, turned off his supply and let him sit dry and uncomfortable on top of a hot pile of stones.

Grace sat down and began to eat her ice. Before she was halfway through it the city clocks struck three and she was left alone with the faint chatter of falling water and the hungry chirp of questing sparrows for company. The sun was hot and a comforting wave of warmth radiated from the dry walls of the garden. Everything was so bright and full of early summer happiness that Grace's spirits, in febrile contrast, began to droop lower and lower. Before she had finished her ice she was sure that she would never get another job. At least, not a job with a pleasant employer, for Mr. Rage—no matter what else he had been—was a pleasant man to work with. Maybe she would have to take a job in a large office with about fifty other girls typing away all day around her, hard, efficient, unsympathetic girls— like the lot who worked for the Granada Finance Corporation. She would have to go away from Fountain Inn. She discovered that she did not want to leave the place. She found, what so many people who had worked in the Inn had discovered, that the place had developed in her an affection which even the misfortune that made her abandon her place there could not warp. And it was hard upon this discovery that she remembered poignantly that it was still Friday, but now she would not be going home with her wages to take her mother out for their weekly jaunt. She would be going home penniless, out of a job, never to return to Fountain Inn. The combination of misfortune and unhappiness was too much for Grace. After the happy start of that morning, she was unable to sustain so much distress. She took out her handkerchief and, pretending to wipe her nose, began to cry into it quietly.

At first she just sobbed gently, dabbing at her eyes. But the tears, once let loose, gathered and very soon she had to hold her head lower to hide her wet eyes and the sniffs and gulps that escaped from her as she tried to conquer her sorrows.

It was at this point that Helen Brown found her. Helen, on her way back to General Factotums, heard first one of Grace's convulsive gulps and then saw the small figure hunched up on one of the fountain seats. Helen knew all about crying. She knew, too, that generally people want to be left alone with their sorrows. But Helen found it difficult to leave people alone with their troubles. Outwardly efficient and with little time for sentiment, she was inwardly a creature of compassion and quite unable to resist any appeal to her emotions. She recognised Grace as the typist from Mr. Rage's office and, without knowing any more about her, she decided that she could help her. She went over and sat down beside Grace, touching her on the shoulder.

"You mustn't let yourself go like that. Come on now—think of your complexion."

Grace turned a very red face towards her and said dolefully: "Please let me alone."

"That's just what I'm not going to do. You don't want to be left alone. Come on now, wipe your eyes and stop sniffing." Her voice was faintly peremptory and the authoritative tone had an effect on Grace. She did wipe her eyes and her sniffs became less pronounced.

"There you are," Helen went on triumphantly. "You see, it won't seem half so bad when you stop and think about it. What's your trouble?" She smiled cheerfully, as though her optimism could banish the trouble before it was even explained.

"I'm sorry." Grace gave a last sniff. "It was silly of me."

"No, it wasn't. You've got every right to cry if you're in trouble. Only you mustn't keep on too long—that's when it becomes silly. You're the girl from Mr. Rage's office, aren't you?"

"Yes. At least—" for a moment Grace felt her depression returning, then she went on more normally "—at least, I was the girl, but I'm not any longer. You see that's why I'm so unhappy. Mr. Rage has gone off and left me."

"Left you?"

Grace explained the position to Helen, finishing: "You see, it was the thought of going home to mother without any wages or a job that suddenly seemed so awful. But, of course, it's not really so bad as that. I shall get another job soon. There are always places to be found for typists in London."

"How much did Mr. Rage pay you?" asked Helen.

"Three pounds, five shillings a week."

"Well," said Helen slowly, "I think we could manage the three pounds, but you'd have to wait a few months for the five shillings, and we want a typist. You'd better come along and work for us. Come on!"

Helen started off and Grace, hypnotised by her firmness, followed her and in ten minutes she had been installed in the outer office of General Factotums, not eight yards from her old office, and it was here, half an hour later, that Ben Brown found her when he returned feeling a little less antagonistic towards the firm which he had helped to create.

He entered the room and was confronted with the sight of Grace sitting before her table. She had cleared all traces of sorrow from her face. But tears leave even a pretty woman looking plain for an hour, and Grace, who was not pretty, looked very plain. She smiled at Ben and, because she liked the look of him at once, was glad that she was wearing her brown skirt with the pleats and had put on the best of her silk blouses that morning in honour of Friday.

"Who are you?" asked Ben, surprised into brusqueness.

"I'm Grace Kirkstall, the new typist. You're Mr. Brown, I know. Your wife is in the other office."

Ben said no more, but plunged straightway into the other office, shutting the door behind him. Helen was sitting at her desk.

Ben drew himself up impressively and, pointing backwards to the door, said dramatically: "What is that woman doing out there?"

"You must have been taking lessons from old Hindle," said Helen admiringly. "She should be typing some letters I gave her. Why?"

"Don't be evasive, Helen Brown! Don't be evasive!" Ben came threateningly towards her. "I leave this office in the morning, leave it functioning perfectly and I come back in the afternoon to find what?"

"To find it still functioning, only perhaps a little more perfectly, because we now have a typist."

"So we now have a typist, and what do we want a typist for? Your typing was slow, I'll admit, but it was fairly accurate. And who appointed this typist? Who appointed her without consulting me?"

"I did, and I had a perfect right to appoint her, as you know."

"You had not! No woman has a right to appoint a typist when there's a man equally concerned in the business. The appointment of a typist is a man's affair. Oh, I know what you're going to say—you're going to say I'm annoyed because she isn't good-looking. You're wrong. I'm annoyed at the overriding of a deep-seated principle. I should have appointed a typist—supposing we'd wanted one. I should have had the pleasure of interviewing a stream of girls, some would have been good-looking and the others plain—like that girl outside, and I should, no doubt, have appointed a plain, efficient creature, but at least I should have had the pleasure first of all of interviewing a few good-looking ones. I should have had that pleasure, at least. Anyway, we don't want a typist. This business can't afford it!"

"It can and it is going to afford it. Listen to me, Ben. I'm sorry I didn't have a chance to consult you, but I knew you would understand. Miss Kirkstall was with Mr. Rage across the landing until this morning. Mr. Rage has disappeared because his business wasn't all it should have been and the girl was out of a job. You know how often both of us have to be out of this office, well with a girl here to look after things we shall keep the business that we lose when the office is empty. And how often have we had to hire a woman to carry out some commission like meeting a child at a station? Miss Kirkstall can do jobs like that for us. In fact, she can do a hundred different things that will save us money. This business is growing steadily and it's a cautious and a wise way of encouraging success to take on a typist. We should have done it long ago. I don't think we shall ever regret the three pounds a week we are to pay her."

"Three pounds!"

"It's the usual wage."

"Three pounds! Now I know you're mad. No." Ben halted suddenly and looked at his wife through narrowed lids. "No," he said softly, "I was wrong. I see what it was. I should have guessed sooner. You found this girl somewhere. I can see it. She was sobbing on the stairs or in some dark corner because she had lost her job and you—you who like to think yourself cold and precise in business, you, the efficient martinet, continually chiding me because I have no business sense, because I am too extravagant— you, I say, were touched, your emotions were aroused and you took this creature to your heart and contracted to give her three pounds each week of our money. Deny it, if you dare!"

"Of course I deny it. It was purely a business arrangement. I heard she had lost her job and I went and offered her this one." Ben ignored Helen's denial. "Well, she's here and she must stay, I suppose."

And Grace did stay. She went home that evening with half of her next week's salary in advance. Helen had insisted on this. With her went George, whom she had met on the stairs. She told him what had happened to her and she could see that he was interested. She did not mention that she had given way to tears. George heard her in silence and when she had finished he said deliberately:

"Well, I hope you have made a change for the better, Miss Kirkstall. There are a great many rogues in this life and I was never overfond of Mr. Rage. This General Factotums business seems to me a very unsound affair, but maybe I'm wrong. I hope for your sake I am."

"Oh, you wouldn't say that if you knew Mr. and Mrs. Brown. They really are very nice, and it's almost inspiring to see a man and wife in the same business. You know a real kind of partnership."

"From what I have heard of married life, Miss Kirkstall, I should imagine that the first resolution of any married man would be to keep his wife away from his business. A married woman's place is in the home."

"Oh, you are a Victorian, Mr. Crane," Grace teased him.

"If you're thinking to annoy me with that epithet, Miss Kirkstall, you're vairy wide of the mark. I take it as a compliment. There was a great deal of common sense amongst the Victorians, even if some of their buildings were a little injudicious."

* * * * *

Punctually at sunset that evening, old Hindle came out of his little office recess in the side of the archway and, with the help of his younger son, Ralph, began to shut the great gates. They were heavy wooden gates and young Ralph, a small, thin boy of eight was hard put to push his section forward.

"Muscle, my son, muscle!" Hindle boomed at him as he swung his section shut. "Always keep your body fit."

The gates were closed and the bolts shot and then the two walked across the court towards the ornamental wrought-iron gates by the fountain to close them. This done, there would be no exit or entrance to the Inn save by knocking at Hindle's doorway. There were not many men who could from sunset each night until sunrise each morning lay claim to so large or so pleasant a domain as Hindle's.

The gates shut, Hindle went back to finish his pipe and the evening paper before commencing his rounds. He sat on a backless chair outside his house, looking across to the lawn on which Ralph played with Elizabeth and her family. The rest of the Hindles—Mrs. Hindle and two children—had gone to the pictures, a practice which Hindle, who swore by buskins and boards, deplored but could not prevent.

Chapter Three

A man wearing a navy blue suit and carrying a cane stick came out of the offices of the Society for Progressive Rehabilitation and, as the door closed behind him, he stood on the landing, staring at the floor reflectively. He stood for a moment, holding this pose, then he raised his bowler hat to his head and began to walk down the stairs, letting his legs drop jerkily from one step to the other in the manner of a man in no hurry to reach the outer world, where his thoughts would have no tranquillity.

He stopped once or twice on the way down, each time shaking his head gently and muttering to himself. When he was in the entrance hall he halted, his eye caught by the notice board showing the occupants of the stairway. He stared first at the slide which carried the name of the Society, then after a time his eyes moved away from the name to the others. He went, working upwards, from one to the other and by his facial expression it was easy to see that none of the other names perplexed him. You could almost hear his thoughts: "Yes, finance corporation. That's all right. Hire purchase. Architect, nothing unusual about that. Eastern Imports, eh? That might be anything or nothing." The Society's board he skipped with a momentary darkening of his brows and then he was murmuring to himself gently. "General Factotums? What the devil can that be?"

It was so that Hindle, coming to see Mr. Parcross, found him. The stranger's stance before the board seemed to indicate a difficulty and it was Hindle's pride to help people in difficulty over matters pertaining to the Inn.

"Can I help you, sir?" he asked quietly. "Perhaps you've got the wrong stairway?"

The man turned and saw Hindle, and guessed that he was someone of authority in the Inn from his green baize apron and the brass buttons of his jacket.

"What in the name of Pete is this General Factotums?" he asked.

Hindle smiled and without a word pulled a little brochure from his inside pocket and presented it to the man. He always carried a copy with him since he had found that many of his friends were not disposed to believe in the existence of such a firm. The printed brochure dispelled their doubts.

The man took the brochure and began to read.

"You'll find all about them in there," Hindle volunteered and then began to move away. "You can keep the brochure, sir, and if you want their offices—you'll find them right at the top."

He stumped up the stairs towards the offices of Eastern Imports, leaving the stranger reading.

A few moments later the man was climbing the stairs, his face still wrapped in the meditative expression, but his pace more brisk and determined.

The man gave his card to the young lady in the outer office.

"I'll see if Mr. Brown is disengaged," she said and left the room.

The stranger liked the appearance of the outer office. It was neat and efficiently free of superfluous furnishings.

Ben looked at the card which Grace had brought him. Mr. Robert Halifax, he read. The address was in Pall Mall.

"John Halifax was a gentleman," he said; "What does Robert Halifax look like, Miss Kirkstall?"

"Well," Grace paused to consider. This was her first Monday morning at General Factotums and she was anxious to be efficient. "Well, Mr. Brown, I wouldn't like to say for certain. He's got nice eyes, but I should think he was a rough diamond. But if you know his brother—"

"His brother died a long time back. Anyway, show Mr. Halifax in and if Mrs. Brown comes back while he's here warn her not to break in on us."

Mr. Robert Halifax entered. He looked, Ben thought, rather like a naval reservist who has settled in Cornwall to farm, up in London for the day. His face was red, crude, and innocent of guile; his chest was broad and capable of carrying without complaint enough sorrow to kill two ordinary men, and his arms hung away from his sides as though they were maintaining some feud with his body and refused to touch and be contaminated. When he smiled he opened his mouth very wide and panted, gently, dog fashion.

Ben welcomed him, made him comfortable in a chair and waited for him to take his own time coming through commonplaces to his business with General Factotums. Business affairs, like love affairs, begin always with polite, tentative skirmishes. There must be no hurry, no forcing and no point at which, in retrospect, one can say there ended politeness and began business, any more than there is a point when one can say there ended friendship and began love.

Mr. Halifax came to his business rather quicker than most people would have done. But having got there he revealed a persistent trick of wandering off side-paths as though he considered progression along a direct line a sin.

As he talked, Mr. Halifax kept his eyes on Ben's face. He had liked this young man at first sight. He liked the set of his mouth and the hint of a smile that flickered at the back of his conscientious air of efficiency.

"I'm an Australian, Mr. Brown, as you may perhaps guess from my accent. That was one of the things my uncle disliked most about me. Funny thing about accents. Some accents you're allowed to have and people envy you for them—they're like that about the Scotch and the Irish—any others they shake their heads over and consider you've been born with a great drawback. There's that feeling with some people against the Australian accent. Not that I care a damn what people think of my voice."

"I agree with you," said Ben. "A lot of people have the same dislike of the Oxford accent. It doesn't do to worry about people who regard certain voices as though they were vices."

"Too right, it doesn't! Anyway, Mr. Brown, that's wandering from the point. I've come to you for help—that's what your firm specialises in, isn't it?"

"Service is the word we use, which means that within certain limits we will do our best to help anyone. What's your particular trouble, Mr. Halifax?"

Mr. Halifax paused and eyed Ben across the desk. Then he said seriously, "Before I begin I must have your confidence, Mr. Brown." He said it as though Ben's confidence was something tangible to be pulled from a pocket and handled between them. "Of course. Anything you say here, Mr. Halifax, goes no further. This firm fully appreciates the delicate feelings which motivate many of our clients."

"Well, my particular trouble, as you call it, happens to be a dead man. Perhaps I'd better begin at the right end. I always like to take things in the proper order."

"It has the merit of avoiding confusion."

"Too right, it has!" Mr. Halifax grinned and exposed a pink epiglottis. "Well, this is it. My father was the younger son of a pretty wealthy family over here, but he never got on with the old folks and finally he cleared out to New Zealand and they forgot all about him. He married an Australian girl and had a son. He died, as everyone expected, of alcoholic poisoning. His wife—my mother—died not long after I went into the timber business. That's my line. Five years ago I took a holiday and came over to the Old Country and called on my father's only and elder brother who had inherited the family fortune. The old boy disliked me from the beginning. He thought I should have turned up from Aussie dead flat so that he could have been charitable—he liked being charitable. A lot of people do, I guess. It didn't please him to find someone who could have bought up him and his little estate in Kent a couple of times over and felt nothing about it. That's not boasting—I just wanted to give you some idea of the old boy."

"He's dead now, I take it?"

"Sure. He's dead. That's the point. After my first visit, I came again once more before his death. It was last June—this time last year, and he died in the following December. Well, this time I felt that I was obliged to show him that my feelings for him pretty well coincided with his feelings for me. My oath, the lad had a temper on him! Before I left, he told me three or four times that I needn't expect any of his money. He was going to leave it all to the National Playing Fields Association. He was nuts on anything to do with physical fitness, and was always playing around with food reform societies and other such bunkum. Why a man can't be content to eat and drink the stuff which Nature works hard to produce and leave the worrying to his digestion, I'm damned if I know. Well, he died last December and he left me five hundred pounds, and apart from a few minor legacies all his cash and effects went to an affair called the Society for Progressive Rehabilitation."

"Which has offices in this same building," put in Ben, wondering what was coming. Mr. Halifax was beginning to be interesting.

"That's so. Now, I don't want you to get me wrong, Mr. Brown. I never expected a penny from the old man—but I won't be such a hypocrite to say that I wouldn't have taken it if it had come my way. No man in his senses turns down hard cash. But I had my own money and the old boy was entitled to leave his just where he felt inclined. But when I heard about the will I wasn't altogether happy. The old man had told me how he was going to leave the bulk of his cash. After I left him, he'd even written to me—to add a few more nasty remarks he'd thought of after I left him—and he mentioned again that I was to get nothing and that he was leaving his cash to the National Playing Fields Association. He said nothing about this Society, although I know he has been interested in it. He was always taking up some new stunt. But I knew the old man—he had all the family traits—once he'd dropped a thing he'd dropped it. Like my father—and in a way myself—once we've finished we don't begin again. And the old boy was getting tired of the Society when I last stayed with him. There were exercises and other nonsense the members carried on with and I could see he was beginning to cool off. That's why I felt it was curious that he should leave all his cash to them—only five months after I had visited him and seen that he was beginning to drop the affair. The most I should have thought he would leave them would have been a couple of hundred."

"If your uncle was so eccentric it doesn't seem unlikely that he might change his mind four or five times within five months?" suggested Ben.

"Don't you believe it. He was eccentric, but in his own way, and with him it was always off with the old love and on with the new. He never went back to things he'd tried once. Now, I've got a feeling about money, especially when there's a lot of it in one place. So, when I came over this year on business I thought I'd take a look at this Society. From what I'd heard about it from my uncle I was sure it was a crazy business. I didn't like the idea of all that money being wasted, or being hooked by some phoney operating a fake society. Well, I took a look this morning. I

called on the head man in the office below this one."

"You mean Mr. Tomms?"

"That's the man. I didn't say who I was, just pretended to be a colonial interested in the Society and asking for information."

"And what were your impressions?"

"The fellow Tomms talks like the genuine article—but if he were a fake that's the first thing he would do—and the Society seems pretty big. But I wasn't satisfied."

"You weren't?" Ben found himself glad that Mr. Halifax had not been satisfied. It might mean much.

"No, but that's the trouble. I felt I wasn't satisfied because I didn't want to be satisfied. Giving all that money to a lunatic society seemed wrong to me, and I would be glad to find there was something fishy somewhere. That's no spirit to start any enquiry. You've got to be impartial, and I couldn't. Besides, I was prejudiced against the whole affair from the moment I saw

Tomms. The man wears a wig."

"A wig!"

"Yes, a wig. It's a good one, I should know because I worked in a barber and wig-maker's outfit in Melbourne for a year and I can tell at once. It's a kind of second sight. Yes, sir, he wears a wig—but it's a wig of white hair that makes him look older than he is. Now why should a man wear a wig to make him look older—it's usually the other way round. That made me very curious."

"So it might. Why did you come here, Mr. Halifax?"

"Well, when I left Tomms I saw your notice board. The janitor explained what your business was and I came up. I thought maybe you'd take a look at this Society and let me have a report about it."

"We're not a detective agency."

"I know that, and I'm not asking you to be. All I want is information about the Society. I could get the stuff myself, only

I can't spare the time. I shan't argue with you about the fee. You do a good job and I'll pay. I never mind paying for work well done."

Ben was silent for a while. "Have you seen your uncle's lawyer?" he asked. The question followed a thought which had occurred to him.

"I have."

"And what did he have to say about the Society?"

"He was satisfied that the will was in order. So it may be—but that doesn't make the Society genuine."

Ben nodded agreement with this and tipped his chair backwards gently as he considered the facts with private elation. It was the first affair since the inception of General Factotums that held a possibility of excitement. He decided to accept the commission and took a few necessary details from Mr. Halifax.

When the Australian had gone, he sat back in his chair and stared at the illustrated calendar on the opposite wall. Considered calmly, there was little to be excited about in the commission. All he had to do was to make a few formal enquiries and then report his findings. But that was not all; behind the enquiries was the possibility that he might find out something which would point to the Society's being incorrectly run, that Tomms might be … What might he be?

He wondered, in a moment of lucidity between wild conjectures, how one started to make enquiries about a Society. He called in Grace.

"Take five shillings from the petty cash," he told her, "and go along to the Theosophical Book Shop—you know the place?—and get all the pamphlets and literature they sell about the Society for Progressive Rehabilitation."

"Their office is just below, wouldn't it be quicker to get it all from them, Mr. Brown?"

"Quicker, but not wiser." A thought occurred to Ben. "You've worked in this building a long time, Miss Kirkstall—do you know much about the Society for Progressive Rehabilitation?"

"Not a lot, Mr. Brown. They're a queer set, I think. Mr. Tomms—he's the head—he's a white-haired gentleman. There's only him and his secretary in the office. She's a quiet, dried-up sort of thing."

"Is that the complete staff?"

"Yes—but there are always people coming and going. I've never seen stranger sights than some of them. I saw an Indian with a turban come out one day. Some of them come pretty regular. There's the purple lady, for instance."

"The purple lady?"

"Well, I call her that. I often meet her on the stairway coming or going to the office. She's a plump, elderly body and she always dresses in purple. Hardly a becoming colour for anyone her age, I think."

"How long have the offices been here?"

"A long time, I think. They were here before I started with Mr. Rage."

It would be worth while, thought Ben when Grace had gone off, getting Hindle's opinion of the Society. Caretakers are privileged persons and often see and hear more than is generally known.

Ben told Helen about the commission as they had lunch. He was not surprised to find her a little opposed to the whole affair.

"We are not a detective agency, Ben. I hope you made that clear?"

"I did, although I believe that I gave the impression that I shouldn't object to a certain amount of dignified snooping around. After all, it's rather a pleasant thing to be curious."

"It seems to me that you are hoping for a lot more from this than can ever happen."

"Maybe, but it's such a long time since anything did happen to me that I fancy I see the adventurous hand of Fate in this, a thin, rather dirty hand which pushed Mr. Halifax through our doorway. And now I must be off." He rose, leaving Helen with her coffee.

"Off where? The office?"

"No, darling, that's your responsibility this afternoon. I'm going to Somerset House."

"Whatever for?"

"To have a look at the will of Mr. Halifax's uncle, Colonel Hasted-Halifax, late of Hormenden in the County of Kent. If you had met Mr. Halifax you would know that he would approve of beginning right at the beginning."

Helen watched him go. Why was it, she wondered, that men wanted to go on playing long after they had outgrown physical boyhood. Here was Ben, a man with an Oxford degree and connections that should have seen him safely into the diplomatic service, careering off in the hope of turning up a scandal connected with some grubby little society, dramatising himself as a modern Sherlock Holmes, wanting to play at Robin Hood like a young boy—yes, young boy, for the older boys certainly never saw themselves as bowmen in the good greenwood. She supposed it was the result of being born without any real sense of class distinction. If Ben had been a snob, he would have become a diplomat—not that diplomats were necessarily snobs, but they had a proper sense of the fitness and right place of things. She stopped herself suddenly. This private examination of Ben was an old trick with her. It generally ended with a decision that she must really make an effort to reform him, to convert him into a sober, sensible citizen employing his talents where they would be most appreciated; a decision from which rose an immediate doubt of her power to do any such thing.

"Grace," she said when she was back at the office, "when you marry, see that you pick for yourself a nice, solid, sensible young man who has a proper idea of the necessity for working hard and settling down to a comfortable family life—there are such men, so I'm told."

"Of course there are, Mrs. Brown," Grace agreed eagerly; "and that's just the kind I shall have, I hope."

Chapter Four

Grace enjoyed her lunch hours. They represented the few periods when London imposed no duty upon her. It was only in the lunch-hour that she was released from the necessity of going somewhere definite, from the economic obligation of reaching a certain point before a stipulated time. She made full use of her liberty. Even in the winter she felt no need for a substantial midday meal—that could wait until she was at home with her mother. Besides, if she did not have an evening meal at home, it meant that her mother would never bother to cook for herself, and Grace did not want that to happen.

In company with thousands of other girls, Grace would content herself with a bun and a glass of milk, or in the very hot weather just the glass of milk, and then sally forth to enjoy an hour of London liberty. She would wander up Oxford Street looking into the shop windows and planning the purchase of an autumn ensemble that was far beyond the reach of her purse. She would stand outside the chromium splendour of beauty parlours, wondering what she would look like with red nails and plucked eyebrows and think of the plain little saloon at home where she occasionally had her ends permed. A pet-store with a restless fox-terrier pup in its cage, convulsing the window crowd with its antics, would set her wishing that her mother liked dogs. Sometimes she had no desire to spend her time window shopping. She would buy a threepenny ticket on a bus and ride north, south, east or west, wherever the bus was going and from the top deck watch the crowded passing of streets and pedestrians, dreaming of the homes through whose windows the elevation of the bus gave her entrance. When the striking clocks gave her warning that she must turn about, she would catch another bus and ride back to her work, listening to the chatter of the passengers around her and wondering about a hundred queer things that came into her mind. When it rained she would go into a museum or art gallery and walk reverently past canvases and cases of exhibits, easily stirred to admiration and, underneath her religious awe, be impressed by the fine polish on the floors and the sparkle of the glass and brass. "Only a man understands the cleaning of brass and boards." Her father used to say that. He was a naval man and had been killed in the War when she was a baby. And as she went out she would look to see whether the attendant, who nearly always seemed to wear ex-Service ribbons, looked naval or military.

But there were times when she wanted to do no more than cross the lawn of Fountain Inn and sit by the pool, listening to the fall of the water and watching the pigeons and sparrows that gathered there to take the crumbs from the men and women who ate their lunches on the fountain seats.

She was sitting there today and next to her sat George Crane. It was not George's wish that they should be sharing the quiet and sunshine of the little garden. He had gone with his book to read during his lunch-time and Grace had found him there and sat beside him. It was here that she had first met and talked with him—that was nearly a year ago now—and she nourished a gentle sentiment about the fountain for this blessing. She liked George, even though she was aware that there were times when he acted as though he was not altogether pleased to see her; but she explained that strangeness by his nationality. All Scotchmen were shy.

"Got an interesting book?" she enquired brightly after he had politely greeted her and then immersed himself in his reading.

"I have," he answered. Women, George decided, had not that natural reticence that men have of intruding upon one another's reading. He had somewhere, probably in a newspaper, seen the point psychologically explained by the theory that a woman's whole life is directed towards attracting the attention of the male and she resents the book as a rival.

"It's nice to see a man deep in a book," Grace went on, happy to be allowed to talk to him. "A book and a pipe —they're two manly things."

Grace stopped talking as she saw George frown. Then she said gently: "I'm sorry, I didn't mean to interrupt you."

Despite himself, George smiled. There was a childish pertinacity and blindness about Grace which infuriated him at times and made him long to be rude to her. Yet, the moment he seized courage to turn and tell her his thoughts, the sight of her face, her lips ready to tremble if anyone hurt her or repulsed her good intentions, evoked a swift head of toleration and kindness which quite killed his desire to be frank with her. He had made up his mind that she must be treated as though she were an enquiring nephew, a small boy who refused to be repressed.

"You are not interrupting me, Miss Kirkstall. It is only that your desire for conversation is making it difficult for me to read."

Grace chuckled; "You do say such things. I can't think how people can hold that you Scotch have no sense of humour. And anyway, you should be glad someone wants to talk to you. Lots of people are very lonely. I was thinking only yesterday—"

What Grace had been thinking yesterday was never revealed for at that moment a shadow fell across them and a woman's voice enquired sweetly:

"I wonder if there's room for another on that seat, my dears? All the others are in the full glare of the sun and I can't stand too much sun at my age."

The seats were actually intended to take four people, but Grace and George had been so disposed that unless anyone had sat rudely between them, first removing Grace's handbag, there was no space save a tiny margin of board at each end of the seat.

George moved up hurriedly and found himself sandwiched between Grace and the newcomer. She was a large woman and, as she sat down, George, finding that he had not made enough allowance for her bulk, slid a little further towards Grace. As he did so the book he had been reading fell from his knees to the ground. Before he could retrieve it, the newcomer bent and picked it up. For such a plump woman, she displayed an unusual agility.

"Why, it's a book on architecture," she said, glancing at the title as she handed it back to him.

"Thank you," said George, taking the book. He disliked the strong perfume she used.

"Are you interested in architecture?" the woman asked.

"I am." George's answer was curt, and Grace, anxious that he should not give the impression that he was rude, leaned across him towards the woman and added in a friendly way:

"He's an architect. A very good architect. I shouldn't doubt it that some day he'll be famous."

She had recognised the woman at once. She was the purple lady about whom she had told Mr. Brown. She had often met and nodded to her on the stairs.

"How interesting. How very interesting. You know, my dears— of course, you'll excuse my calling you that, but I'm so much older than you it seems so natural—my father was an architect. At least he was a builder."

"It is not the same thing," said George decisively.

"No, perhaps not, but the two are so close. It quite cheers me up to talk to someone who is interested in buildings. But I mustn't start talking like this to you. You're young and you won't want to be bothered with a silly old woman like myself. I know you both by sight. I often come to the Inn on business and I've seen you here. I suppose it was just that you two looked so happy sitting there, enjoying the sun in your lunch-hour, that I couldn't resist the temptation to come and sit with you. I hope you don't mind?"

"Why, we don't mind at all, do we?" Grace looked at George firmly. The woman's plea had touched her and she was determined that George should not have a chance to hurt her by some blunt expression of feeling.

"Why, no. Of course not, madam." Long afterwards George wondered with what impotence Grace had managed to infect him at that moment so that he followed her lead meekly.

"How kind you are, and how unlike most young people of today! They have no time for anything or anyone but themselves and their own interests. They don't know what loneliness is. And I hope they never do. I hope, my dears, that you never know what it is to be lonely. But you won't, of course. I can see that you have one another."

George frowned at this gigantic assumption and refused to look at Grace.

"You mustn't mind him when he frowns," said Grace, noticing that the woman had caught George's fierce look. "He always does it when you've said something that pleases him.

He's Scottish, you see, and very contrary."

George sat, his helplessness growing, as the two women exerted their influence over him. Grace he could have managed, but the two of them were a sudden and strong problem before which he was pitifully inadequate.

The woman laughed. "How you two understand one another. It's so nice to see it. And your friendliness, how pleasant that is.

The moment I saw you sitting here I knew you were both the kind of people I should like at once. You work in the Inn, don't you? That's why you don't seem quite like strangers to me." She ran on, her words coming quickly as though she were afraid that if she did not speak now she would never regain the courage needed for her request; "I wonder if you two would like to come and have some tea with me this Sunday? Now, don't say Yes if you don't want to, but it would be so nice to have some young people in the house. You could see the photographs, too, of the buildings that father put up. I'm sure that would interest you. But, of course, you won't come, and it was very wrong of me to ask you … I couldn't help the impulse."

She broke off, embarrassed by a sudden sense of her indelicacy, and in that moment her plump face tightened into an expression of unhappiness that stirred Grace immediately. The poor old thing, it was so little that she asked, really.

"Why, I'm sure we'd be glad to come. It's very kind of you to ask us, isn't it?" Grace turned to George quickly and that unfortunate saw for the first time a vigour and threat in Grace's eyes that were new to him. She was bullying him by the determination of her lips and the small frown of her brow into acting like a good Samaritan, and George, although he held strong views on the subject of conversing with strangers, and stronger views on accepting the offer of their hospitality, found himself without the courage to be honest.

"No, I can see he doesn't want to come. And he's quite right. It was improper of me to ask. Never mind."

Then George spoke, and he wondered at his own voice. "You're quite mistaken about my feelings, madam. I take your invitation vairy kindly." He did not see the grateful look that Grace gave him, but he was not unaware of a faint sense of delicious immolation. After all—he commenced to argue with himself and then broke off. He had committed himself. Let that be enough foolishness for one day. Grace and the woman were talking across him now, but he heard little they said with any comprehension.

Later as he walked across the turf with Grace towards the stairway, she expressed her pleasure to him.

"I wouldn't have blamed you, if you had refused. After all, it was a lot to ask. But I'm glad you didn't refuse, Mr. Crane."

George frowned at Grace and said: "Sometimes, Miss Kirkstall, a man does things deliberately of which he disapproves. It is a kind of paradox which arises out of sentiment, and, as I've told you before, I think, I'm no great lover of sentiment. Did the lady think to tell you her name and her address?"

"She did. She gave me her card and she wants us to be there about four next Sunday. Look." She held the card out to him.

George took it and read it. It announced

Miss Victoria Logan,
The Hollies,
Sheldon Road, Ealing.

After George and Grace had gone back to their offices Miss Logan sat on at the fountain, her hands folded in her lap, her eyes following the soft fall of water from the Neptune.

Once or twice she made a move as though she would leave the seat, and after each start she would sit back, her face drawn into plump puckers as though her thoughts were worrying her, touching her with anxiety.

Long after Grace had settled down to the afternoon work, Miss Logan got up and crossed the Inn to Number One stairway. Her mouth was set in a determined line, and she was so obsessed by some private problem that she almost trod on Elizabeth the cat.

She went up to the office of the Society for Progressive Rehabilitation and asked the secretary if she might see Mr. Tomms.

The secretary gave her a chair, passed a pleasant few words with her and then went into Mr. Tomms's room. There was no doubt from her manner that Miss Logan was a welcome visitor. She came back quickly.

"Mr. Tomms will be glad to see you, Miss Logan." She held the door open for her.

As Miss Logan came through the door Mr. Tomms rose happily to meet her, his great face corticated with smiles, his hand extended in a warm greeting.

"Come in, my dear Miss Logan. If you knew how welcome was the sight of your dear face here you would honour me more often. You have always a special place in my heart, Miss Logan, for was it not through you that Ealing was conquered for the Society. Pioneer work! Pioneer work! Had you been a little earlier you would have caught me at my afternoon exercises. What a glorious day, a day that was made for Man. The earth rhythm was particularly pronounced this morning. You no doubt noticed it? We near the solstice—that's the reason."

He propelled her to an armchair by the window and forced her into it gently. He always felt more sure of himself if people sat down and he was allowed to stand.

Miss Victoria Logan accepted his greeting with a little nervous smile of pleasure, a timidness mixed with apprehension at the warmth of his welcome, and she handed him a long envelope.

"I had to come to Town on other business, Mr. Tomms, so I thought I would bring in these returns. You know you wrote to me about them a few days ago. And, of course, it's always such a pleasure to come and see you personally. Coming to the fountain-head, I always call it."

They both laughed at this faint joke and as Mr. Tomms took the envelope from her his eyes surveyed her swiftly and critically. He knew her well, so well that this afternoon he was instantly aware of a change in her. For some reason she was nervous.

Miss Victoria Logan might, as the result of a quick glance, have been dismissed as one of those numerous women well past middle-age who have plenty of money and little to occupy their minds. She looked like that. She was plump and her skin, though it sagged in places, was as fresh and clear as a girl's. She was wearing a purple toque and a purple dress with a high lace collar. From the toque dropped a white net veil which she pushed back while talking to Mr. Tomms. About her neck and on her breast and wrist jangled various ornaments; a Wedgwood brooch mounted in silver, a little watch in an ebony case on the end of a long gold chain, and a bracelet made from a curiously carved matrix. She had an opulent, over-blown look; ripe and rich with bloom. But although it was true that she had plenty of money and not enough work to keep her mind healthily occupied, Miss Logan refused to be dismissed so summarily on that account. There was a presumptive, assertive atmosphere about her presence that forced attention and made people remember her long after the normal personalities of casual meetings had been forgotten. She was one of those women who had just missed being a Force, but her passage through the shadows of so near a destiny had left a mark upon her. She could never be casually put aside as an elderly, meddlesome woman.

Mr. Tomms, as became a man who was the founder and autocratic head of a Society that numbered five thousand members in the British Isles, realised Miss Logan's peculiar powers and for that reason he was vaguely worried at the obvious change in her manner this morning.

"And how is the great work progressing, Mr. Tomms?" Miss Logan asked. She was trying to make her voice seem natural, for she had suddenly become dimly aware of his recognition of her nervousness.

"Soon, soon now every member will have an opportunity of seeing."

"You mean all the plans are ready? I did hope that if you had them in the office I might be allowed a tiny peep—just for a moment, that's all."

Tomms nodded benevolently. Was that why she had acted so nervously, because she had wanted to get a peep at the plans before the other members of the Society? He smiled to himself at this evidence of feminine weakness.

"My dear Miss Logan, what enthusiasm! You and I and the thousands of others who have found the new way of life—we all share this enthusiasm, but it is a hard task to inspire the lay folk outside our circle with the same glorious infection. Plans must be made by architects, and Craddock and Couch—the firm of architects in this building who are doing the work—refuse to be hurried. And perhaps they are right. Building is an act of creation and it is a sin to force natural laws. I had hoped that the plans would be ready for tomorrow night's meeting, but it could not be. We must be patient. The plans are almost completed and—but this is a secret between us—I hope to have them exhibited at our next weekly assembly."

"I'm so glad to hear that, Mr. Tomms, so glad indeed. I'm sure that when the new homes are ready more and more people will turn to us for the light and renewed vigour which is needed in this dark chasm of modern life. You see how much I think about you, I even find myself using your phrases in my speech ... 'the dark chasm of modern life.' It is indeed a dark and mysterious chasm, Mr. Tomms."

Mr. Tomms stirred a little at this compliment. Then he rose, rubbing his large hands together, twining his fingers over and under themselves and he boomed in his resonant voice, "Dark it is, Miss Logan, but do not let us commit the sin of pessimism, the sin against the future. Let us remember that there is comedy and laughter as well as sorrow and despair in that long valley of life. It is good to laugh."

"Oh, how true that is, and how glad I am to hear you say that. There are so many amusing things in life, Mr. Tomms. Why—" she broke off for a moment and stared at him "—that reminds me of a very amusing thing that happened to me and, in a way, you, Mr. Tomms. It was most strange."

"You fill me with curiosity, Miss Logan."

"Well, so I might when you hear. You see I have a sister who lives in Canada and last month when I wrote to her I sent her one of the photographs of yourself—the ones that are sold at the weekly meetings. She's very interested in the Society. And what do you think? She's written back to say that she's sure she's seen you before and what's more that she's sure it was in Toronto— that's where she lives. She never forgets a face—I will say that for Janet—but I'm positive she must be mistaken this time. Have you ever been to Toronto, Mr. Tomms?"

Mr. Tomms shook his head gravely. "Never," he said smoothly. "Except for a few trips to the Continent, I am a poor, insular creature."

"Well, it just shows, doesn't it, how easy it is for people to get fancies in their heads. Now I must go. You are a busy man and I mustn't detain you."

Mr. Tomms showed her to the door and then returned to his room. He stood at his window and watched Miss Logan cross the Inn and go out into Chain Walk. His eyes followed her purple figure, but his thoughts were very far away from Miss Logan. He was wondering why it was that in so large a world the shifts of time and travel, of birth and accident, should more often unite people than separate them. Perhaps, in fact, it wasn't so, but it certainly seemed like it, and this drift towards association was stronger if you had any reason to disown the past. Toronto and Fountain Inn, Miss Logan and her curious sister and then himself ... He went back to his desk and, unlocking one of his drawers, pulled out a private ledger and began to work on it.

From Fountain Inn, Miss Victoria Logan walked a few hundred yards to Chancery Lane and entered the offices of Spenser and Trout, her lawyers. There was no Mr. Trout now, and his memory had long faded from the firm which was ruled by Mr. Ederley Spenser.

Mr. Spenser saw Miss Logan at once. She was shown into a wide, low-ceilinged room full of shadows, the smell of old leather and the suggestion of grave secrets. Two small windows looked out into Chancery Lane and its traffic. The only touch of colour in the room, before Miss Logan's purple appeared, was a bowl of red roses standing on Mr. Spenser's desk.

Mr. Spenser welcomed her. He was a thin, brittle little man, with wide, projecting bone arches over his eyes that cast his narrow face into shadows and emphasised a broad forehead that was already unduly exposed by the recession of his pepper-andsalt hair, which he wore cropped very close. His eyes moved in their deep sockets with a gentle flicker. He always wore a dark grey cloth and nothing his tailor could do helped to hide the bony length of his wrists and hands. They projected over the desk now with a splayed, protesting movement against their indecent exposure. They were ugly wrists and hands.

"Something's worrying you, Miss Logan?" The question had authority, the authority which was always part of his speech and offset the brittle defence of his body.

"Yes, Mr. Spenser, I'm very worried, very worried indeed. That's why I've come to see you. You know how much I value your advice." Miss Logan appeared almost breathless with agitation.

"If I can help you in any way, I will. But what is it?"

"It's about the Society for Progressive Rehabilitation."

"You surprise me. Aren't you yourself a member?"

"I am, but it isn't that. I don't mean there's anything wrong with its ideals. Oh, no, the ideals are beautiful and they really do help one to live a better and fuller life. No, it isn't that …

Oh, I wish I could explain myself without appearing to be so very unkind." She hesitated for a moment, searching for the right approach and Spenser watched her closely. He was interested in people. He saw so many different kinds in his office and heard them deliver themselves of secrets and expose the dark places of their beings. He had never exhausted his curiosity nor lost his sense of amazement at some of the things he heard. It was a pity almost that one couldn't collect people as one collected books ... Miss Logan went on:

"The trouble is really, Mr. Spenser, that I'm a very suspicious and unworthy person. I've fought against it, but I can't help it. I'm so inclined to doubt people. I get a feeling about a person and I simply can't shake it off. It's just as though somewhere inside me there's an electric bell and when I meet some people they start the bell ringing, a warning bell. It may not be the first time I meet them that it happens; it may not happen until I know them very well, but when it does I just can't ignore it and I start looking for reasons."

"I hope I've never rung the bell," put in Mr. Spenser with a smile. His joke was intended to ease her embarrassment.

"Of course not," she answered seriously.

"Well, who has made the bell ring? May I ask that question?"

"That's what I came to tell you. It's Mr. Tomms."

"Mr. Tomms, the head of the Society?"

"Yes. During the last year I've fancied I noticed one or two minor discrepancies in the Society's affairs."

"Go on, Miss Logan." Spenser encouraged her.

"Well, the moment the Society inherited the Colonel's money, I began to have this feeling very strongly about Mr.

Tomms. He, of course, looks after the Society's financial affairs. I began to feel that he wasn't a trustworthy person. It was such a strong feeling that I couldn't ignore it, and each time I met him it grew stronger."

She paused, exhausted for a moment by her vehemence. Her large bosom stirred with the effort of her breathing and little beads of perspiration starred the corners of her mouth. Spenser took advantage of her pause to speak:

"You know, Miss Logan, I don't want to seem flippant or unappreciative of your feelings, but it doesn't always do to follow one's intuitions too far without insisting upon a few facts. I know it was a lot of money for the Society to inherit. In fact, no one knows it better than I do, because, as you know, I handled all the Colonel's affairs, and I may say that when I realised just what measure of autocracy this Mr. Tomms exercised over the Society and just what opportunities the inheritance might offer to a dishonest man, I was very careful in my approach to him. But I must say he seemed a very genuine person to me and deeply involved in the Society's ideals. He was at once full of plans for using the money to foster the growth of the Society in a way which would be in the spirit of the bequest."

"Dear Mr. Spenser, how ashamed you make me feel, but I had to do what I did. I felt that I owed it first to the dear Colonel and secondly to the Society. I felt I had to be sure of Mr. Tomms. So—"

"So, Miss Logan?" Spenser rubbed his bony wrists.

"So, I paid a firm of private detectives to make enquiries about Mr. Tomms for me. That was three months ago. I got their full report two days ago. Here it is." She took a long envelope from her bag and handed it to Spenser. He took it, drew out the report and leant back in his chair reading it. He read it carefully and Miss Logan watched his face as he read. If she had expected him to show any emotion, she was disappointed. Mr. Spenser knew how to control his features so that by now they took no part in the subtleties of emotion and feeling that might be awakened in him. His practice demanded that he should be to his clients a sphinx, an unemotional custodian of secrets.

He put the report down and faced her, his long hands cupped about his face, drawing the flesh tight as he concentrated in thought before speaking.

"We must not be too ready to condemn a man for his past sins, Miss Logan, especially when those sins have been expiated in a statutory way, as have those of Mr. Tomms apparently. But I must say that this is a serious revelation. Have you approached Mr. Tomms at all?"

"Yes, this morning. I didn't say anything to him, of course, but I mentioned Toronto to him and he definitely lied about having been there. I had to tell him a lie about having a sister there who had recognised his photograph, but I thought that was excusable in the circumstances. I then came straight to you for advice."

"Quite, and I hope you have not mentioned this matter to anyone else? It's not a crime in itself for a man to have a criminal record, and you might find yourself mixed up in a slander case if you weren't careful. But certainly, from this report, it seems clear that the matter should be taken further. Only we must remember that Mr. Tomms may have genuinely cut away from the past and is living a life of absolute probity. In fact, it is more than possible that the foundation of his Society arose from a genuine desire for rehabilitation, the rehabilitation of his soul, Miss Logan. As a lawyer, however, I feel that it is not wise for Mr. Tomms to have such absolute control of the Society's money. If you will leave it to me, I will see him. Our best plan is to be honest with him in the hope that he will be honest with us. If he is genuinely desirous of advancing the Society, it should not be difficult for him to agree to an arrangement whereby the financial matters are subject to the authority of a second person as well as himself. But until I have seen him and—for my own satisfaction—made a few enquiries, might I suggest that it would be wise if you would mention nothing of this to anyone else?"

As he made this request for secrecy, Spenser knew that he was asking Miss Logan the impossible almost. She was—he could not prevent the vulgarism from coming to his mind—literally itching to spread her news confidentially amongst the other members. He made the request seriously, hoping she would be silent for a while at least, until he could go into the matter fully.

"Of course, Mr. Spenser. Of course; and I do hope that it does prove that Mr. Tomms is really a different man from what his past suggests. I cannot feel that a man who has given the last five years of his life to the Society can be motivated by selfish ideals."

Mr. Spenser saw her out and then went back and read the report again. When he had finished it he leaned back in his chair and shut his eyes, pressing the tips of his fingers against his temples as he thought. He sat very still for a long time.

Chapter Five

Early that Tuesday evening a young man came from below to the forward deck of the *Lorora*. The *Lorora*, a cargo boat of nearly three thousand tons, lay alongside the wharf of Pilcher's Warehouse, a tall, grey building hung with derricks that were now idle. The other front of the warehouse formed part of that almost continuous cliff of buildings which made up one side of Wapping High Street. Only rarely is there a break in the buildings showing you a narrow chasm leading down to the river, or a falling away of the tall warehouses to make room for some channel to slip in from the Thames to a sheltered basin.

The young man, who wore a grey suit and a dark jersey with a high, rolled collar and a greasy cap, walked to the side, carrying in one hand a large, imitation leather suitcase. He put the case down in the bows and then, leaning over the rail, wrinkled his nose distastefully at the pungent smell of oranges which came from the wharf. Then he glanced upstream at the pale silhouette of Tower Bridge. His face, which until then had carried a hard, rather mean look, softened and he almost smiled, revealing a sensitiveness which was in strange contrast with his habitual expression.

It was evening, yet quite light. Against the western sky Tower Bridge was almost a black outline, a cut-out in a toy-scene. Its fairy, mediaeval towers reached to the pale pearl sky and across its span moved a dwarf procession of cars and people. Between its arches spun the dirty Thames, its water touched into metallic beauty by the late sun, its surface untroubled by the traffic of the day. The young man watched the river. A pleasure steamer came down on its way to Greenwich, her rails crowded with tourists, who pointed and sent echoing cries across the water. A police launch came upstream, close in and the officer nodded friendlily to the young man, who faintly moved his head in reply. He watched like one who has come back to a familiar scene, come back to engage with his eyes once more details and movements which had filled his dreams.

"You look as though you was in love with the blinkin' river!"

He turned to find the watchman behind him. He was one of the crew who had been kept behind when the others were paid off for the voyage.

"There's nothing wrong with the river." He was about to say more, but he stopped and stared across to the far bank as though he were searching for something over there.

"I've heard you say you didn't care if you never saw old London town agin."

"Well, maybe I've grown out of that feeling."

"And was you aimin' to make a long stay in the Metropolis?"

"I don't stay long in any place."

"Then you'll be signing on agin?"

"Not in this orange crate. I never did like oranges. And the company isn't all that I could wish." This was directed at his questioner, and the young man's lips were curled with his meaning. "I'll find myself another berth when the time comes."

He picked up his case and walked away without saying more.

The watchman eyed him as he went. The weight of the case made more pronounced a slight limp in his left leg. He went off the boat, across the wharf and disappeared towards the High Street along a narrow alley-way.

"Nasty-tempered swine," the watchman muttered. He began to fill his pipe and walked back along the deck whistling gently to himself.

*   *   *   *   *

Ben ducked as the cushion came towards him and caught it with one hand. He returned it at once with a jerk. It took Helen, unprepared, in the middle and she collapsed on to her bed.

"There are times," she said with dignity and difficulty, for her breath had gone from her, "when I see in your love of horseplay an alarming indication of the state of your mind. I thought I'd married a civilised man; apparently I've got myself a

Neanderthal monstrosity."

"You threw the cushion first," Ben pointed out.

"That's got nothing to do with it. You deliberately irritated me."

"So you are curious! You said just now that you didn't want to know."

"Naturally, I was lying. You should have known that. When my husband comes home wearing a false moustache, thick eyebrows and glasses, do you expect me to accept it as an ordinary event to excite no comment?"

"It's a lovely disguise, isn't it?" Ben got up and surveyed himself in the glass. "Paddy fixed me up—you remember Paddy,

of course. He's starting rehearsals again soon."

"But what's it for?"

"To disguise myself, of course. Maybe I'd better begin at the beginning. I'll begin with Colonel Hasted-Halifax's will."

"I thought it was all something to do with that business. You know, Ben, I wish you wouldn't let yourself be carried away so much by it. It's probably only a very ordinary affair after all."

"That's not proven yet. Nothing is. Anyway I had a look at his will. I went to Somerset House … You know, Helen, other people's wills are most interesting documents. All of us have to leave this world at some time or other and a will is properly a testament to life. It gives men and women a last chance to settle their accounts for better or for worse. A will survives death like an echo."

"Must you?"

"Well, if you aren't interested. Anyway, I saw the will. It's quite a straightforward affair drawn up by his solicitor in Chancery Lane. There were two witnesses; one a Ronald Lambert, who was probably a family servant, for his address is that of the Colonel's house at Hormenden, and the other a Dorian

Ballard—does that mean anything to you?"

"Isn't there an author of that name?"

"There is, and I believe it's the same. Don't you read your Sunday papers? Dorian Ballard, author of *Gold Goes Begging*, now in its fortieth thousand in England, over the hundred thousand in America; film rights sold at a fabulous figure. Mr. Ballard's work, I believe—I never read bestsellers these days, they're so long it's become a full-time occupation—takes up a thousand pages and details the history of a family of American financiers from the seventeenth century emigre to the twentieth century industrialist. He was the other witness—probably a friend of the Colonel's. The Colonel left five hundred to our friend, Mr. Halifax, nothing at all to his servants, some furniture to his lawyer, the three oil paintings in his study—whatever they were—to my dear friend, Miss Victoria Logan, whoever she is, and the rest to the Society for Progressive Rehabilitation. That means the Society got about fifty thousand in cash and whatever the Colonel's small estate and house are worth. They are now for sale, so Halifax tells me."

"There's nothing wrong with all that."

"Perhaps not, but it's satisfying to know exactly where you are in an affair like this."

"You're not forgetting that it's the Society Mr. Halifax wants reported upon, not his uncle's will?"

"Not at all. I'm coming to that. I've digested all the available literature about the Society—and very interesting it is. As far as I can make out, the idea is that the soul, or spirit of man, grows through one stage to another just as his body does, that man's body and spirit must always be changing and the great thing is for the change to be progressive—always towards the ultimate perfection. The Society maintains that there are exactly seven stages, seven distinct rehabilitations of body and spirit and, according to them, most people—naturally those who don't belong to the Society—seldom get beyond number three. If you join the Society and carry out its rules and exercises then you have a good chance of getting into the sixth form—the seventh apparently is only reached by a few exceptional individuals."

"It sounds a lot of nonsense."

"It's caught the imagination of quite a lot of people. It's not a small society."

"And the disguise, you haven't explained that."

"There's a weekly meeting of the Society each Tuesday night at their hall, which is near King's Cross Station. All are welcomed—and we're going tonight."

"But why disguised?"

"You needn't be disguised. We can separate before we go into the hall. But I don't want Mr. Tomms to see me."

"Why on earth not? It can't mean anything to him. And, anyway, I shan't be disguised. He may see me."

"You don't matter. I want to talk to the people there and find out what they think of the Society. It's my job to do that and I feel I can do it best by casting off my real personality and going as a stranger. Besides, I haven't had an excuse for wearing a disguise ever before in my life."

"You mean you want to play."

Ben shook his head hopelessly at Helen's lack of imagination.

"Say this thing did turn out to be fishy. It would be an advantage then if Tomms had never seen me at his meeting."

"I give in," said Helen. "You want to wear a disguise. Go ahead."

The meeting hall of the Society was in a small street, a turning off Gray's Inn Road, close to King's Cross Station. It looked as though it had once been a chapel. The main door was a gloomy, Gothic affair, the roof of ugly Welsh slate and the brickwork gone that dingy colour that London's atmosphere works upon all masonry after a few years.

Helen and Ben separated outside the hall and entered singly, finding seats in different parts of the hall. There were about a hundred people there, but, as the hall could have comfortably seated three hundred, the audience had a scattered appearance. Little groups were isolated towards the back of the hall, while the front three rows of seats were filled completely.

Helen took a seat in the middle of the hall. She looked round and saw that there were more women than men present. She was not surprised. The Society's influence was wide. The audience held women who were obviously well-to-do and women who had that contained, pinched look of those who live by themselves in bed-sitting-rooms. The men seemed either fat, simple folk with the bright, expectant eyes of the credulous or else elderly, angular creatures who wore glasses, frowned seriously and fingered their chins. Helen wondered if anyone present had reached the seventh stage. Once or twice she found people looking at her and she was uncomfortably aware that most of the audience knew one another by sight and were curious about her. Perhaps, she decided, they had some way of telling into which stage people had struggled and she might be an obvious member of the first stage, attracting attention by her under-development. Across the hall she could see Ben rubbing his false moustache—the gum was probably making his skin itch—and waiting calmly for the meeting to begin.

The curtains were drawn from a small stage at the end of the hall to reveal a grand piano at which sat a young woman, her hair coiled into earphones. On the stage was set a long table behind which sat three people; a short, dumpy man with a long beard, Mr. Tomms, and on his left a plump, elderly woman with a friendly face who was in purple and wore a toque with a white veil.

The girl at the piano began to play and everyone rose and sang. The song was obviously known to all the members but their singing did not make the words clear enough for Helen to catch. The singing had that sibilant, panting quality as though everyone were quietly hissing at the piano.

The song finished, everyone sat down and then Mr. Tomms rose and read a few announcements about the Society's affairs which meant nothing to Helen. Helen decided that she liked Mr. Tomms. Amongst this odd collection of people, none of whom seemed to have much vigour, he stood out forcibly as a man in whom worked a tremendous vitality and sense of life. His voice boomed confidently around the hall, his eyes moved quickly from face to face and he held himself loosely yet boldly before them, assured of their favour and ready to prove himself capable of protecting them if the need arose. He spoke like a father to a rather large family of children who were somehow colourless and slow.

"Tonight we have with us," he was saying, "Leader Rackman of the Chelmsford Circle. Leader Rackman was one of the very first members of the Society and it is to his influence and labour that we are indebted for the lusty growth of the movement in Chelmsford. Leader Rackman is going to talk to you of a subject which has considerable topical interest and I know that you will give him your intelligent interest and sympathy."

He introduced Leader Rackman, who was the man with the beard, and then sat down.

To Helen's surprise Mr. Rackman had a strong, cultured voice and spoke well. For the next hour she listened, interested despite her amazement. Leader Rackman began with a brief résumé of the Society's progressive exercises for mind and body.

He explained their purpose and the benefits which came with them.

"There is a feeling amongst those who know little of the Society," he explained, "to see in us a cult of sun-worshippers. Nothing could be farther from the truth. We worship, as other people worship, the Great Mystery of Life. The One who is Eternal. But that does not preclude us from intelligently estimating the beneficial influence upon the mind and body of the sun's rays. The labourer in the fields knows the value of the sun for his crops, the convalescent by the sea-shore knows the strength which comes to him in the sunlight—they do not worship the sun, no more do we. But we try to understand the part played in life by the sun. From it comes light, and light is the essence of sight, and from seeing clearly comes the distinction of right and wrong, and to be right is to have might, the power of truth …"

Helen listened carefully, not always following Leader Rackman's logic, but interested in his words. He explained that the Universe moved to a definite rhythm. Every planet, every atom had a rhythm and it was only when the human body and mind could fall into rhythm with the general earth swing that it really functioned completely. It was necessary for each member to ascertain by experiment his or her proper rhythm length. He pointed out that with the sun this month nearing its solstice a conjunction of sunshine and exercises based upon each individual's rhythm length brought greater good than at any other time during the year. He proceeded to demonstrate a new rhythm exercise designed for this month and invited the members to stand up and practise it with him to the piano.

In a few moments the body of the hall was like a penguin rookery. Men and women bowed and swung towards one another, following the Leader's directions. Helen, to avoid being conspicuous was forced to join in the exercise. Across the hall she saw Ben, dipping and swaying from side to side. She saw too that he was having trouble with his moustache. The jerking of his head had loosened it and once she saw him come up from a low forward bow with a clean lip. The next time he straightened up the moustache had been restored, but it was now cocked a little on one side, giving him a rakish look.

"One! Two! Three! Four!" cried Leader Rackman enthusiastically, and the members dipped and jerked, their faces set in grim lines, their breath grunting from them as tight body belts and waistcoats pinched them, and the piano tinkled thinly at a tune which Helen recognised as having some relationship to "Pop Goes the Weasel." It was on every pop that they bowed forward vigorously. She was glad when the Leader raised his hand to indicate an end of the exercise.

Leader Rackman got a round of applause and there was no doubt that he had stirred his audience. A few people got up and asked him, breathlessly, questions which he answered carefully and conscientiously. When these had finished the lady in purple rose to her feet and explained that before the meeting broke up she would like to make a special announcement.

Helen had no idea what the special announcement was to be, but she could see that the woman was excited. Her voice shook with her excitement.

"I want you all to make a particular point of being here next week," she said. "Our dear Leader—" and she turned to Mr. Tomms "—has told me that next week he intends to make known his plans for the new rest homes for members which have become possible through the generosity of one of us who has now passed away. I won't say any more now, except to urge you all to be here."

The meeting broke up and for a while the gathering was animated as people stood about talking and greeting each other.

The young girl who had played the piano came across to Helen before she could get away and welcomed her.

"We're always glad to have newcomers. I hope you enjoyed the talk. Leader Rackman is such a force. You mustn't be disappointed because there are so few people here. That really means nothing. You see, this is only the meeting place for the Central London Branch—there are branches all over the country and in almost every suburb. It's summer, too, and people sometimes prefer to stay away from the meetings in order to

catch all the sunshine they can."

Helen murmured unintelligibly, and the girl went on:

"I wish I could be sure that I had found my right rhythm length. It's so important to get it exact. You've no idea what a difference it makes to you."

"That's true," said Helen, and she wondered if Ben were being interrogated about his rhythm length.

The girl left her, and a fat man, his face glistening still from his exercise, gripped her arm confidentially.

"You're fourth stage, aren't you? I can tell—it's a gift with me."

"I'm hot," said Helen, politely freeing herself.

"Earth emanations—very good for you ..." The man drifted away.

A tall, distinguished man, his teeth flashing constantly in a rictus, bowed to her and said sonorously: "Welcome."

Helen smiled nervously, not sure of the correct response, and was immediately involved in a monologue by the man giving a counter theory to Leader Rackman's about solstice exercises. She gathered that the Society was not without its inner critics, and was aware that the dignified gentleman strongly objected to the bowing part of the exercise as being "abdominally disturbing and without ethereal significance."

A question from her about Mr. Tomms brought a flood of praise. The dignified gentleman was enthusiastic about the Founder. Helen was surprised that a man who obviously enjoyed criticising should have nothing to say against Tomms, not even an insubstantial comment that might have been allowed to the faithful.

Helen got away at last and waited for Ben at the corner of the street. It was some time before he arrived.

"Well?" she questioned.

He was silent for a moment. Then he spoke, rather dolefully, Helen thought. "I talked to about half a dozen different people after the meeting. They're all screwy, of course, but they're sincere and they don't seem to have the slightest doubts about the good faith of Tomms and the Society. You can tell that. Quite frankly, I'm a little disappointed. I expected to find something wrong—but there isn't anything. It's just a rummy little society, that's all. It's sad, isn't it, to find that life is just a dull affair after all. There's madness, but no mystery. This moustache is the very devil, too!"

Helen said nothing. It was no time for words. She took his arm and they walked slowly along. Cars and buses rolled by them, people jostled them on the pavement. London turned noisily around them, but they did not hear it.

*   *   *   *   *

Mr. Pilchard was spending the evening with the Kirkstalls. It was a weekly custom. Mr. Pilchard was a butcher, not in a big way, but—and so much more desirable, Mrs. Kirkstall thought—in a comfortable way. Mr. Pilchard, like so many butchers, was round and plump, red-faced and good-natured, and a little husky in his speech, as though his breath, exhausted by the labyrinthine journey from his body, had little power left to spare for his voice. When he laughed it was a long and soft grunt, a wheezy, infectious expulsion of air as though some unseen force had gently pressed his great sides as a child presses a rubber ball with a hole in it.

Mr. Harold Pilchard was a widower of long standing, but he was no lover of the celibate life. For five years he had wanted to marry Mrs. Kirkstall and for five years Mrs. Kirkstall had been trying to make up her mind about him. Grace, who was used to her mother, was not surprised that she had not made up her mind about marriage in so many years. It frequently took her from waking until nearly noon to decide whether she should have any breakfast; and marriage, being a less urgent affair than breakfast, naturally admitted of much lengthier consideration.

"I could understand your mother, Grace, if it was a question of not wanting to marry an uninteresting butcher after being used to a naval man." Mr. Pilchard's proposals had reached the point of intimacy where they could be, and were, discussed with interest amongst the three of them. It was a topic which often lasted them a whole evening. "After all, once you've been used to a Navy man then other men must seem pretty dull fish. Well, I'll admit I ain't—" there was an occasional suggestion of illiteracy in Mr. Pilchard's speech which he could not conquer "—never climbed any rigging, nor know much about boats. I used to scull a bit when I was a boy. But there's nothing about steel you can tell me. Handle a cutlass? That would be child's play to me."

"They don't use cutlasses in the Navy now," put in Mrs. Kirkstall dreamily.

"'And-to-'and fighting—it still comes to that at times. If you know the right place to stick a pig I reckon there isn't any difference when it comes to stickin' a Chinee."

"Mr. Pilchard! You are a blood-thirsty one!" Grace shivered as Mr. Pilchard waved an imaginary knife and thrust his thumb at her dramatically.

"Ah, well," Mr. Pilchard sighed and cast a puzzled look at Mrs. Kirkstall. "She won't give me a 'Yes' and she won't give me a 'No.' Can't you help her decide, Grace? I'd be a good father to you. You haven't never had cause to grumble about the joints I send up. The best, they are …"

"Second marriages …" Mrs. Kirkstall's voice trailed away, leaving a cryptic silence.

"What's wrong with second marriages? Man was made for woman and woman for man."

"Mr. Pilchard!"

"Well, it's true, Grace."

"A woman should have time to think these things over. After all …"

"After all—what, Mother?"

"Well, as I was going to say, dear, after all, it isn't everyone that has to face a second marriage, and although I like Mr. Pilchard, I do feel I ought to think it over a bit more."

"But you have been thinking it over for five years, Mrs. Kirkstall!"

"That's not long. Some people are engaged longer than that, and, anyway, I'd rather take ten years deciding and be sure of not making a mistake. There's no drawing back once you've decided, you know."

"You make me hot!" cried Mr. Pilchard vehemently. "If I didn't know you was the only woman in the world, I don't know how I should have stood it all these years. Make up your mind quickly."

"I'll think about it while I'm getting the supper."

"I'll get the supper, Mother. You stop and talk to Mr. Pilchard." Grace got up and left the room. The supper would have been a long time coming if her mother had begun to get it.

She went into the kitchen and lit the gas stove. Mr. Pilchard had brought a packet of sausages. Grace began to fry them. She liked Mr. Pilchard and she thought her mother ought to marry him, but she knew it would have clone no good to try to influence her mother to make up her mind before she was ready. Vaguely, she had the feeling that her mother did not intend to make up her mind until—Grace hesitated to frame her thoughts with words—until things were different. She wanted to see her settled in life first. Their life together was very happy, and Mrs. Kirkstall saw no reason strong enough to prompt her to alter it until ... Next Sunday—how far away it seemed yet. It would be the first time she had gone anywhere with George.

She looked up and her eyes went to the kitchen window. She started and nearly dropped the frying-pan. From the gloom outside a pair of eyes, the pupils lit with the light from the room, stared in at her. She put her hand to her mouth and stopped a cry. The eyes disappeared.

Grace stood there, her heart thumping violently. Then she put down the pan and moved to the garden door. She was no coward and, her fear slipping from her, she was angry at the silly prank. If it was one of the boys from the neighbourhood she would have something to say to him. Why, anyone with a weak heart would have had a nasty turn.

She went out into the garden. There was no one there. She walked round the side of the house and saw that the front gate was off the latch. Someone had been in the garden. She leant over the gate and looked up and down the road. She could not see far in the dark. There was no one about. She stood there for a moment and then, as she was about to go back to the house, far down the street a figure moved from out of the shadows into the pale circle of a lamp's light. It was a man and he passed through the cone of light quickly, so quickly that Grace was undecided whether her eyes had tricked her when she fancied she noticed that he limped slightly.

He had limped, and she knew that walk well. Or had she imagined it, tricked by the play of light and shadows by the street lamp?

She was tempted momentarily to run after him. It couldn't be ... No, it couldn't ... She stood undecided. Then she went back to the kitchen, her mind active with speculations, her face pale and thoughtful.

When she took the supper in she was her usual self, but her mind for the rest of the evening was far from the conversation. She said nothing to the others about the face which had looked through the kitchen window.

"'Pon my Sam, Grace," said Mr. Pilchard, "you cook well. If your mother doesn't give me an answer very soon I'll be blowed if I don't set my cap at you. You wouldn't be so long making up your mind. I always say that sausages is delicate things. Most people will try to go cooking them in a rush and bustin' their jackets, but not Grace—she's got a proper sausage touch, and that's a compliment coming from a butcher."

Chapter Six

Grace and George went to Ealing. For part of the way they travelled on the same line by which they went to Town on weekdays, but the journey had no resemblance to those crushed morning passages for Grace. It was an adventure into romantic probability, and she had dressed herself in the spirit of the day. It had taken her—and her mother—more than an hour of doubt and renewed consideration to effect the final settlement of what would be right. She wore a silk lemon-coloured dress and over it a light summer coat that hung half-length. The light coat was an accommodating oatmeal colour and hid the iron singeing which marked the lemon dress just below the right shoulder blade. For hat Grace wore a little straw plate with a pleasantly curved brim, a hat which she had bought because it matched the dress, but which she never dared to wear at the saucy angle indicated by the girl in the millinery department. Grace wore it, as she felt all hats should be worn, so that it would protect her from rain. There was good sense in Grace's attitude towards hats, but little sober consideration of facts. Her straw hat would not have withstood five minutes' hard rain, so why bother to wear it fair and square?

If George had been on more intimate terms with her, he might have made that point. As it was, he merely wondered, without any desire to go deeply into the subject, why it was that a hat was attractive on one girl and not on another. And, for a girl who did not use make-up, yellow, he decided, was a dangerous colour. If Grace could have known all his thoughts during the first five minutes of their meeting, she would have left him for ever and returned desperately unhappy. Happily George kept his own counsel and did his best not to show that he was still irritated because he had promised to go with her.

As they sat in the electric train that was taking them to Ealing Broadway he pulled out a pipe and pouch.

"Why, I didn't know you smoked," said Grace, who had never seen him with pipe or cigarette before.

"It is a habit in which I take pleasure, but of which I do not altogether approve," answered George. "I have not so much money that I can afford to burn more than a very little of it. I smoke only on Sundays. Do you mind?"

Grace liked him for asking her permission, even though the carriage was a "smoker." George lit up and Grace, no expert, guessed from the smell that even on Sundays George's conscience would only allow him to smoke cheap tobacco. A man opposite confirmed this opinion as he moved further away with a look of reproach, a look that asked what he, a stranger, could have done to have deserved such an acrid attack.

"It is impossible to buy it in London," explained George as Grace coughed. "My father sends it for me from Kirkcudbright. It has a fanciful name—Tartan Mixture—but it is good tobacco and costs sevenpence the ounce."

"I like to see a man with a pipe," said Grace, her eyes on George's face as he puffed gently, releasing pungent clouds of smoke into the compartment.

At that moment Grace would not have bartered her place at George's side for any money or privilege. She was filled with the tingling elation that comes with true happiness. She felt suddenly and almost unworthily important and mature. Whatever their real relation, in the eyes of the world George belonged to her. People looked at them and saw them as one, as man and woman. For the first time in her life Grace knew that swift uprising, fierce and possessive, of pride which men and women stimulate in one another when they slip out of the casual contacts of life into the inner circle of intimacy and growing affection.

In her own thoughts Grace could liken the heightened awareness of every nerve in her body only to that exotic exhilaration she had known at Christmas, when Mr. Pilchard insisted on her drinking sherry—and even then the comparison was hopelessly inadequate.

They left the train at Ealing Broadway Station and walked out into the main road. Grace looked at Miss Logan's card and then at George.

"I wonder where Sheldon Road is? We'd better ask someone the way."

"There is no need."

"Do you know where it is then?"

"No, but I have the means of finding out. I have always found that it is not good sense to ask people the way. They are always too obliging, Miss Kirkstall, and, to avoid disappointing you, what they don't know they guess."

George pulled a small blue book from his pocket. It was an atlas and guide to London with an index of street names. He looked up Sheldon Road and traced its reference on the sectional map.

"There we are," he said. "You see it is not far."

It was not far and four o'clock was just striking as they stood outside "The Hollies." It was a small house in a quiet side road of detached houses. Fronting the pavement was a breast-high stone wall, at the back of which grew a thick holly hedge, screening the road save where the gateway was placed. From the gate one had a view of a small, creeper-covered house, baywindowed and slate-roofed. Before it ran a long stretch of lawn. A line of laurels and lilacs flanked the lawn on either side and marked the division from the neighbouring houses. It was one of those ordinary, comfortable little houses, well-kept and unpretentious, that can be found down any side-turning of a long-established suburb.

Grace and George went up the garden path to the door. Under the windows were beds of budding polyanthus roses and sweetsmelling stocks. George tugged at the brass bell pull and they heard the clangour deep within the house. It rang for a few seconds after George's hand had left the pull, a lingering sound. No one came to the door and there was no sound of movement within. They waited for a while.

"Ring again. They may not have heard," Grace said. Obediently, George pulled at the bell. He pulled longer and more vigorously. Grace put up her hand to stop him. She knew how annoying it was to have someone tugging at your bell a second time when you had heard their first ring and could not get away immediately to answer it. Perhaps they didn't have bells in Kirkcudbright, she wondered.

"But if they're not in the house, they're maybe in the garden at the back and they'll not hear it unless I pull it hard," protested George.

"Anyone could hear that noise," said Grace firmly.

This time the bell died hard. It jangled to a slow beat and ended in three distinct and solemn notes, released reluctantly, a thin echo of a bell tolling a tragedy.

No one came. A sparrow flew from the roof to the lawn with a quick whirring of wings and hopped towards the two curiously and across the houses came the noise of Sunday traffic along the main road. The house was still, wrapped in a hot silence. A faint smell of blistering paint came from the windows and doorway.

"It doesn't look as though there was anyone at home." Grace frowned.

"Are you sure she said this Sunday?" asked George.

"Quite sure. At four o'clock. It's just gone four. Do you think maybe she's given the maid the afternoon off and gone out herself, meaning to be back at four, and is late?"

"It's possible," said George and went on: "We'll go away and walk around the streets for ten minutes and then come back. Maybe she'll be back by then."

They went away and came back after a quarter of an hour. There was still no answer to the bell.

"Either she's forgotten about us and gone off to tea somewhere or else she's just a mad creature who goes about asking people to tea and then makes a point of not being in when they come." George was annoyed. He had no use for people without any sense of punctuality or of their proper obligations.

"I'm sure she's not forgotten us." Grace defended Miss Logan. "And she's not mad either. I'm going round the back. She may be asleep in the garden."

Before George could stop her, she had gone round the side of the house. He waited for her to return. She was not long.

"She's not there. Do you think we ought to go inside the house and see if she's there? Maybe she lives all alone and has had an accident. It would be awful to think—"

"We'll not go into the house," said George firmly. "In my opinion she is just a forgetful woman. As you know, I am not overfond of the sex, but I reserve my greatest antipathy for those who add forgetfulness to their other annoying traits."

"But she may be in there ill."

"You're being melodramatic, Miss Kirkstall. It would be unlikely that she lives alone in this house. Consider the number of rooms it must have—she could not keep them clean herself, and the garden—she obviously has a gardener. In my opinion she is a poor demented creature who has forgotten she ever met us."

"She was as sane as I am!"

For a moment George was tempted to make use of this opening. Then he controlled himself.

"Maybe, Miss Kirkstall. I'll admit that the whole question allows only of doubtful conjectures. I think we'd better go."

Grace had to agree with him. After all they could not go into the house and look round on the vague and remote chance that Miss Logan might be alone and ill. Besides … she was not sure that she wanted to go into the house. She looked at George for a moment as though she would say something. She decided to keep her own counsel. In their talk she had told Miss Logan where she worked. Tomorrow, she thought, there would be an apologetic letter from her … She followed George, half-angry, half-curious.

She cheered up, however, when he suggested that they should have their tea in Ealing. He had been aware of her disappointment. For her, Miss Logan's forgetfulness was harder to bear than for him. She had been anxious to please the old lady and now the absent-minded creature had rebuffed Grace's generous nature. George had a great respect for generosity. He took Grace to tea in a salmon-pink parlour with shaded alcoves and deep divans and forgot his dislike of such trimmings while she ate three fancy cakes and he explained carefully, and as simply as possible, the difference between the baroque and the rococo in architecture. Grace listened carefully and intelligently and quite forgot Miss Logan. When George talked his forehead contracted into little furrows that gave his face a serious, forceful look, a feeling of integrity and soundness.

"Did father smoke much?" Grace asked her mother that evening.

"Continuously," said her mother. "He always had a pipe in his mouth."

"I like to see a man with a pipe, don't you?" Grace asked the question dreamily.

"Not in bed, I don't," said Mrs. Kirkstall with something like vigour. "Your father used to burn the sheets. He was badtempered, too, when he couldn't get his proper tobacco. He used to have it sent to him from away somewhere ... Mrs. Kirkstall was dreaming too.

"Was it Tartan Mixture?" asked Grace gently.

"It was not. Your father was very particular about his tobacco. It was African Nigger Cut at sixpence an ounce and it smelt terrible, but I got to like it. I can still fancy I smell it about the house now ..."

Grace went to sleep, forgetting to tell her mother of Miss Logan's strange behaviour, and her mother quite forgot to ask about her outing.

Mrs. Kirkstall heard the full story at breakfast the following morning, and Grace went off to work teasing herself with the problem.

She could not understand why Miss Logan had asked her and George to tea and then, apparently, forgotten all about the invitation. She sought to find some reason, an hypothesis, however strained, that would account for the spinster's curious behaviour, but there was no suggestion which entirely satisfied her.

George, whom she happened to meet outside the station, walked with her to the office. He made no mention of Miss Logan and she realised that, with typical masculine practicalness, he had almost forgotten the woman. But she could not forget her. It was so strange and so impolite. She fully expected a letter of apology to be awaiting her at the office —Miss Logan knew her only at that address. There was no letter for her. There was, in fact, no letter of any kind. The post office authorities had left General Factotums alone that morning.

"No letters—no commissions—no work," said Ben almost happily, for it was a fine day for being lazy. "Don't think I'm glad about it," he said quickly seeing Helen look at him. "This business is moribund and I regret it, but facts are facts and I see no reason why I shouldn't face them cheerfully."

"That being so you intend to go out and do what?" asked Helen, seeing him reach for his hat.

"I don't know," was the reply. "I have been known to spend a whole morning just sitting on the Embankment staring at the river. But this isn't a river morning. I feel as though I shall go to the Zoo. I might even buy a couple of pounds of onions for the monkeys."

He went.

"I didn't know monkeys liked onions," said Grace when he had left. She and Helen were in the outer office.

"Well, they do."

"That's funny, because I don't suppose any onions grow in the hot countries where you find monkeys."

"I wouldn't be sure of that. Anyhow, quite a lot of English people like bananas, but they don't grow in England. It's an acquired taste. What are you looking in the dictionary for?" Helen, who was busy at a filing cabinet, looked across at Grace.

"I'm looking for a word—the word 'moribund' that Mr. Brown used. It's a thing I always do. Whenever I hear a new word I always look it up. I call it going on with my education, though I do think there's quite a lot of words that seem only another way of saying something very simple."

"I'll save you the trouble. It means dying, dead from the neck down. But you mustn't believe all Mr. Brown says about this business. It's doing very well and it's going to do better. Unless a thing is succeeding marvellously, Mr. Brown can't believe it's any good. He's one of those men who have to be managed—without his knowing it."

"I think George is a bit like that—"

"George? Who's George?" Helen asked quickly and saw Grace drop her head a little to hide her eyes.

94

"He's Mr. Crane."

"Oh, I know—the young man from the architect's office down below. I saw you going off home with him one night."

"That's the one."

"He looks a nice, sensible young man."

"Oh, he is, very sensible. He's Scottish. I went to Ealing with him yesterday."

"To Ealing—whatever for?"

"Well, we went to tea with someone. At least, we were going to tea with someone, but then we had it alone—in a café place." Grace, who had been longing to tell someone about her Sunday adventure, found herself confiding the whole story to Helen. Helen listened with real interest. She liked Grace, liked her for her common sense, her good nature, and for the ordinariness of her mind. She was the good, solid stuff that made comfortable clean homes and cooked satisfying, healthy meals for menfolk. She was the kind who would have three children and worship them in between scolding them; who would have a dog and a cat about the house and call them Spot and Tibby; who would visit the cinema once a week with her husband, leaving the children with a neighbour, would attend church fairly regularly and take in a picture paper for the sake of its strip cartoon. She was destined to be an English house-wife, a fond wife and a loving mother. Helen liked her for all these things. She saw—with a less sentimental eye—that, with the help of the right clothes and apt cosmetics, Grace could be made to look smart and attractive. George—she could read his reluctance in Grace's account—was a fool to be so slow; but then he was a Scot, and that for Grace, apparently, made a great deal of difference. One made allowances for foreigners.

"You mean to tell me that this good lady asked you to tea and then forgot all about you and went out?"

Grace nodded. "Yes, isn't it strange? I thought the least she might have done would have been to have written to me and explained.

I expected a letter this morning. She was so nice and kind, I can't understand how she could have been so rude. It worries me a bit, because—" Grace hesitated.

"It shouldn't worry you. Old ladies often do peculiar things."

"She wasn't like that, Mrs. Brown, really. But it isn't that.

You see, I'm sure there was someone in the house all the time."

"You're what?"

"Yes, I'm sure. I didn't say anything to George at the time, because he was already cross about the whole affair and, anyway, there wasn't anything he could have done. But, you see, when I went round the back of the house to see if anyone was there I distinctly saw the curtains in one of the rooms move and a man's face draw back. I'm sure of it. There was a man in the house and he was watching me. I know you'll probably think I imagined it— that's what George would have said—but it's the truth. There was a man in the house."

"Perhaps this Miss Logan has a brother who lives with her?"

"I don't think so. She said she was lonely. Anyway, why couldn't he answer the door?"

"Well, that is strange, I must say. This Miss Logan. Good Lord!" Helen exclaimed suddenly, a thought striking her. "Miss

Logan, you said her name was? Miss Victoria Logan?"

"That's it. But why?"

"What does she look like? You did say she came into the Inn on business with the Society for Progressive Rehabilitation, didn't you?"

"Why, yes, Mrs. Brown. But I don't really know much about her. I only learned her name when she invited us to tea. Before that I always called her the purple lady. She was big and plump and always wore purple."

After that Helen scarcely listened. This Miss Logan, she was fairly sure, was the same person she had heard give out an announcement the week before and, what was more interesting, the name had a familiar ring which she recognised now. It was one of the names in Colonel Hasted-Halifax's will; his "dear friend" to whom he had left three oil-paintings.

"Do you think there might be something wrong?" Grace finished.

"You can't tell." Helen moved about, getting her hat and gloves. "Probably not. There may be a letter of apology for you tomorrow morning. But, anyhow, I shouldn't worry. There was nothing you could have done. Now be a good girl and hold the fort here, will you, until I get back?"

"You're going out?"

"Yes, I'm going to the Zoo."

Helen went, leaving a mystified Grace. The Browns, she decided were nice people. Yet they had their faults. They were apt to lose interest in a subject quickly and their movements were so erratic that it was often impossible to divine what reasons lay behind them.

Chapter Seven

Helen went to the Zoo. She lagged a while through the Botanical Gardens, admiring the Russell lupins and the early roses. Some day, she thought, she and Ben would have a house with a garden—perhaps in the country—and not a flat with a couple of window boxes that reluctantly nourished spindly mignonette. They could go and live in the country now, of course, only Ben wasn't a countryman and he would rebel from boredom in a month. It was not enough to love the country; you had to learn how to live in it before you could be happy, and the best learners were old people. One was either born and stayed in the country or one retired to it. Her hair would go white rather nicely since it was fair, and Ben would have a couple of dogs who would be the curse of their lives going off rabbiting, and he would be enthralled by the mystery of brussels sprouts and cauliflowers. She walked through the turnstiles, planning a bucolic end for Ben.

Ben was not in the monkey house, so she went straight to the sea-lion and seal pool. Ben was there, leaning on the railings watching the smooth performance of the seals. It was a joy to watch the way they moved round their home, swiftly, effortlessly, on the surge of a long, shining sweep of water.

"How man has the impudence to perform his splashing antics in the water after watching these paragons of grace, I cannot imagine," he said when he saw Helen. "From this moment I swear I will never swim again."

"You always say that after you've been here, and you always do swim again," Helen pointed out as she led him away to a vacant seat.

"Man is a clumsy imitator." Ben ignored her. "He swims badly and he flies noisily. Where do we go from here—and why aren't you working?"

"I am working; sit still and listen to me. The name Victoria Logan means something to you?"

"It does. She was left three oil paintings by a now dead Colonel; subject of paintings unknown, but I am prepared to make guesses."

"Never mind the guesses. You remember the good lady in purple who spoke at last week's meeting of the Society?"

"I do. She urged everyone to come along to the next weekly meeting, which takes place tomorrow night. But what of it?"

"That good lady was Miss Victoria Logan."

"I am not surprised. She probably met the Colonel through the Society. I repeat—what of it?"

"Have you made up your mind about that Society?"

"I have. I intend to dictate my report this afternoon to our quite unnecessary typist and to post it to Mr. Halifax this evening."

"Then listen to this." Helen told him about Grace's visit to Ealing. Ben listened politely, his eyes on a distant laburnum tree, where a family of Zoo sparrows were holding revel. Some day, he decided, some poet would pay homage to the London sparrow, to the little black-chested bullies who fight and scramble over their quiet brown mistresses amongst the rumble of wheels and the hoot of horns, to the ubiquitous pillagers who steal from lion's den and hotel dustbin, to the noisy gutter-pipe serenaders of morning, foggy or clear. And the sparrows would block the poet's drain-pipe with their nests and pick the petals from his crocuses for thanks.

"Now doesn't all that seem a little mysterious to you?" Helen looked at him. His face, in profile, was set calmly, his mouth pursed a little forward.

"Odd is a better word, but I could think of a hundred different explanations. Apart from that, what has it got to do with us?"

Helen did not answer and Ben looked at her and smiled. He knew exactly what she was up to. "You know my feelings about the Society," he said. "You know I think it's a one-eyed affair, but, for all that, there is nothing wrong about it. That meeting and the talk I had with some of the members told me that, and that's the kind of report I shall send it. I'll admit that I hoped to find something very different, but I didn't. I was disappointed, but it's no good ignoring facts. And now you come along trying to work up my hopes all over again. Don't protest, dear! It's very sweet of you and that's one of the reasons why I love you—you're always trying to make things happen as I want them to happen. But you can't turn this goose of a Society into a phoenix. This Miss Logan is probably an eccentric who forgot all about those two. You see—she'll be at the meeting tomorrow night. You go along and see if I'm not right—and I should take Grace with you. I'll bet the old lady will either apologise handsomely and make another invitation or else she'll not recognise Grace."

"Will you come?"

"I will not. I shall stay at home and try to work out my proper earth rhythm."

Helen made no protest. Ben was right, of course. He knew what she was doing. In her own heart she felt that there was nothing wrong with Miss Logan. It was only that the affair had turned out so tamely that she had snatched at the slightest chance of its developing into a mystery, a task to suit Ben's hopes. It was irritatingly unnecessary of Ben, however, to tell her what she was doing.

"You see," Ben went on, "we both suffer from a very common and modern disease. We're restless. We want to do something different from what most people have to do. Unluckily for us, we are forced into the immediate compromise of earning a living at one thing while we scout around for the right thing. We have a living, our bread and a certain amount of butter and jam, and when we started General Factotums we thought we'd found what was wanted. Well, it was a good starting point, but unfortunately once we were started we found that it was a familiar old track that we were following. Life's just refused to do a song and dance for us especially. It's the same old life, without much excitement, without much mystery. If you want those you've got to go to fiction. Still, in our way, we do a certain amount of good and get a little more fun from things than we should in most other jobs, so let's be cheerful about it and remember that you either die of the disease or become inured to it—there's no cure that I know of."

"Let's go and see the vultures," said Helen. "I feel rapacious and predatory."

That afternoon Ben dictated his report for Mr. Halifax on the Society. Grace took it down and was quietly curious about it all. She had known nothing of the commission. Now she knew why Mr. Brown had sent her out for the Society's literature. Half-way through the report Ben stopped and looked across at her seriously.

"I don't know whether my wife has made it clear to you, Miss Kirkstall, but you understand that all the official matters you deal with in this place are entirely confidential."

"Of course, Mr. Brown. I wouldn't dream—"

"Naturally, Grace, naturally, I didn't think you would, but I felt I ought to mention it formally." Ben smiled and Grace smiled back. He had called her Grace instead of Miss Kirkstall. She felt as though she really were part of General Factotums. She went on writing shorthand as Ben delivered himself of his findings.

" 'To summarise the whole report, it would appear that the Society for Progressive Rehabilitation is a perfectly legitimate organisation—its theories may be peculiar—but its conduct seems open to no suspicion. That its affairs seem to be largely in the hands of one man is not unusual—the position is ultimately the same in nearly all such organisations—and it is only right to add that Mr. Tomms seems to enjoy the confidence and goodwill of all the members so far as it is possible to ascertain this.' That's all, Grace. I want that typed separately and sent with the letter I gave you." Ben leaned back in his chair and shouted through the open door into the outer office to Helen.

"I said our fee was three guineas. Do you think I should make it five? He seems to have plenty of money."

"What do you think? Has he got three or five guineas' worth of information?" Helen called back.

"Being truthful, I should say it was worth about ninepence."

"Better say five guineas, then. The figure five is better than three. It'll hypnotise him into thinking he's got something good for his money. Figures always impress rich men—the right figures, that is."

"Make it five, Grace," said Ben.

When Grace came out and began her typing Helen shut the door on Ben and, motioning to Grace to continue her work so that the noise of the keys would make her voice less distinct, she said:

"When you've finished that report and Mr. Brown's signed the letter, Grace, I don't want you to post it. just put it into your desk and keep it there until I ask for it."

"But, Mrs. Brown, I—"

"It's quite all right. I know what I'm doing. And, by the way, if you're free tomorrow evening, I would like you to come to a meeting with me. We shall probably meet your friend Miss Logan there and we can ask her what happened to her on Sunday. Can you manage it?"

"Why, I think … Well, I don't—" Grace did not like things to happen too quickly to her. She preferred to have time to sort them out.

"If you don't want to come, you must say so." Helen told her what the meeting was.

"I shall be glad to come," said Grace, not sure whether she was telling the truth, but feeling that Helen wanted her to come and that it was her duty to comply with her employer's request. The question of the meeting made her lose some of the curiosity she had originally felt about the delaying of Ben's report on the Society.

She went on with her typing, her fingers following the keys automatically, but her brain was busy with thoughts of Miss Logan, of the Society for Progressive Rehabilitation, of this Mr. Halifax … There was something going on. To Grace any suggestion of goings-on was like the scent of a laid-up game bird to a pointer. She stiffened mentally, came to a point and waited, tremulous with a delicious uncertainty and excitement.

She was still thinking about it when she arrived home. She and her mother were going down to watch Mr. Pilchard playing in the local bowling tournament. Mr. Pilchard swore that he played better when they watched, though Grace knew it was only that he wanted to show off before her mother.

"That Mr. and Mrs. Brown," she said as she waited for her mother to finish her toilet; "they're a funny couple. I don't know that I've got the depth of them yet."

"No, dear. Do you mind if I borrow one of your hankies?"

"No. It seems that I've got myself into a confidential business— not that I mind, but it makes you curious at times. You can't help being curious, one way and another."

"I'm sure it's all right, dear …" Mrs. Kirkstall looked round weakly for her hat which Grace was holding for her.

"I hope it is," said Grace, slightly disappointed that she had not roused her mother's real interest, "because I like the job and I don't want it to finish yet. Yellow does suit you, mum. I'm sure when Mr. Pilchard sees you he'll be put right off his game. Dazzled by your beauty, as they say …" She giggled and together they left the house to dazzle and encourage Mr. Pilchard.

*   *   *   *   *

Mr. Tomms enjoyed public speaking. He never felt that a man was being privately immodest to acknowledge in his own heart the pleasure which came from having and holding the attention of a meeting. He was proud of his Society, proud of its history and proud because it was from his brain, by his work, that it had grown. He had made it; it was his. What a man has made he can destroy. Mr. Tomms knew that. He realised that without him the Society would lose its focal point, would have its character weakened and gradually lapse into the dusty death that waits for all organisations which have lost their spirit.

These thoughts were going through his mind as he spoke now.

"You have waited long and patiently," he was saying, "and I—and the rest of the Committee—am grateful to you for your restraint. I don't have to recapitulate to you all the details which have made this thing possible. Most of you know who was our benefactor. Tonight, you are to witness the beginning of the work which Colonel Hasted-Halifax made possible for us. We are planning to build and maintain six Homes of Rehabilitation, to be placed in various districts, not yet decided upon. These homes will be centres of rest and re-energation." They loved a word like that, and so did he. "To these homes, members who are out of tune with life, who have lost their faculty of rhythmic synchronisation will be able to withdraw in order to rehabilitate themselves for world life once more. These homes have been designed to our demands by an excellent firm of architects and tonight you have the first plans for your inspection." Mr. Tomms pointed to the sides of the hall. Along each wall stood three easels, draped with black cloth. As he spoke, the young girl who usually played the piano moved down the right-hand side and removed the draperies. Another member did the same for the easels on the opposite side. The boards were revealed, bearing large plans in various elevations of the Homes of Rehabilitation. The members stirred. Mr. Tomms passed one hand over his long white hair and went on.

"They are for your approval, for your criticism. Sites, of course, have still to be found. It is a long task, but it will be done. You have seen the beginning and I pray that we shall be granted the joy of witnessing the end."

He sat down in the luxury of robust applause and then the meeting broke up and members crowded around the easels. The plans were in duplicate sets on each side of the hall.

Helen and Grace moved to the left-hand side. The largest crowd was round the middle easel which showed a general perspective sketch of the Home.

"It's very modern, isn't it?" whispered Grace, peering over the shoulder of a tall, thin man. "But what's it all for?"

"It's a kind of convalescent home," explained Helen. The Home was really a splendid building, plain and functional, and yet with a simple beauty. The drawing suggested that inside there would be light, rest and comfort … Around her the members were politely elbowing one another and talking excitedly.

"Excellent! Excellent!" exclaimed one man, bereft of any other word by the wonder of the building. Helen heard him swallowed into the crowd, thrown up and again submerged, his voice dying and falling.

"And the door. See it, my dear. The door is the focal point of the whole building—and so it should be. Into that doorway go the weary, the unhappy, and the maladjusted. And out of it pass those same people, healthy, happy and in rhythm with life."

"Yes, that was the aim of the Committee, to focus the whole design upon the door. I know some people say the fireplace is the focal point of a room—so it may be, but of the complete building it must be the doorway. Dear Mr. Tomms. Did you notice how happy he looked tonight?"

Grace and Helen had by now been forced into the front line of people about the easel. The crowd was moving now from one easel to another and there was more room.

Grace caught Helen's arm suddenly and pointed to the plan.

"Look, Mrs. Brown. Look!"

"What's the matter?"

"It's him. See there's his name."

At the bottom of the plan were the words, "Craddock and Couch, Architects," and then, in the right-hand corner, in very small print, the sign, "del. George Crane," and a date.

"So it is," said Helen.

"What does 'del' mean?"

"It means that your George drew the plans. Aren't you proud of him?"

Grace did not answer. She was looking at the plan again, but this time with an entirely new interest. She wanted to impress upon her memory every line, every hatching and detail of the sketch. George had done this. She had no idea he was so clever. Until this moment architecture had been a hazy affair of buildings; now it was an art, a mystery that was far beyond her reach, but somehow very near to her, because George understood it and practised it. To meet the plan in this hall was like suddenly meeting George himself …

Helen drew Grace gently away. She could understand the girl's feeling. She had felt something of the same emotion when she and Ben had gone to Germany together for the first time and Ben had begun to speak German with a fluency that almost made a stranger out of him. It was pleasant to make discoveries about a man you loved, discoveries that increased his uniqueness.

"You mustn't forget that we want to find Miss Logan," Helen reminded her.

"She can't be here," said Grace. "I've looked all around and I can't see her."

"Neither can I. I wonder—" Helen broke off as the young girl pianist came gushing towards her.

"Oh, so you've come again this week. How lovely! And you've brought a friend. Isn't that just the way! First the ideals of the Society attract you and then you must pass on the good news to your friends. Isn't this a wonderful night? Do you know—" she was suddenly confidential and it was difficult for Helen to prevent herself leaning her head forward in the conspiratorial bow that the girl's tone demanded "—do you know, I knew this morning that this was to be a happy day. For the first time, I really felt that I had achieved my proper rhythm length. I swayed so—" she began to teeter "—and suddenly I knew that I had it right. From that moment everything was changed …" She broke off in an ecstasy.

Grace looked at Helen curiously. There were some funny people about, to be sure.

"Your friend, here." The girl indicated Grace. "Does she know all about rhythm?"

"I like dance music," offered Grace uncertainly.

"Ah, music. What a pity you did not hear Leader Snelgrove of Bristol last month. He called his talk 'The Music of the Spheres'— so original." She took a deep breath preparatory to plunging into an explanation of the music of the spheres, but Helen took advantage of the pause and said:

"I don't see Miss Logan here tonight."

The girl turned a quick look on Helen. She did not answer directly.

"She seemed so anxious last week that everyone who could should come that I fully expected her to be here," went on Helen.

"Yes, I know," the girl answered. "I can't think why she hasn't come along. It's so unlike her. And she's a third stage person—they seldom miss appointments or break promises. She was so keen, as you say …" She drifted away from them as though she had no real desire to discuss Miss Logan.

Grace travelled home convinced that it really did take all sorts to make a world. If she hadn't been to the meeting she would never have believed that people could have been so silly as to be serious about such nonsense. From which it will be seen that Grace was profoundly practical in her outlook. She had no time for any more mysticism than was permitted by the Church which she supported vaguely.

"What it all comes to," she explained to her mother as she undressed, "is that they're just a lot of men and women who have more time and money than they know what to do with. I almost wonder at Geo—Mr. Crane—bothering to design their silly rest homes for them."

"Mr. Crane is the young man you went to Ealing with?" Her mother raised her head from the woman's magazine she was reading until Grace should get into bed. "You must bring him to supper one night, Grace dear. I'm sure he and Mr. Pilchard would get along very well."

Grace did not answer. She turned her face from her mother, but quite forgot that the mirror permitted her mother to see the flush which had uncontrollably taken possession of her cheeks.

In their flat Helen, too, was preparing for bed. Ben was already in bed, reading and unwilling to talk.

"She wasn't there. I was right about that, you know," declared Helen.

"It doesn't signify," answered Ben absently.

"It does—at least, I think so." Helen brushed her fair hair vigorously. The hard bristles over her scalp made her feel like purring. "Anyway, I'm going to Ealing tomorrow to call on her."

"Whatever for? I've sent in my report."

"That doesn't matter. She was a friend of the Colonel's and she's a member of the Society and—if she's there, which I doubt, somehow—she could give us her opinion of Mr. Tomms. That's what Mr. Halifax wants. We could send in a supplementary report."

"And charge another five guineas, I suppose," suggested Ben derisively. "He's not that gullible."

"We'll see," said Helen. "I think you gave up the affair far too soon. But that was typical of you. Unless things go as you want them to, you lose interest. You've no stamina, no backbone, no imagination. You're a drifter, a worthless, ineffectual nondescript, and why I gave up a perfectly good stage career to harness myself to you for life I cannot at this moment possibly imagine." Helen stopped, exhausted, and she smiled a little foolishly at her reflection.

Ben raised himself upon one elbow and looked at her curiously. "You know, Mrs. Brown, I've had exactly the same feeling about myself at times, and now you've discovered it. But you won't noise it about, will you? It must be kept a family secret."

When Helen was in bed Ben stretched out his hand for the light switch. "Good night, darling." He jerked the switch and there was silence, a silence broken after a few moments by the thump of the book he had been reading falling off the bed. It fell with its covers spread-eagled and, had there been any light, one might have read the title, *Gold Goes Begging*, by Dorian Ballard.

Chapter Eight

At ten o'clock the next morning Helen stood outside "The Hollies," Sheldon Road, Ealing. If Miss Logan were in she meant to pose as someone interested in the Society who had heard of Miss Logan's connection with it and was anxious for more information. It was not a good reason, but it would serve with a woman like Miss Logan. The house did not present quite such a pleasant and reposeful appearance as when Grace and George had visited it. It was drizzling heavily with that dull, determined monotony which is characteristic of summer drizzle that follows a long spell of fine weather. It was a chastising rain—a damping, depressing onslaught that seemed to express mostly the admonition that English people need not think that they could forget their umbrellas in June just because the sun had shone regularly for a week or two, and it was about time that they recognised that the sun was only a flashy sort of fellow who could not be relied upon from one minute to another.

Helen stood on the doorstep, closed her umbrella, and shook a spray of drops around her, marking the step which, she noticed, had been recently hearthstoned.

She tugged at the brass pull and heard the bell ring within the house. There was no answer. She counted deliberately, refusing to scamper the last ten, up to fifty and then she pulled again, vigorously.

This time the door opened while her hand was still on the pull. Helen was so surprised that for a moment she could do no more than stare at the person who stood before her.

It was a woman. A long-faced, tired-looking woman who wore a dirty blue-and-white apron and black gumboots. Underneath the apron was a grey dress with a cheap red brooch at the throat, a throat from which rose a lean, brown neck that inclined forward from the body, so that the shoulders appeared hunched and drawn. The woman's expression was gloomy and spiritless; her flesh fell away from her bones as though it had no life and her face was curiously apathetic. Even her eyes were without sparkle— grey, stained balls that seemed full of sleep. "Hullo," she said, and waited.

Helen recovered herself and decided, from the greeting, that here was one who did not normally answer the door. "Is Miss Logan at home?"

"She isn't," came the answer.

"She isn't?" Helen frowned and, as she regarded the woman, began to think quickly. She was suddenly tremendously anxious to get inside the house and she knew that to do so she would have to have a good reason for passing this incurious, exceptional creature.

"Do you mean to say she's not expecting me?"

"I don't know what she's expecting. She isn't here. She's away."

"But didn't she get my letter on Monday?"

"Not on Monday she didn't. She wasn't here then."

"Oh, then that explains it. I'm a friend of hers—from Manchester—and I said I would call today. I'm in London on a little holiday. But I don't understand. She wrote to me that she ..."

"You'd better come inside. I don't want this rain blowing over the hall. I only polished it this morning." The woman held the door open and Helen went in. She was shown into the sittingroom to the right of the hall.

"Your letter's probably amongst that lot," explained the woman, nodding to a pile of mail that was on the table. Helen looked through it and, picking out a private envelope that seemed addressed in a feminine hand, said, "Yes, this is it." Then, noticing the postmark, which was Oxford, added quickly, "I wrote it from Oxford where I was staying with friends. But where is Miss Logan?"

"I dunno," answered the woman. "I don't live here. Mrs. Dalby's the name. I come in three times a week for her. She don't keep a maid. I come in special when she wants me. Fred does the garden."

"Fred?"

"Fred Dalby. My husband. I married him. He's nightwatchman at Harridges. I go and sit with him some nights. Doesn't like to be alone much. Interferes with your sleep, though." She gave the biographical details without any vivacity. "But where has Miss Logan gone? I was so looking forward to seeing her."

"I dunno. There was a note for me here Monday morning—I've got a key—saying she's gone off on a holiday, but she didn't say where."

"Does she often do that?"

"Can't say as I've known her do it before."

"But isn't that strange?"

"Depends. I suppose it is when you come to think of it."

"I suppose it is," agreed Helen, privately amazed at the woman's incurious nature. To any normal charlady, the sudden skipping of one of her "ladies" on a holiday for an unknown destination would have been rich material. Mrs. Dalby apparently concealed a vigorous originality under her depressing appearance. "But what about her mail?"

"She said she'd write me where to send it later."

"I see."

"I'm scrubbing the kitchen out. I'm going to do this room next."

For a moment Helen did not appreciate the depth of suggestion behind this utterance. Then she realised that Mrs. Dalby was implying that she would like her to go so that she might return to her kitchen and get on with her work.

"Well, I'm disappointed. I did so want to see her. I wonder if you'd mind if I sat down and wrote her a note before I go."

Mrs. Dalby signified her assent by a nod and walked across to the little escritoire that stood by the window. Helen followed her and took a sheet of note paper. She sat down and, taking her pen from her bag, unscrewed it. Mrs. Dalby watched her.

Helen scribbled a note to Miss Logan. She made it as real as she could. Mrs. Dalby might seem incurious, but, after she was gone, there was always the chance that she might get busy with a kettle and steam the letter open.

Helen sealed her note and placed it on top of the escritoire. She noticed that the top of the desk was littered with tiny ornaments as was the whole room. It was a crowded, carpeted, curtained room, the walls plastered with pictures and photographs, the chairs cushioned and antimacassared.

"Have you worked for Miss Logan long?" asked Helen as she stood up.

"Nearly a year."

"I thought I didn't remember you from the last time I was here. That was more than a year ago."

"That was in Mrs. Raikes's time."

"Yes, I remember."

"She left because she couldn't put up with Miss Logan's ways." Mrs. Dalby was suddenly almost communicative and Helen realised that a discussion of her predecessor made her voluble. "She was sacked, really. Smoking it was. She liked a quiet whiff in the kitchen sometimes, and you know how Miss Logan hates smoking in the house."

"Is she still as particular?" Helen played up to Mrs. Dalby, hoping to lead her on to more illuminating subjects.

"Particular—that ain't the word. There's no one ever smoked a cigarette in this house that I can remember. None of her friends would dare, and she never let any callers smoke. Why, she don't like my Fred to smoke his pipe in the garden hardly …" Mrs. Dalby was stirred at this thought. She turned to the door suddenly. "I must get back to my kitchen," she said and Helen saw that she intended to gossip no more.

Helen was moving to follow her when she remembered her bag was still on the escritoire. She turned back to get it —Mrs. Dalby went out through the door—and as she picked it up Helen noticed what had escaped her at first. A little glass pin-tray stood on top of the escritoire and it had been used as an ash-tray. In it lay half a cigarette.

When Helen joined Mrs. Dalby in the hall, the half-cigarette was in her handbag.

"You'll see Miss Logan gets my note when she returns?"

"I will," said Mrs. Dalby and she pocketed, without comment or change of expression, the half-crown which went with the request. "But when she'll be back goodness only knows. It's nice to be some people."

With this cryptic remark Helen was shown out. She walked down the road very much occupied with thoughts of Mrs. Dalby. The sitting-room had not been dusted for at least two days. She had noticed that on first entering it; and the pin-tray had probably not been emptied for some time. Mrs. Dalby probably hadn't been in the room to clean up that week. But somebody had smoked in the room recently and somebody who had been no friend of Miss Logan, for her friends were sure to know about that foible. Suddenly Helen was in a hurry to get to Ben.

"I think," said Ben when Helen told him her story, "that you've got a bee in your bonnet about the whole affair. There are plenty of ways that cigarette could have come innocently into Miss Logan's house, and there's no reason on earth why an eccentric old lady shouldn't suddenly pop off on a vacation without leaving any forwarding address. I've had the same desire myself at times!"

"That's what you say," Helen defended herself vigorously. "But if you knew Miss Logan as Mrs. Dalby seems to know her, you'd believe that it's almost impossible for a cigarette end to get into her house. None of her friends would dream of smoking and no visitor would get the chance. Wouldn't any casual caller ask for or wait until permission to smoke was given? If you admit that, then the only way the cigarette end could have come into the house is from someone who didn't care about Miss Logan's feelings either because she wasn't there or because she couldn't make any protest."

"Poppycock! In a minute you'll be talking about your intuition. I've told you definitely that I've finished with this affair and it's no good your trying to bring me back into it by scraping up odd little, meaningless bits of so-called clues which lead nowhere. I'm going out!"

Ben got up and left the office. He really was annoyed with Helen. Once she got an idea into her head, she worried it to death, bullied it in an effort to make it turn her way instead of the natural way. He knew why she was doing it over this particular case and he felt additionally annoyed because she was playing the traditional woman's part of encourages to a despondent male. It was more the vision of himself as a despondent male than of Helen as encourager-in-chief that gave rise to his annoyance.

He got as far as the little sunken garden by the fountain and sat down on one of the seats. From where he sat he could see the window of General Factotums and the open door of Number One stairway.

Life, he thought—and when Ben was in the mood for analysis he found it convenient, as most people do, to start with a generalisation about life—was for the majority of folk a pleasant, but by no means exciting, affair. It so seldom ran as colourfully and interestingly as it appeared in books. There were an awful lot of people and concerns in Fountain Inn, for instance, but nothing tremendously exciting ever happened to them. Even amongst the inhabitants of Number One stairway, what could a novelist find to make fiction from? The girls in the Granada Finance office were just girls, full of their little hopes and fears, muddling and smiling through life. There was no future film star hidden amongst them. In Craddock and Couch's office there bent over drawing-boards, no coming Wren or Lutyens, but only pleasant, capable assistants who would go on in their pleasant, capable way for the rest of their lives—until what? Until they were as settled and confirmed in their daily business as was old Parcross, who had been around the Inn for donkey's years. Even Mr. Rage, who had been a rogue, had little colour about him. All he could ever do would be to set into movement a sordid court case for fraud.

And Mr. Tomms! Ben grinned to himself, his good humour returning, so that he was quickly ashamed of the annoyance he had held against Helen. Poor old Tomms! It was unfair to the man the way Helen was trying to work up something against him for his sake. He thought of the cigarette she had brought back from Ealing. It was a hand-rolled cigarette, and had been rolled by someone who was expert at the business. Whenever he tried to roll a cigarette the thing finished by looking like a young bolster with the stuffing trailing out of the ends. Rolling cigarettes was an art, and the Ealing cigarette had been the work of a master. The half that remained was tight, well-packed with a dark, closely cut tobacco, and the paper was of a brand new to Ben. On the butt end was a small, six pointed star encircled with the words *Etoile d'Or*. Out of the hundreds of cigarette ends lying around, how could one particular brand ever be isolated? Ben looked around the paving by the seat, and within a radius of a few yards there were, he counted, thirty cigarette ends. He was suddenly conscious of the general untidiness of smokers.

He sat, thinking about cigarettes and smoking for a while and priming himself to return and apologise to Helen for being so rude about her attempts to gain his interest in Miss Logan and the Society for Progressive Rehabilitation—for she insisted on linking the two firmly together. And as he sat there, his eyes on the doorway of Number One stairway, he saw in the space of ten minutes four people emerge. First came Mr. Parcross, an umbrella on his arm, who slipped away into Holborn through the gate. Then Mr. Tomms, bare-headed, and conducting to the gateway a tall, broad-shouldered man whose face was shadowed by a wide-brimmed hat. Tomms came back after a while and as he entered the doorway, was passed by Hindle, who moved across to his quarters.

As Hindle disappeared into the lodge at the gate, Ben got up and moved across the lawn. He walked slowly, his eyes on the ground, his mind still occupied with the untidiness of mankind. Even in the Inn there were bus tickets blown in from Holborn, empty match boxes and the inevitable cigarette ends. He entered the hallway of Number One stairway and began to climb. He had not mounted more than a few steps when he stopped. There on the next step up was a half-smoked cigarette, but this time, an added breach of tidiness, the cigarette was still smoking where it had been inadequately screwed out by someone's heel. Ben raised his foot to extinguish the cigarette. His foot never fell on the cigarette. Something caught his eye and he bent swiftly and picked up the end. On the butt, the gold showing clearly, was a six pointed star and the words *Etoile d'Or*.

Ben held the butt, his mind suddenly awake to several exciting inferences. The cigarette had not been on the stairs long and he himself had seen everyone come in and out for the last fifteen minutes. He began to race up the stairs to the office.

An hour later that morning Helen was sitting at the inner window of General Factotums, the window which looked out to the carefully polled lime trees and the lawn of the courtyard. She was sitting watching the entrance gateway —which she could only do by squeezing into the side of the slightly rounded window seat and craning her neck. At her side were her hat, bag and gloves.

She was alone and excited and happy. Ben had returned to the fold in a way she had never imagined. Four people—Mr. Parcross, Mr. Tomms, old Hindle, and a broad-shouldered stranger—and one of them had been in Miss Logan's house and, either against her wishes, or unknown to her, had smoked an *Etoile d'Or* cigarette. Ben was already out, getting into touch with Hindle and through him Parcross. She could not believe it was Hindle. He looked like a pipe man.

She leapt to her feet suddenly, grabbed her hat and bag and flew from the room.

Helen clattered down the stairway, out into the courtyard and ran through the great gateway and on to the Holborn pavement. For a moment she stood still, questing on either stretch of the pavement. Then, walking briskly Citywards, she saw the middlesized, portly figure of Mr. Tomms, a black Italian hat set on his white hair, one hand swinging a thin cane and the other raised to his lips holding a cigarette. Helen started after him. She meant to follow Mr. Tomms until she got his cigarette end.

Although he is a person one seldom meets in life—and then, in those rare moments rather disappointing—the detective enjoys a great deal of our affections and admiration. His statue among literary figures, although the cement is scarcely dry, is accepted, and if his monument lacks the superior elevation and weathered charm of others, it does at least commemorate an aspect of life which enchants by its gloom and evil. We have grown to like and understand him. Sometimes he is a laughing, bold figure moving outside the law, a Robin Hood, to do the work of the law. Then it is that he is blue-eyed and has an insouciant way of being most humorous when death is closest. Other times sees him a cultured, unexcitable young man stamped Debrett and Oxford and full of erudite quotations and directing the clumsy attentions of the proper authorities to the esoteric yet convincing clues of guilt.

Helen knew all about detection. Some of her details were hazy, but in broad outline she knew about fingerprints, poisons, the seven approved methods of disposing of bodies, the permutations possible in the locked-room crime, the credence to be given to Lombroso and his later detractors, and she had read so often of men being shadowed and followed that to put this operation into action gave her no anxiety—until she started to do it. And then Helen found that to follow a man, even so conspicuous a man as Mr. Tomms, was not easy.

Mr. Tomms went away down Holborn towards the City at a smart pace and Helen kept about fifty yards behind. But even so she was constantly losing sight of him, for the broad pavement was beginning to thicken with the lunchtime crowd and there were always a great many people outside Bruce Brothers. She had a good view of him as he crossed the open road under the shadow of the Old Bailey and entered Newgate Street. But in Newgate Street Helen lost him. She was blocked for a moment by three Marines in royal scarlet who bore down upon her and forced her to the wall, where she found herself being importuned by an old lady to buy a pair of shoe laces. Helen dropped a penny into the old lady's box and realised as she looked up the pavement that she had lost Mr. Tomms. She hurried forward, dodging in and out of the crowd, hoping to catch up with him. She had reached the top of Cheapside before she had to admit that she had lost him. She stood back against a shop window to avoid the pedestrians and cursed herself for not keeping closer to him, and it was as she stood there that Mr. Tomms came briskly along Newgate Street and crossed into Cheapside. Under his arm was a small paper parcel.

Helen decided that he must have slipped into one of the shops—a possibility which had not occurred before to her—and she had passed him. She followed him now quickly, keeping closer now and hoping he would not look round and see her. She noticed that he was still smoking.

They went down Cheapside into Poultry and it was as he was making use of a pedestrian crossing at the Mansion House confluence of roads and traffic that Mr. Tomms threw away his cigarette. Helen was within five yards of him, waiting for the moment, hawk-eyed. She groaned inwardly as she saw what happened. Mr. Tomms, unlike most men, did not drop his end quietly to the ground and pass on. No, he took a last puff, a reluctant Goodbye and then, with a graceful gesture of his right arm, he tossed the butt out into the roadway, where it fell, sending up a momentary jet of spark, and was immediately subjected to a pummelling, squashing, grinding, tearing and rending by the wheels of omnibus, lorry, car and motor cycle. Helen watched dismayed. Within the space of thirty seconds, the cigarette was mangled and scuffled deeper into the road without her getting a chance to retrieve it.

She had to decide quickly between the chance of getting the end in a condition which would be useful to her or losing Mr. Tomms, who might start another cigarette. She went after Mr. Tomms, who was stepping it out along Lombard Street. Helen soon caught up with him to find that he had lit another cigarette. Mr. Tomms, she soon found out, believed in exercise. London people are not fond of walking far, and Helen was soon praying that Mr. Tomms would reach wherever he was going and throw his cigarette away. Her high-heeled shoes already hurt her.

Mr. Tomms walked like a man with an objective. He went down Lombard Street, crossed into Fenchurch Street, slipped away to the right into Great Tower Street and, half-way down this street, with the open sweep of Tower Hill and its crowd before him, he threw away his cigarette, half-smoked, and without any oratorical gesture. He dropped it into the gutter and went on.

Helen hurried forward to get it. A yard from it she hesitated. The pavement was busy with clerks and warehousemen walking towards Tower Hill for their lunch-time entertainment, and she was suddenly conscious of the odd figure which she would present. Well-dressed young women were not to be seen every day in London picking fag-ends from the gutter. Her hesitation lost her the cigarette butt. As she stepped towards it, a dirty, ragged tramp shuffled across the road, his eye drawn to the smoke of the substantial butty, and he snapped it up, sticking it between his lips. He stared at Helen, who was face to face with him, stretched his unshaven face into a grin and then, with a bright nod to her, he shuffled away, drawing contentedly at his free smoke.

For a while she debated with herself whether she should follow the tramp and buy the cigarette end from him. The receding figure of Mr. Tomms decided her. She went after him. She did not have to follow him for long.

They came out into the crowd on Tower Hill. Helen was sure she would lose him in the crowd until she saw that he was making straight for a portable rostrum which was standing on the edge of the crowd. A board on it announced—SOCIETY FOR PROGRESSIVE REHABILITATION, and beside it stood a shabby man who greeted Mr. Tomms with a nod, took some coin that was handed to him and slouched away presumably to have a drink until it should be time for him to come back and carry away the stand which Mr. Tomms had now mounted.

Knowing that Mr. Tomms was safe for a while, Helen hobbled to a wall on one side of the open space and sat down, glad to be still.

It was the first time she had been on Tower Hill for many years, and she had almost forgotten what it was like. It was a warm day and she was content to sit in the sun after her walk from Holborn. Behind her was the river and Tower Bridge. She could hear the distant boom of a cargo boat as it cleared Wapping Basin and the stir of traffic across the bridge. Between the wall on which she sat and the Tower Gardens the roadway was blocked with parked lorries and drays, whose drivers stood at the coffee stalls taking their lunch or mixed with the crowd which was packed tightly before her over the space between the wall and the towering block of warehouses.

About here, not so long ago, men had lost their heads to the executioner and the crowd had found entertainment in the spectacle. Now the crowd still found entertainment here. They came each lunch hour from their offices, their factories and shops, and lingered for an hour, passing from one speaker to another, arguing sometimes, often chaffing and seldom taking any of the oracles seriously. Here, within sight and sound of the dirty Thames, who had watched and served the city so long, men and women were offered everything. Religion cried to them from different stands in voices that ranged from a lusty bellow to the husky, whispered plea of a pale young man who fought for his breath between each mouthful of oratory. Politics—friendly, inimical, red-tied and black-shirted—shouted for their attention and, gaining it, held it with vituperation or patient explanation. There were men who proved that all doctors were quacks, and quacks who had no doubt that they were doctors. There were men who inveighed against the sappy degeneracy of the modern music-hall and the plugging of inferior dance tunes, men who recalled the glory of the old comedians and improvident Edwardian and pre-jazz personalities whose songs were still sung, and they asked for charity with wit and derision—and got it. There was a quiet, mannerly speaker with a bowler hat and a genealogical table who proved that he was entitled to the Throne of England; and a couple of brawny men in dirty trousers and greasy singlets who invited members of the crowd to rope them up so that they might wriggle free and pass the hat for coppers. It was an open space and nobody had laid claim to it. The speakers and the crowd had found it and made it theirs. Demos was still curious, but there were no more tumbling heads for him, only a tumbling, rumbling spate of words and jokes, fantasy and fact, a chuckling, refreshing passage of time between morning and afternoon labour.

It was into this babble that Mr. Tomms entered. Helen watched him from a distance. He began to speak and soon had a crowd around him. Helen saw that he was by no means as large a draw as some of the others. She waited. She waited for two hours and she only let Mr. Tomms out of her sight once when she was compelled to slip across to the nearest stall and have a coffee and a sausage roll. Mr. Tomms talked solidly for two hours and then, as the crowd began to thin, his henchman returned, wiping a draggly moustache, to lean nonchalantly against the stand, waiting for the end.

Mr. Tomms got down, said a few words to his man and then, still briskly, his shoulders square with the pride of a man who has done a good work, he started away from Tower Hill, taking a cigarette from his case and lighting it as he went. Helen followed after him. At the Mansion House Mr. Tomms stood by a stop, waiting for a bus. Helen kept close, ready to follow him.

He got aboard a bus bound for Holborn. Helen caught the same bus and went inside, while Mr. Tomms, because he was smoking, had to go aloft. The bus rumbled back along the way Helen had come and, as she guessed, when it stopped by Bruce Brothers Mr. Tomms got off. Helen slipped after him. He was still smoking. He went up the pavement and as he turned smartly into the gateway of Fountain Inn he threw away his cigarette end. This time Helen made sure of it. Disregarding all onlookers, she jumped for it and picked it up. She stood staring at it dismally. It was a cork-tipped butt of a popular make.

"Is anything the matter, Mrs. Brown?" Hindle, who had seen her standing in the gateway, came forward.

Helen jerked back to life. "No," she said evenly. "No, there's nothing the matter."

She went on to the office, feeling that Mr. Tomms had let her down.

"Well," said Ben as she come into the room. "What luck?"

"None," said Helen a little viciously and she sat down and slipped off her shoes.

"Tell me about it."

When Helen had finished he said:

"And I tackled Hindle. He's a confirmed pipe-smoker and he swears that Mr. Parcross never smokes. So with Tomms out of it that leaves only the broad-shouldered man that Tomms conducted out of the Inn. Which, if you see what I mean, really brings Tomms in again. It's extraordinary how my interest in Mr. Tomms—and Miss Logan —has increased since this morning.

It's beginning to look like a mystery." Helen looked up, her eyes brightening.

"You mean you're really glad I didn't send that report in, Ben?"

"I still disapprove of the principle, but I must say that I commend that particular practice. Yes, I'm interested. Assuming—and it's a big assumption for which we have very little ground, really—that Miss Logan has been made off with—a lovely phrase—and by someone in some way connected with Tomms, where would she be?"

"How should I know?"

"That's what I said. Then I decided to give life a second chance to let this affair develop as it should. I've been disappointed once. But I'm being magnanimous and giving it another chance. I said that it was no simple matter to hold a fullgrown female like Miss

Logan and then I thought of the Colonel's house which this Society has and which—so Halifax told me—is for sale."

"The place at Hormenden?"

"That's it. I've got an awful curiosity coming over me about it. I feel I must have a look at it, and I was wondering if you would care to spend the weekend at Hormenden with me? I've an idea that there's quite a nice little hotel there."

"Ben, it's a grand idea."

"Good. But, remember, if nothing happens, then I send in that report on Monday morning without fail." Helen agreed with a nod. Monday morning was a long way off yet. It was something to have got Ben interested in the affair again.

*   *   *   *   *

It was a quarter-past seven that evening as Grace, who had walked from the office, turned into the station entrance. She was not late because she had been busy. She had seen that George had not gone off to catch his usual train home and she had guessed that he was probably working overtime and would catch a later train. After Ben and Helen had gone, she had sat in the office knitting and reading, the door open so that she could hear anyone coming out of Craddock and Couch—they had a door with an automatic spring closer which squeaked unmistakably. She could not miss it. But George had shown no sign of moving. Three times Grace jumped up, ready to follow, but the squeaking door had let out other members of the staff. A simple calculation showed Grace that George was probably the only one now left and that if he did not stir within the next five minutes she must go off, otherwise she would miss the train and have to wait another hour—which she was not prepared to do for she had promised her mother that she would not be too late. George had not stirred and Grace had gone off without him.

She was wondering what he could be working so hard on as she entered the station. He'd probably forgotten all about the time—some men were like that over their work, and she was glad that George was such a man.

She walked towards the bookstall and as she did so, someone caught her arm gently and a young, familiar voice said quietly to her, "Hullo, Grace, darling …"

Grace turned to find at her side a young man in a cheap grey suit, a dark jersey with a rolled collar and wearing a greasy cap pushed back to expose his fair hair. He was half-smiling, halfsneering at her.

"Didn't expect to meet me, did you?" he questioned, chuckling.

"As a matter of fact," said Grace, fighting down her alarm, "I had an idea you were about."

"You did? Then I wonder you didn't welcome me more lovingly. I've been waiting here over an hour for you."

"Let go of my arm," said Grace firmly. "I've got no time for you. I must catch my train."

"Your train goes at twenty-five past, as I know well. That gives us a good five minutes, and I can say all I want to in that time. Come on. There's a waiting-room over here."

Grace followed him, wishing now that she had remembered that her watch always gained. She need not have left the office so soon. She might have missed this … She tightened her lips and said firmly:

"Anything you want to say you can say here, and you'd better be quick."

There was no mistaking her tones. The young man laughed and then whistled softly. "A proper spitfire, eh? You've changed, Gracie. But this'll do as well as the waiting-room. It was for your sake I thought you'd like to go there. Listen …"

A steam train began to fill the vault of the station with an echoing scream and a loud speaker began to boom details of departure platforms, people streamed into the great hallway and a dog, lost in the scramble of legs, began to howl unhappily. Grace found herself leaning forward to hear what was being said to her, but even as she listened her eyes were on the station clock. She did not mean to miss her train.

At twenty-four and a half minutes after seven George came hurrying into the station. A glance at the clock showed him that he had timed himself properly. He was pleased. He liked his calculations to work out accurately. Then, as his eyes travelled down from the clock he saw Grace and with her a young man. They were talking together. At almost the same moment as he saw her, Grace saw him. She snapped at once to the young man:

"All right. I'll meet you outside Bruce Brothers at half-past one tomorrow." She was moving away from him as she spoke.

For a second the man was tempted to follow her, but as he stood there he saw her met by a thick-set, solid-looking young man and he decided to hold his ground. The next minute Grace and her friend had passed on to their departure platform. The young man shrugged his shoulders and turned away.

Grace said nothing for some time after her "Hullo" in greeting to George. Her heart was beating quicker than it normally did and her mind was given over to the exercise of an emotion which was part anger and part alarm.

"Your friend seemed a little upset at the way you left him," George made the observation as they settled down in the compartment. He was aware of an odd feeling about Grace's friend. The sight of her talking to another young man, although it was a young man of the class that wore cheap cloth caps, was disturbing, and he could not understand why. It didn't occur to him that he might be faintly jealous. It was more that he had come to suppose he must be about the only male acquaintance Grace had; she never spoke of anyone else and the way she pursued his company seemed convincing proof of this lack in her life. Apparently, however, she did know other young men—and George was curious.

"My friend?"

"Ay, the young man you were talking to as I came into the station."

Grace laughed gently. "That wasn't a friend. It was some stranger who wanted to know if I could direct him to the platform for Caterham. I had to leave him hurriedly because I might have missed my own train."

"I see," said George, not convinced. "You're later tonight than you usually are."

"So are you," countered Grace, she was almost ready to be angry with George for his remark about her friend.

"I was working," answered George.

"So was I."

George wisely said nothing more. They sat side by side and the electric train clacked out from London towards Bromley. After a time Grace began to feel her normal self, though she still had a small core of unhappiness within her that she could not disperse.

"I was at a meeting of Mr. Tomms's Society on Tuesday night. Did I tell you?" she asked.

"You did not, and I was not aware that you took any interest in such matters."

"I don't really. I went with Mrs. Brown. Can you guess what I saw there … *Del*. George Crane?" It was the first time she had spoken his full name before him, but she felt safe under her artifice.

It was a moment or two before George understood.

"Oh, so you saw the plans we did for Mr. Tomms?"

"The plans you did."

"I did some of them, it's true."

"And I think they were beautiful. I can't tell you how clever I thought they were, and everyone there was full of them.

Since I've known you, I'm beginning to be really interested in buildings."

"I don't know whether to take your last remark as a compliment, Miss Kirkstall ... However, I'm glad the plans were well received and I'm not so foolishly modest as to deny that I don't think them very good. By the way, did you ever hear from that creature who got us dragged all out to Ealing on her behalf?"

"Miss Logan? No—I expected to see her at the meeting, but she wasn't there, but Mrs. Brown heard from someone that she's gone abroad suddenly on a holiday."

"She must have been in a mighty hurry, or very forgetful," said George.

George got out at his station and as he walked towards his lodgings he found himself wondering who the young man in the grey suit had been. He seemed to remember, too, the impression he had of him, as he turned away and walked towards the station exit, was of someone with a slight limp. He was not sure. Miss Kirkstall, he decided, was a curious young woman and not unpleasant company, and if she knew nothing about the finer points of architecture it did not detract from the satisfaction he got from her thinking him a good architect. Ay, she had a small, almost impertinent face, and her lips were a wee bit thin, perhaps, but they were well formed, and her mouth had a proper balance.

He let out an exclamation of disgust as he discovered that his contemplation of Grace's features had made him walk past his own lodgings.

Later, as Grace walked up Fisher Road to her home she was not thinking of George, but of the young man she had met at the station. Her face was set into a severe frown, which stayed there until she entered the house. It was gone when she came into the parlour to greet her mother and Mr. Pilchard, who had come up for the evening.

"You're late, Grace."

"Sorry, Mum, but I had to finish some work." It was not often that she lied to her mother. She looked at the smiling, rather tired face of her mother and she was suddenly decided.

"Well, Grace, I'm glad you've come. I always said you had an eye for colour," boomed Mr. Pilchard. "Your ma and I have been trying to decide how I shall have the new delivery van painted. Now, your ma's all for a pig's head on a plate with a kind of garland of sausages. But I prefer something more countrified—gives people the idea of freshness—with a pig and its little ones in a field with a tree and a pond in the distance.

Now then, what do you say?"

Chapter Nine

Ben and Helen went to Kent late on Saturday morning. The previous day Ben had rung up Halifax to tell him that he hoped to let him have a report very shortly and at the same time he had got from him the name of the agents who were handling the sale of the Colonel's house. The agents had their offices in Maidstone and a telephone conversation with them revealed that, if Ben and his wife wished to look over the house, they must make a definite appointment so that the caretaker would know when to expect them. Ben arranged to visit the house at three o'clock on the Saturday.

"I wonder why," mused Helen as they drove down, "the caretaker insisted upon having a definite appointment?"

"If you'd ever tried to sell a house you'd know," said Ben, keeping his eyes on the broad track as they dipped down a hill and had a vast sweep of plain, wooded with orchards and pinnacled with the red points of oast-houses, open before them. "People looking for a house to buy have the most odd idea of time. They think nothing of coming just as you're going to bed, or when you are about to sit down to lunch. No, it's always wise to insist upon appointments. You can have the place looking its best then."

"In other words—it gives you time to make proper preparations?" Helen looked across at Ben, but he refused to be moved by the bait. The car roared forward. Although it was an old car, it bore a respected name and age had not impaired its capabilities. Indeed, it was a car which, while enjoying the ease of main roads, was always game for a scramble over ruts and potholes.

Helen enjoyed the ride to Hormenden. For a long while they had the main-road company of motor coaches heading for the coast, great coloured monsters bearing their load of holiday folk. Then there were the motor cycles—angry, waspish affairs that flashed by the car, scarfs streaming, driven by goggled fiends who were encouraged by gay girls who clung to the pillions and swayed and shouted to one another. The main road had little time to dally with the country, and it was only when they had turned off it that the true Kent crowded around them. They passed down lanes bordered with the new green of fruit trees, by long stretches of hop gardens where the brown earth showed thin green lines of the young hops already started on their way up to the maze of twine and pole, and twice they swept by hillside fields of strawberries where aproned women bent to the earth gathering its fruit.

Hormenden itself was a quiet, well-kept village that had grown up round its church and its green. The green sloped gently down from the church to the main road. The church was reached by a small, narrow road that encircled the green.

Ben and Helen found the Bull Hotel, an old, red-roofed inn facing the road. At its side stood a pleasant garden, noisy with the courting of pigeons from a dovecote, a garden that overlooked the green. Early roses trailed over the garden palisade.

Ben and Helen had their lunch and then drove off to find the Colonel's house. Harden Hall—for that was its name—was a mile from the village on the coast road. It stood back about a hundred yards from the road and was approached by a gravelled drive and protected from the gaze of passers-by with a line of poplars and a thick undergrowth of rhododendrons. The hall itself was a compact, Georgian, red-bricked building, its brickwork hidden and its beauty disfigured by a rampant ivy growth over nearly the whole of its front.

Ben rang the bell. It was answered very shortly by a tall woman, young and good-looking. She was dark-haired, her skin a warm brown tan and she smiled at them pleasantly.

"Is Mr. Burns, the caretaker—" began Ben, but she cut in with a spontaneous

"I'm Mrs. Burns. I expect you're the lady and gentleman the agent told us to expect. I'm sorry my husband isn't here, but I think I can show you round and answer any questions you might

want to ask. Will you come in, please?" Helen and Ben entered the hall.

"She's very young for a caretaker," whispered Helen as Mrs.

Burns, murmuring something about keys, excused herself.

"And pretty," said Ben. "It's a pleasure to see such a caretaker. I wonder where her husband is …"

Ben's query was answered by Mrs. Burns herself as she began to show them round.

"My husband would have liked to show you round himself. But he's at cricket. He plays for the village and he never likes to miss a match. But I'll do my best. This that you're standing in, of course, is the hall. Over there is the morning-room. Will you follow me?"

She began to show them round. Ben and Helen followed her obediently. They went over the ground floor and then climbed the wide stairway. As they went up, Mrs. Burns said:

"The place is furnished now, but, of course, as soon as the sale is made all the furniture will be auctioned unless the purchaser wishes to make an offer for the whole lot as it stands. My husband tells me—I don't understand these things very well—that there are some very good pieces here. As a matter of fact, he was in the antique trade himself for years, but business went against us, so we had to take this job …"

She talked on as they went round and Helen had to admit to herself that it seemed very unlikely that this young married woman could have any dealing with a possible abduction of Miss Logan. She talked artlessly, frankly and without the slightest hint of a false inflexion.

There were twelve bedrooms, the beds bare in all but the one used by the Burnses.

"Above this floor there are several attics and a long box room," she explained. "I don't suppose you'll want to see those."

"Oh, yes, we should like to," said Helen quickly. "You see, my husband is a keen photographer and he would want one of them fixed up as a dark room if we decided about the place."

"Of course." Mrs. Burns showed no signs of distress. She led them up to the attics. Helen let nothing escape her, but she could see no signs of abnormal use. All the attics had narrow windows that looked out on to the roof-top which was surrounded by a narrow balcony. The box room had no window except a long skylight that stretched between the two chimney stacks. It was bare and clean. Two of the attics were full of boxes and broken furniture thick with dust.

"It's a big job cleaning up everywhere, and you'll see that there are some of the attics we haven't got round to yet," pointed out Mrs. Burns. "Though, of course, we're not bound to do any cleaning up here, but my husband is rather conscientious about such things."

When they had finished with the house, Mrs. Burns took them around the grounds. There were about ten acres, a great deal of it given up to shrubberies, lawns and orchard, and, away from the house, set in a belt of alder and oaks was a small lake, scarcely a hundred yards in breadth at its widest point. In the centre of the lake was an island, fringed with mace reeds and tangled willow shoots. Facing them from the island as they stood on the edge of the lake was a small summer house, built chalet fashion, its windows shuttered, the water lapping under its narrow verandah.

"What a charming little house!" cried Helen, delighted at the seclusion the place suggested.

"Yes, it is pretty, isn't it. I believe that Colonel Halifax used to be very fond of sitting out there."

"Can we go over and see it?" asked Ben, and as he spoke he kept his eyes on the woman's face.

"I'm afraid not," she said easily, shaking her head. "I've often wanted to go there myself, but the only way is by water and there's no boat. There was a punt—it's further down the bank there—but it's so rotten that it wouldn't keep out the water for ten yards."

"What a pity!" cried Helen. "It looks such a lovely island."

Mrs. Burns laughed, a gentle, commiserating laugh as though she understood and appreciated Helen's disappointment.

Ben and Helen did not speak as they drove back to the village. Ben put the car away in the *Bull* garage and they walked out to the village green and stretched themselves on the grass at the church end. The road around the green was now thinly marked with parked cars and spectators. In the centre of the green was the white movement of cricket players.

Ben eyed the players and said slowly: "Well, what do you think of Mrs. Burns?"

"I don't know." Helen was honest. It was useless to let one's imagination distort one's sense of truth. "She seemed a nice, sensible sort of creature to me."

"And we went over every inch of space in that house—Oh, a nice stroke!" Ben broke off and clapped his hands gently as a batsman opened out his shoulders and sent the ball whizzing across the green with a perfect off drive.

"In the house, yes. But we didn't get over to that little island."

"Neither could Mr. or Mrs. Burns. You saw the rotten punt for yourself as we went by."

"I did. But they might have another boat, a small, collapsible one perhaps that they could keep hidden somewhere in the shrubberies. I should like to go to that island."

"What is there about islands that always makes one want to visit them? It's an itch that we all have to impose ourselves upon a state of beautiful isolation. I feel that I want to visit that island, too." Ben's eyes were on the players; the hot sun touched the back of his neck and he stretched himself luxuriantly. Village cricket, a Saturday afternoon, and all the world seemed at peace, at least all the world comprised by the green. For a few hours everything was secondary to a game. You could forget everything except the necessity of making a ball break in sharply from leg. The world could stand still while you trembled to see whether the ball you had skied would be held or not … It was all very pleasant and very English but it was only the surface. Underneath moved a host of harmless jealousies, business rivalries and little meannesses. Men and women could be villains, but they were seldom detached in their villainies. Few of them ever went into it in a big way. Ben began to wonder … he stopped wondering as he caught Helen's eyes upon him. She was smiling.

"The best time to visit an island like that," she said softly "would be this evening—late." "I think it would," agreed Ben.

At nine o'clock that evening, Helen was alone in the lounge reading a faded copy of *Little Women* which she had found there. Ben was sitting in the *Bull* bar, his pipe drawing sweetly, his hands clasped round a tankard of beer while its brother was held by an old man at his side who had kept him company for the last hour. He was an interesting and entertaining old man and was proving most useful to Ben.

136

"Ay, it was last year the Colonel died, all right," said the old man. "I know'd him well. He was a hasty tempered man—but fair. I likes a man who's fair. He couldn't stand didikies, though."

"Didikies?"

"Gypsies you folk probably call 'em. They be didikies to us. He wouldn't have any near his place. I well remember old Lambert."

"Who was Lambert?" asked Ben, remembering the Ronald Lambert who had witnessed the Colonel's bill.

"Lambert? He was the Colonel's butler. That's what I was going to say about these 'ere didikies. They said as how Lambert's wife was from a didiky family and he didn't like the way the Colonel used to chase 'em about. Still, Lambert's dead now and it don't matter. 'E died about a month before the master. They were both pretty old—though I would call 'em young. It's a pity about the house being for sale, but there 'tis. Once things begin to change they change quickly. What kind of weather have 'ee been havin' up London way? 'T'as been kind and dry down here, but us could do with some rain now to fill out the peas and strawberries."

The old man went on, mumbling contentedly about the weather and the local news. He seemed set to talk without stop as long as Ben saw that the bottom never showed for long in his tankard. Ben listened to him and his eyes moved over the crowd in the bar. It was Saturday evening and well crowded. As Ben watched, a man pushed his way from the counter, holding a glass of beer. He made his way to the wall and set the glass down on a chair and standing up began to search his pockets. He was a middle-aged man, strongly built, his face a cheerful wrinkle of firm muscle lines and his chin flat and slightly spatulate with a dip in its centre. He had steady grey eyes and a well-combed head of crisp, fair hair. There was something friendly, solid and trustworthy about his appearance, a quality of worthiness and good humour that made him stand out from the labourers and men about the bar. He was dressed in a light flannel suit, in the coat pocket of which he was feeling as Ben watched him.

He stood talking to an acquaintance seated by him, and as he talked he pulled out a thin pouch and a packet of cigarette papers. With the dexterity of the habitué he rolled himself a cigarette, his firm fingers shaping and tapping at the paper. Ben watched the process, fascinated. It made his own occasional efforts at cigarette rolling so childish.

"Who's the gentleman who rolls his own cigarettes?" he asked the old man, nodding across the room to the man.

"Him?" the old man peered through the smoke. "Oh, that's Mr. Burns. Rare hand at that cigarette game, ain't he? He's a newcomer to these parts. Caretaker at the hall. But he's wellliked from what I know of him. He bowls for the cricket team and bowls pretty smartish, too, I can tell 'ee. Why only last week now—"

Ben was not listening. He was looking at Mr. Burns, who had now lit his cigarette and was seated. Ben was suddenly very anxious to have the stub of the cigarette when Mr. Burns had finished, though even as he felt himself filled with a subtle excitement he also found that he was warning himself that this cheerful middle-aged man and his young wife looked a very unlikely pair to be mixed up in anything so fantastic as the abduction of an old lady.

He sat patiently, watching the cigarette burn away. For the first time he realised just how long it took a cigarette to burn away. He kept looking across to Mr. Burns, but he was careful not to catch the man's eye. Eventually the cigarette was finished and he saw him toss it to the ground and, standing up, crush it absently with one foot. Then he nodded "Good night" to his companion and moved across the bar towards the door. Ben watched him go and, the moment he was from the room, he was on his feet and moving towards the counter. When he was

138

standing by the stub-end, Ben stopped, took out his matches and pretended to light his pipe. As he struck at the box with a match he dropped the lot in such a way that some of the matches were spilled. He bent down, with an exclamation of annoyance, and began to pick them up. When he rose, the cigarette end was safely in his match box.

Five minutes later he entered the lounge and sat down at Helen's side. Helen looked up from her book, gave him a cheerful grin, and dived back again into the story which was restoring to her the lost memories of her early childhood. Ben said nothing. He placed a cigarette end on her page. Helen looked up at him quickly, a frown forming on her forehead. Then she looked at the cigarette end. It was the remains of a handrolled one and on its tip was a golden star surrounded by the circle of words—*Etoile d'Or*.

"Mr. Burns," said Ben quietly—for there were other people in the lounge—answering her unspoken question, "was kind enough to leave it in the bar a little while ago. He's now on his way home. We'll give him an hour's grace and then follow him."

They gave Mr. Burns a good hour's grace and then left the *Bull* to make their way to Harden Hall. The weather which the old man had described as kind and dry had changed during the evening and it was now spitting intermittently with rain, soft showers coming and going with a quickening frequency that threatened to develop into a continual, steady drizzle.

Ben and Helen walked along the road, the rain running off their mackintoshes. A few late travellers passed them on bicycles, wobbling pools of light that came up to them and disappeared in the night.

They passed the main entrance to the Hall and a little lower down the road swung to the left along a narrow lane that marked the boundary of the estate. The lane passed within two fields of the small lake.

Helen followed Ben blindly. She was not very good at finding her way and the, to her, uncanny way in which Ben moved through the darkness filled her with admiration. She followed him over a gate, across a field, through a tangle of barbed wire where she tore her skirt, across another field, this time sinking into soft plough and conscious of lines of growing stuff, probably mangels. And then, almost before she was prepared for it, they were standing in the cover of the trees that surrounded the lake.

"Here we are," whispered Ben. "Not much of a night for a swim, is it? I wish I'd got a costume with me. But it's dark enough for me to undress without being immodest. You'd better stay here and watch my clothes."

"I'll do nothing of the sort," said Helen vigorously. "I'm coming with you."

"There's no need for both of us to go in," protested Ben.

Helen ignored his plea and began to slip off her coat. "You needn't think, Benjamin Brown," she whispered intensely, "that you're going to have all the fun of swimming out to that island alone while I stand here doing nothing."

"I was only being chivalrous." Ben began to strip.

"I wish I could believe it. You didn't want me around. I know you."

Ben said no more. In a few moments they were both ready. Ben in his ultimate underwear and Helen, he guessed, trying to persuade herself that a silk shift would make an excellent bathing costume. Had it not been that they both thought they might find someone on the island—Miss Logan, perhaps—they would have discarded even these flimsy concessions to a convention which the night rendered unnecessary.

"Who's going first?" asked Ben, feeling the water with his foot. A shove from behind told him that he was. He stepped forward and felt his feet sinking into rich, velvety slime. He moved forward more and then let himself drop quietly into the blackness. The water came up around him, warm and confiding. He trod water and waited. In a little while Helen came alongside.

He could just make out the shape of her head beside him.

"Have you got a torch?" she asked.

"Yes." Ben flicked it quickly and then they began to swim outwards. The rain hissed down upon the water. Now and then their hands felt long streamers of weed and once Helen had difficulty in stopping a cry of alarm as her foot found a submerged snag, the foreign touch in the blackness sending a quick fear through her.

Ahead of them, outlined against the grey night sky, rose the black bulk of the island. As they neared it, they both swam with less noise, gliding forward on their strokes.

Ben felt his feet on mud and, with a caution to Helen, he paddled himself forward into a foot of water, his body dragging unpleasantly over the slime. His hands found reeds and clutching their roots he pulled himself upwards. The slime was too soft to give any firm purchase to his feet. When he was free of the mud, he turned and groped for Helen. His hand caught hers and he pulled her forward. She had been standing on the slime and she came reluctantly at first and then with a suddenness that sent them both toppling backwards. They lay still after their fall, listening. Through the night came the noise of the rain and the momentary squawk of a moor-fowl disturbed in its roost.

"Clumsy," said Ben quietly, but with feeling.

"Clumsy yourself. How did I know I was going to come out like that. Ugh, I'm all muddy."

"Probably good for the skin," said Ben, picking himself up and flashing his torch to give himself bearings. "Come on."

He led the way forward slowly. Neither of them could have moved quickly in their bare feet. They proceeded, keeping the water within a few feet of their left hand, knowing they must strike the summer house very soon. Helen forgot that she was muddy, that her shift clung to her shamefully and that her hair was draggled into her eyes. No one could see her except Ben and if an occasional flash of the torch did make her condition evident to him she had no worry. He loved her and was far beyond the stage where lovers imagine there is some peculiar magic about their loved one which enables her to be always attractive and lovely. Ben had thrown off that superstition some years before. She still remembered how grotesque her face had looked, bulged on one side with toothache, and she still remembered Ben's laughter … This moving through the darkness, feeling her face touched by wet trailing branches and dropping her feet into muddy slime, thoughts of leeches and other odious creatures crowding into her mind, was like some adventure from *Martin Rattler*—or was it *Midshipman Easy*? She was always a little resentful of the fact that these were known as boys' books. Most of the girls she had known enjoyed them. She bumped into Ben's outstretched hand.

"Here we are."

She looked, and slowly from the murk there emerged a dark, rising shape.

"Stay here," whispered Ben and he was gone before she could protest. Men were all like that—they thought there was something about their sex which gave them the right to handle the torch and take all the initiative. She grinned in the dark as she recognised what Ben called the Pankhurst in her.

Once or twice she saw a momentary flicker of light ahead of her. After a while she heard Ben returning.

"Come along," he said, his voice less guarded. He took her hand and very shortly they were at the back of the summer house. Ben flicked on his torch, showing her a small door which he pushed open. They entered and he held the torch on permanently.

"The windows are all shuttered," he said. "No one can see the light. You see, there's nothing in here."

Helen looked around. She was in a small room, empty but for a cane chair in one corner and an almanack on one of the walls. In front of her was another door which evidently led out to the balcony overlooking the lake.

"No—there's no one here," she agreed. "But there has been someone here."

"How do you know?"

"Haven't you noticed?"

"What?"

Helen shook her head. "Smell!" she commanded.

Ben raised his head and sniffed. A new look came into his eyes. "Scent," he said; "and it's not yours."

"Quite right. It's scent all right, and not mine. And it's strong enough to show that someone who uses it pretty liberally was here today."

"Perhaps it was Mrs. Burns?"

Helen shook her head vigorously. "I'd have noticed it when we met her. You always notice another woman's scent. Besides, this perfume is—" she expanded her nostrils delicately, savouring the air "—I should say a Chypre and used too heavily.

Now what kind of person might use scent in that way?"

"Miss Logan. But how'd she come to have scent with her?"

"Supposing they did abduct her. They probably did it politely and gave her time to pack a few things. Yes, Mr. and Mrs. Burns seem pretty strong on courtesy."

"But if she were here today, where is she now?"

"A fair question. I'd say she was back in the house. They probably shifted her out here when they heard we were coming. They must do that every time someone comes to see the house and that's the reason they insist upon an appointment first. I'll bet if we looked we'd find that collapsible boat I mentioned." "We might," agreed Ben. "But it's still a big assumption. Burns is connected with the Society—it's their house—and he may have some connection with

Miss Logan which is quite innocent and would account for his cigarette end in her room. As for the smell of scent in here—well, maybe the Burns woman didn't want the fag of bringing us across, but someone else might have called later today, some woman who uses scent as you say, and she insisted upon coming over here because she happened to spot the collapsible boat somewhere in the shrubberies. You see!"

"I do—and it seems a pretty long-winded way of discrediting the obvious."

"I'm merely pointing out how the reality may prove you wrong. Life isn't an affair of logical sequences. I'm suspicious of life— especially where Miss Logan and this Society are concerned."

"You talk as though you weren't interested."

"I am interested. Very. Things are all pointing so consistently towards something fishy that I'm just being cautious so that I shan't be too disappointed if—"

"If. There's one way to try that 'if.' We must have a look in the house and see if she's there."

"But not tonight!" Ben flashed the light over his muddy B.D.Vs. "We've got to get back to the hotel and get warm. Miss Logan will keep until tomorrow night."

An involuntary shiver made Helen acknowledge that Ben's suggestion was wise. They left the summer house, swam back to the shore and stripped in the darkness.

"Here's a towel." Ben jerked the towel from his raincoat pocket. They wiped as well as they could in the rain and very soon were on their way to the hotel. A hot bath and hot drinks and the comfort of their beds soon put their adventure into the realm of fantasy. It was hard to credit that little more than an hour before they had been squelching through rain and mud in their underclothes. If Miss Logan were at Harden Hall, thought Ben, as he felt himself slipping into the kind meshes of sleep, he hoped she was as comfortably bedded as he. Tomorrow evening … tomorrow evening he would know perhaps. It was a strange world, and yet a familiar, happy little world that refused to let its strangeness obtrude too indecently upon the ordinary show of existence.

Chapter Ten

House-breaking is a very serious offence. And very rightly, too. Only very broad-minded and quixotic people are willing to regard the house-breaker as a guest. His is the least romantic of crimes. He is a creature of rain spouts, roof gutters, knifed window catches and darkness. For him houses are as tills to a bank robber, as purses to the snatch-and-run man; and when a man gets into the way of seeing houses like that, it is a great loss to his sense of proportion.

You may walk off openly from a man's house with his best umbrella, take his expensive homburg and leave him your cheap masquerade; unbeknown to him, you may borrow his first editions and hope never to return them, you may pilfer plants from his rockery as you leave and successfully filch from his collection of hotel ashtrays … All these things you can do and when found out still hope to retain his friendship. But if your friend comes down at night to find you alone in his library, your torch focused on so much as a box of matches, your hand clasped about so small a thing as a cheap piece of crested ware from a seaside town—then you are no longer his friend. You are a house-breaker.

And for house-breakers, when caught there is the Law. And it was the Law which Ben was thinking about as he approached

Harden Hall that Sunday evening. Helen he had made stay at the hotel. One person, he had successfully argued, could get into a house easier than two. It was not the getting into the house which worried him—his schooldays had given him quite a lot of practice in the handling of window catches and the climbing of drain pipes. He might be caught inside. That was a very real problem and, if he were caught, and if Miss Logan were not in the house, then he was in for an awkward time. He drew only the vaguest comfort from the thought that if he were caught and started on an awkward time then he would be able to blame Helen for the enthusiasm which she had stirred in him for this rash adventure. It would be her fault—but he would have to take the consequences.

There were no dogs. He had learned that from the old man at the *Bull*. Mr. Burns apparently did not like dogs. Ben was glad of that. He was not sure that he could have dealt with a dog.

Getting into the grounds of Harden Hall was easy, and a careful survey showed him that there was a light in the rear of the house, where Mr. and Mrs. Burns were sitting. That was as he had wished. As long as they were safely in their own quarters, it left him free to examine the rest of the house. If he had left the search until later when they were in bed, he would have felt less confident of moving about without disturbing them, as they slept on the second floor.

He went round to the front of the house, his footsteps cushioned by the grassy lawns, taking advantage of the cover of the clumps of shrubs. Then he crossed to the house-front, making for a window to the right of the door. A few minutes probing with his knife and he heard the catch fall back inside. The noise was tremendous in the night and he waited anxiously. Nothing stirred and there was no sound beyond the booming of a night bug that came clumsily through the air, banged into him, buzzed angrily and was away again. From the flower border below him came the strong spicy smell of pinks, their white mop heads showing palely in the starlight.

Ben got his hands to the window frame and pushed it up gently. He raised it until there was a space large enough for him to enter. He waited again, wondering whether the movement of the window might have set off an alarm. A period of silence, broken once by the distant hoot of a car along the main road; then he was inside and the window closed again so that it should not attract attention from outside if Mr. Burns decided to take a stroll around the garden after supper.

Ben knew where he was. He had a good head for house details. He went forward, flicking his torch once to locate the door and a few moments later was standing in the dark hallway. He made at once for the stairway and began to mount. He had decided to start with an examination of the attics and work his way down. He was on the first landing when he stiffened. From his right had come the sound of someone stirring, a faint, momentary scuffle of noise. Ben stood tensed, one foot still poised, not daring to move. He stood like a statue until his limbs began to ache with the strain. The noise was not repeated, and he decided that it must have been a rat or mouse scuffling away over the boards. He lowered his foot and began to move forward. He took one step when from behind him, at the bend of the stairs, a hoarse voice cried loudly:

"Heil Hitler! Heil Hitler!"

Ben flattened against the wall and swung about. There was a silence while through his mind raced a score of probabilities. He waited, his torch ready. He heard something stir before him then a low chuckle rippled across the darkness and the same voice cried soothingly:

"Okay! Okay!" and then suddenly, as though regretting its submission, "Heil Hitler! Heil Hitler!" in a series of piercing cries.

Ben only had one thought in his mind now. He switched on his torch quickly and as quickly had it off, the sudden burst of light dispelling his fears. On the other side of the landing, standing on a low table, was a cage and he had a glimpse of the beady eye of a stout, vociferating parrot, dancing along its perch, cackling. Ben turned and sped up the stairs, followed by a chorus of "Heil Hitlers!" At the next landing he stopped. The noise from the parrot was filling the house with echoes.

From the hallway there came the sound of a door opening and then the click of a light switch, the stairway was bathed with light that died weakly into grey shadows around Ben. He looked cautiously over the balustrade down the staircase well and saw Mr. Burns, in shirt sleeves and carpet slippers, a pipe in one hand and a book in the other.

"For Pete's sake, Micawber," Mr. Burns yelled up the stairs to the parrot.

"Heil Hitler! Heil Hitler!" flung back the parrot.

"Micawber!" There was an angry note in Burns' voice. "Did you hear me?" He began to mount the stairs and the parrot, seeing him and probably guessing his fate, dropped suddenly into a conciliatory "Okay! Okay! …"

"You can cry 'Okay' as much as you like," said Mr. Burns, talking loudly to the bird; "but if you think I'm going to stand for your outbursts you're wrong. Take that, you nasty little Nazi!" and he dropped a blanket over the cage and silenced the bird.

He went back, grumbling to himself. The hall was dark and the bird silent, and Ben, smiling to himself, despite his scare, found that he was up on the top floor. He gave Mr. Burns five minutes' grace to get settled again with his pipe and book.

There were four rooms on the roof level, the three attics which had small dormer windows giving on to the leads and a box-room lit by a skylight. The door to the boxroom was at the end of the L-shaped corridor which connected the attics. Ben went from one room to another. There was no one in the first two attics. But as he stole quietly down the corridor towards the doorway of the third, his eyes caught sight of a thin sliver of light coming from under the doorway of the box-room. Ben stopped dead. Then he went back along the corridor to the first attic. He went through the room and out on to the roof. A glance showed him a patch of light coming from the skylight. He dropped on to his knees and began to climb the slight slope. He reached the edge of the panel of glass and looked in.

He was to remember that moment always, to remember it with fondness when his days were dull. For in that moment the tenor of his life began to run swiftly, exhilaratingly, and he was propelled into a spontaneous recognition of life's power to touch ordinary affairs with strangeness and cross stable lives with unexpected evil and fears; and he was to remember without shame that he was also a little apprehensive of his thoughts as he looked down into the box-room.

The room was not the same room into which Mrs. Burns had conducted Helen and himself. Its bare boards were now partly covered with a red carpet. In addition to the odd packing cases around the walls, there was now a narrow, white-counterpaned truckle bed. A small oak table stood in the centre of the floor and on it a reading lamp with a green shade. There were other small pieces of furniture. The whole assembly could have been cleared away in half an hour and been scattered over the other rooms of the house.

In a comfortable cane armchair by the table sat a woman, a plump, placid-looking woman who was crocheting with deft, even movements and, at the same time reading a magazine which was spread under the reading lamp. She was an elderly woman, her hair greying, her neck creased into mature folds, but her crochet movements were vigorous and her skin still had the odd quality of freshness and youth which some women retain all their lives. She wore a purple dress with a white fichu collar and on her nose was balanced almost incongruously a pair of pincenez, worn with that awkwardness which proclaimed them reading glasses. Ben recognised the woman who had spoken at the Society meeting. Here in this box-room was Miss Victoria Logan.

Ben lay on the roof looking down at Miss Logan. The lighted room beneath him was a great attraction. It was like staring down from an unusual angle on a theatre scene, and waiting tremulously for an entrance, an entrance that would set moving a sharply marked set of incidents and climaxes. Miss Logan went on with her crocheting ant reading, occasionally turning a page, sometimes stooping for her ball of silk. Ben saw that she was making a table-centre. Once she spread it out on her knees to admire the pattern, an intricate succession of whorls and scallops. And the expected entrance came. He saw Miss Logan look up sharply and then Mrs. Burns entered, carrying a supper tray. She stayed for a few moments, chatting with Miss Logan. Then she was gone. Ben was surprised at the evident friendly relationship between jailor and captive—Miss Logan had actually laughed at something the woman had said. Ben watched Miss Logan begin her supper.

He started to move away, conscious that he was stiff with lying tensed against the roof. He had been prompted for a moment to rap on the glass and attract her attention. He had not done so. She was an old woman and he did not want to alarm her.

He slid down the slope and made for the attic window. He felt the need of a consultation with Helen. Miss Logan would not run away.

As he put one foot through the attic window and turned to lower himself into the room, Ben was immediately aware of, yet unable to avoid entirely, the blow that was to come. It might have been that intuitive sense which marks the close presence of the inimical; it might have been the scarcely noted warning conveyed to the brain and relayed to the muscles that came from the smell of a strange tobacco. But, whatever the cause, Ben knew that a man was standing close to the window waiting for him, and as he dropped into the room he ducked and swung aside. He did not entirely escape the blow. It fell on to the top part of his left arm, numbing it. He staggered sideways and saw against the window a dark shape. A man leaned toward him, a hand found his throat and he heard the hiss of breath as the man raised his arm for another blow. He had no thought for fairness. He raised his knee and drove it hard into the other's stomach and as the man jerked towards him, doubling up, he swung his right hand and smashed it against the man's chin. It was the first time in his life that he had ever with bare fist knocked anyone out and, as his opponent dropped neatly, as though it had all been a rehearsed scrimmage, to the ground, Ben found himself flooded with a swift, happy pride. He had no idea that things really could happen in quite such an ordered way. Then he was aware of his damaged knuckles, his stinging arm and his desire to get out of the house before Burns recovered. He dashed from the room and, holding his torch on, ran down the stairs three at a time. He reached the bottom as Mrs. Burns came into the hallway. She switched on the light and ran towards him. Ben avoided her, skidded on a loose mat, and, before she could get to him, had pulled the catch of the main door and was out into the garden racing towards the drive.

He ran without stopping all the way back to the village, regretting that he was not in better training and trying to marshal his thoughts.

"Darling, your hand," cried Helen as he entered their bedroom where she sat, fully dressed waiting for him.

"It's only a scratch," he said, tying his handkerchief round his bleeding knuckles.

"What happened?" Helen was on her feet, her face suddenly alive with eagerness as she watched him panting for his breath. When his lungs were satisfied, he told all that had passed.

"She's there in the house and they know that we know she is. What do we do?"

"Then it is true—there is something fishy going on. Do?" Helen looked at him suddenly, her mind was working quickly, her love of order and precision schooling the position. "Do? We go to the police, of course. She's being kept there against her will. You can prove it. We must go and get her—lawfully. Come on, we'll find the village policeman. We must hurry or they'll be gone."

"Do you think they will?"

"Don't be stupid. Do you think they'll wait quietly for us to come back. They may not bother to take her—realising that their game, whatever it is, must be up—but they'll skip off and leave her most likely."

They hurried into the village street. The church clock was striking eleven and there were very few people about.

"He lives down the other end of the village. I saw the. notice over his cottage this morning," said Helen. "You're sure your arm is all right?"

"It was only numbed. It's coming back now. He must have hit me with a coal-hammer by the feel of it."

The village constable did not bother to conceal his surprise at their late visit. He asked them into his parlour politely and enquired what he could do for them. Helen looked at Ben and left him to do the explaining. He decided that there was little point in fogging the man with his own house-breaking exploits and he told him simply that he was the head of a private enquiry agency who had been investigating the disappearance of an elderly spinster, Miss Victoria Logan of London, who was believed to have been abducted, and that he had just received information of a reliable nature that she was being held against her wishes at Harden Hall by the Burnses.

"And why," asked the constable naturally, "should the Burnses want to do that?"

"That is what we should like to know," said Ben, "but until we get hold of Miss Logan we shan't know."

They could see that the man was not altogether convinced. He said as much.

"You're sure about this story of yours, sir? You see, I know the Burnses and they've always been a respectable couple. I can't believe—"

"Should we come to you if we weren't sure?" put in Helen quickly.

"No—I don't suppose you would," agreed the constable. "Unless," he added, as a thought occurred to him, "unless this was your idea of a joke."

Ben made an exclamation of disgust. "We're wasting time with all this talk."

The constable reflected a moment, obviously in doubt about the story. Then he said: "Very well, we'll go along to the Hall and see what's in this."

The three of them started for the Hall. They walked in silence until they were going up the drive, when the constable turned to them and said, "If you don't mind, sir, you'll let me do the talking to begin with."

"I don't care who does the talking as long as we get Miss Logan," answered Ben.

There were no signs of unusual activity as they approached the house. The policeman pulled the bell. He had to pull a second time before there was any answer. Then came the sound of someone moving in the hall. The hall and door lights came on and Mrs. Burns stood at the doorway, smiling pleasantly at them.

"Good evening, Mrs. Burns," said the policeman. "Sorry to disturb you so late."

"Good evening." Mrs. Burns nodded to them calmly. "Is there anything wrong?"

"So it seems, Mrs. Burns."

"Perhaps you'd better come inside." She held the door open for them and they entered the hall. "What's the trouble?" she asked. The question was addressed to the policeman, but she was looking at Ben. She showed no trace of nervousness. Helen watched her and admired; the woman was an actress. She realised that now—a capable, confident actress, and Helen wondered what was going to happen, wondered with a halfsuspicion that she knew what was about to happen.

"Well," the policeman coughed rather self-consciously; "I'm sorry to have to say it, Mrs. Burns, but this lady and gentleman have come to me with a complaint about you."

"Good gracious me! What can I have done?" The question was asked rapidly and with just the proper amount of surprise, the woman's dark eyes widening with a look that was halfcuriosity, half-alarm.

"They say that you're keeping a lady, by name of Miss Logan, in this house against her wishes. I don't say anything one way or another, mind, Mrs. Burns," he added quickly, "except that I've known you and Mr. Burns long enough now to feel that there must be a mistake about all this somewhere. But I have my duty to perform and I should like to know what you have to say?"

Mrs. Burns' reply was a laugh, a delicious chuckle.

"Why, I've never heard of anyone by that name—and you know yourself that there's only my husband and myself in the house—at least there usually is, but my husband's not here tonight, he's had to go up to London and won't be back before tomorrow night. The whole story is nonsense."

155

"The gentleman says that he's had private information about it. What's more, he says the lady is kept in a box-room at the top of the house or else in the summer house on the island in the lake outside there."

"And I suppose—" this to Ben "—you would like to look for her in both those places?"

"We haven't a search warrant, of course, Mrs. Burns, and I told this gentleman he was mistaken about you. But it would settle this whole affair if you would be kind enough to let us look around. It's giving you a lot of trouble—but it would satisfy everyone concerned if you wouldn't mind."

The policeman, Helen decided, was a sensible person, holding a just balance between both parties, but she was afraid that a search wouldn't do any good now. Mrs. Burns' remark about her husband's trip to London suggested what might have happened.

"You can look where you like. The whole thing is most irregular. If it weren't that I have a sense of humour, I should be angry about it."

"I can assure you, madam," said Ben politely, "that if we are wrong—and it is possible, of course, that my information is false—then I shall not be able to apologise enough and I shall understand that I cannot expect you to forgive me for breaking so rudely upon your evening peace."

"Follow me," was all she said, and began to show them around the house. As she moved off, the policeman looked at Ben and there was a frown on his forehead. Ben looked at Helen. He was beginning to feel very uneasy.

They went over the whole house. The box-room was as it had been when Ben and Helen had first seen it.

"What a curious smell," Helen exclaimed as she stood in the room.

Mrs. Burns smiled. "Yes, it's a patent sprayer my husband was using here this morning to kill the flies. They always seem to congregate up here."

"Of course …" It had successfully killed any lingering odour of scent, too. Mrs. Burns, or perhaps her husband, had a mind which was not impatient of details.

"Well, she's not here," said the policeman.

"There's still the island," declared Ben.

They went outside and by the light of the constable's torch went down to the lake.

"There's a little dinghy over in the laurels," said Mrs. Burns quietly. "We keep it away from the lake so that the village boys shan't find it."

"Oh, there is a boat?" Ben looked at her, a half-smile on his lips.

"Yes, of course." She met Ben's glance boldly.

"It's a long time since I did any rowing," was the policeman's only comment as they got the boat down. There was not room for four people to sit comfortably in the boat so Ben and the policeman went across to the island while Helen and Mrs. Burns waited for them on the shore.

"I feel sure my husband is going to be disappointed over there," said Helen, indicating the torchlight which was now bobbing about the island.

"So am I. I can't think how he could have let himself be persuaded that there was any truth in the information he received."

"Men are easily persuaded where they want to believe, and they're very difficult to manage once they let an idea take possession of them."

Mrs. Burns turned to Helen and in the faint starlight Helen saw a quick look of fear draw her young face into lines, for a moment she had revealed the real woman who lived beneath the composure that had flaunted itself brazenly at them that evening.

"My husband is the same," she said in a low voice. Sometimes I wish—" She stopped, and then said lightly: "Well, we marry them for better or for worse."

The two men came back and the dinghy was hauled back to its hiding place.

"There's no one on the island." The policeman looked at Ben and Helen. "I don't know what to make of this. It's all very irregular. I'm only glad that Mrs. Burns has taken it so kindly."

"That's all right, constable. I'm sure we all make mistakes at times and if, as you say, this gentleman is looking for a missing lady and he thought she was here, well it was just as well to make sure. I feel I should have done the same myself."

"It's nice of you to say that," Ben spoke, his mind chasing an explanation for the disappearance of Miss Logan and Mr. Burns. There were a hundred questions he would have liked to have asked Mrs. Burns, but not one of them could, with any propriety, be put to her. "I can only apologise for the mistake of my informant and ask you to believe that I haven't put this indignity upon you from any frivolous motive."

"Don't worry. I don't bear any malice." Mrs. Burns stood on the hall step and nodded their dismissal. They turned away and the door closed on them. They walked up the drive in silence.

"It's lucky for you that Mrs. Burns took it so well," observed the policeman as they turned into the roadway. "My advice to you is to forget all about the business. If this lady of yours really is missing, the best thing for you to do is to turn the matter over

to the police wherever she comes from." Ben made no reply.

"I think we've got to thank you too for being so patient and understanding." Helen smiled at him.

The man chuckled. "That's all right, madam. It's a part of my duty. 'Tisn't the first time I've been hauled out at night on a wild-goose chase. There's some rummy people in the world, you know, but for all that it don't do to suppose that everything that sounds cock-and-bull to you may not be the truth."

"That," said Helen as they left him, "was a very sensible man."

"Don't talk to me about sense," snapped Ben, irritated with himself. "I should never have left that woman alone in the house. I must say that couple have a pretty good nerve."

"One might almost say that whatever they're up to they deserve to succeed in."

"They won't. I'm determined about that. But I would like to know where Mr. Burns has taken Miss Logan. They can't have bolt-holes all over the country, and it's not easy to cart a woman about against her will."

"I wonder," said Helen, as they moved back towards the *Bull*, "what it's all about?"

"That's what I'd like to know. And, what's more, I'm going to know. It looks as though Miss Logan knows a thing or two which isn't healthy for someone. Which someone?"

"Maybe Burns—or maybe something to do with the Society? I suppose we must notify the police about this?" Ben looked at Helen in amazement.

"Notify the police! We've just done that thing and you see what happened. The police can't help us at this stage. Even if we could convince Scotland Yard of Miss Logan's disappearance they would only stamp around and spoil everything. Besides, aren't you forgetting that the further I carry this thing the bigger will be my bill to Halifax. Where's your business instinct?"

"I was thinking of Miss Logan."

"She's all right. They're treating her well, that's obvious, and I wouldn't mind betting that she's enjoying it."

"That's what you want to believe."

"Are you trying to put me off the thing at this point?" Ben eyed her suspiciously.

Helen was silent for a while. She had a few doubts, but they were easily silenced. And she was still anxious that Ben should go on with the case. After all, she had been instrumental in rousing his interest anew.

"What do you do next?" she asked quietly.

"Have a chat with Spenser—the lawyer in whose hands the sale of the house is—and find out what I can about the Burnses." They turned into the hotel, both silent.

Chapter Eleven

Helen was in the office at nine-thirty the next morning. She and Ben had driven up early from Hormenden. Grace was already in the office. She enquired whether Helen had spent a pleasant weekend and then they got clown to the business of opening the mail. There were fourteen letters and amongst them four commissions, simple affairs that they could do between them in a day. Helen was beginning to appreciate that General Factotums could not expect a steady flow of business from day to day. Their work came spasmodically, and one important commission between a score of minor duties made all the difference between profit and loss. There were days when there was hardly any work to be done and other days when the hours seemed too short for their tasks. It was difficult to organise against such fluctuating pressures of work. Ben was already out on a commission which had been arranged the previous week.

At ten o'clock there was a knock on the door and Hindle entered. He was dressed in his Sunday black. Helen, who happened to be with Grace in the room, noticed his finery, but she did not know that he wore it because he was going to call on Mr. Walter across the Inn and inform him of a strange event which had taken place the previous evening. Mr. Hindle had a great respect for Mr. Walter, and when he had any formal business with him he was always honoured by the Sunday black.

"Morning, ma'am," Hindle greeted Helen.

"Good morning, Hindle."

"Might I have a word with Miss Kirkstall, ma'am?"

"Why, certainly, Hindle." Helen started for the other room, but Hindle went on:

"It isn't exactly private, ma'am, and perhaps you might care to hear about it." He was not anxious to have his audience diminished more than he could help.

Grace wrinkled her forehead and wondered what Hindle could want with her.

"It's about something that happened in these offices last night."

"In here?" Helen was interested.

"Not exactly in this office, ma'am, but in those across the way. The ones that Mr. Rage used to have." He looked at Grace as he spoke and Helen, following his glance, fancied that she saw a troubled shadow pass quickly over Grace's face.

"What happened, Hindle?" Grace asked the question sharply, a quick anxiety waking in her breast.

Deciding that he had worked up the right interest, Hindle swelled his breast and delivered himself of an account of the previous evening's adventure.

It appeared that while on his evening rounds Hindle had noticed a smell of kippers coming from Mr. Rage's room. He had investigated, found the door unlocked and a young man in occupation; a young man who had a fire going from box-wood and his supper grilling.

Hindle had tried to detain the stranger, but he had waited for no explanations and, pushing Hindle aside, had made off over the railings into the darkness of Chain Walk. Hindle watched their mounting surprise and heard their occasional "Ohs!" and "Well I nevers!" with gratification.

"So, you see, I've got to report the matter to Mr. Walter," he said. "I'm going over there in a few minutes to tell him all about it.

But before I go I had to come and see Miss Kirkstall, because there was one thing I wanted cleared up. You see, whoever it was in that room was pretty sure of himself, and he'd been there before that night. In fact, it's my opinion that he'd been using it as a lodging for a little while. He could get into the Inn easy enough and stay hid until I'd locked up—but what I want to know is, how did he get into Mr. Rage's room? It was always kept locked and I had the keys. At least, I thought I had the keys until I came to look and then I found that I only had one key. Well, at first I thought the other one must have been broken until I remembered that it was possible that I'd never had back Miss Kirkstall's key that she used to have when she worked there."

"Oh!" Grace could not keep back her gasp of alarm. Hindle, fortunately put his own interpretation on her cry.

"Now, Miss Kirkstall, I'm not saying I didn't have it back from you. Very likely I did and it was taken from my office at some time. But you see—" he appealed to Helen "—I had to make sure before I put the facts before Mr. Walter, so I thought I'd come up and ask Miss Kirkstall whether she had given the keys back to me."

"Why, I'm sure she did. Didn't you, Grace?" Helen was puzzled by Grace's manner. She knew the girl very well now and she knew that Grace was no Mrs. Burns. Everything that Grace felt or thought was evident in her face. Her expressions were weather vanes that showed each puff and tremor of breeze.

"But I don't know, Mrs. Brown ..." Grace was embarrassed and hesitant. "I can't really say ..."

"But surely you'd remember if you gave me back the key?" Hindle helped her kindly.

"If you don't remember, how do you expect me to?" asked Grace, suddenly suspicious and antagonistic towards him. "I thought I'd given it back to you. But it was some time ago and I may have lost it from my handbag and then forgotten all about it. I can't really say."

"I wish you could remember, miss. It would help a lot. Not that whoever it was is likely to come back, but it's not right that there should be someone going about with one of our keys."

Grace shook her head stubbornly. "I can't remember. I certainly meant to give it to you and maybe I did. But you wouldn't want me to say I had if I wasn't sure I'd given it to you?"

"Of course not, Miss Kirkstall. Well, it's a pity, that's all, because I'd like to know how that key came to be missing. I'm sure I don't know what Mr. Walter will say. It's hardly the thing to have people cooking kippers about the Inn at night."

He thanked them both and turned away to report to Mr. Walter.

When he was safely down the stairs, Helen went over to Grace. Grace kept her eyes on her typewriter keys, but Helen took her by the chin, holding her head up.

"You didn't tell the truth, did you, Grace?"

"Why, Mrs. Brown."

Helen smiled and shook her head. "You can't fool me. I'm not Hindle. I'm not very good at lying myself—" privately she thought she was belittling her powers when she said that "—but you're far worse. Come on, now. Tell me what happened to that key."

"Mrs. Brown, I really don't—" Tears came into Grace's eyes.

Helen said nothing. She went over to the office door and locked it. She didn't want anyone breaking in on this scene. She waited awhile until Grace was sniffing herself back to normal and then she said:

"Come on, Grace. Tell me all about it—that is if you want to.

You know you can rely upon me. What's all the trouble about?"

"Oh, Mrs. Brown." Grace came near to tears again.

"Whoah—no more waterworks," Helen stopped her. "Do you know anything about the man who has been making free with Mr. Rage's old rooms?"

The question was direct, a little severe. Grace hesitated. Then she nodded gently.

"You do?" Helen scarcely hid her surprise. She had not expected this.

"He's my brother," said Grace, calmer now that she had committed herself to the truth. After all, she argued with herself, Mrs. Brown would understand, and, anyway, nothing terrible had happened, really. "He's my brother Gerald."

"And why should Gerald want to sleep and eat over there?"

"He's a sailor," explained Grace.

"I've heard that put as a reason for many things, but it doesn't seem to fit this affair. Why didn't he sleep at home?"

"Because I didn't want him at home and because I wouldn't have let him go home if there was anything I could possibly do to stop it," said Grace suddenly fierce. "I hate him. He's always made me unhappy. Mother used to worry herself sick about him and I didn't want her worried."

Gradually the story came out. Gerald, so Helen learned, was a very unpleasant young man. His unpleasantness had begun in his early years and increased with the passing of time. Once Grace was started on her account of him, she omitted few details. Gerald had been a terror at school. He had imposed himself upon his mother and sister, who were unable to restrain him. Without a father to take the hide off his bottom, he had developed, uncramped, into a wilful, boastful, indolent young man with an easy moral attitude towards money. Poor Mrs. Kirkstall had lived in fear of his exploits, always dreading that he would one day do something that would bring him into the hands of the police and so discredit her and Grace. The end had come when he had forged a cheque in the name of Mr.

Pilchard—a gentleman much interested in Mrs. Kirkstall, Helen gathered —and had got away with fifty pounds belonging to the butcher. Mr. Pilchard had, with true magnanimity, declared that he would take no proceedings as long as Gerald cleared out of England and never came back to worry his mother and sister. Gerald had improved the bargain to the extent of another twenty pounds from Mr. Pilchard and gone off to Australia to farm. That was four years ago. But now he was back in England and had made contact with Grace.

"You can't understand just what his nature is, Mrs. Brown. He knows I'd do anything to keep him from going home to worry Mother. He seems to think that Mr. Pilchard wouldn't do anything about the forged cheque now. It's so long ago. And he's right. Mr. Pilchard would never do anything. He's too fond of Mother. He met me at the station last week. He'd been in London a few days then and he'd spent all his money. He drinks and gambles as badly as he always did, and to stop him from going home I let him have the key to Mr. Rage's room so he could lodge there. You see, I'd promised to draw some money from my Post Office savings—five pounds—and he'd agreed to go off again if I did that."

"And do you think he intended to go off again so easily?"

"I don't know, Mrs. Brown. Really, I don't know. He's a devil, and you can never tell. All I know is that I'd have done anything to stop him from going home. Mother doesn't know he's in England."

Helen put her arm around Grace's shoulder. "I shouldn't worry, Grace. I think I should have done exactly the same as you did."

"But what am I to do now? He's sure to come to me again … Oh dear, Mrs. Brown …"

"Now, don't you worry. If Gerald comes to you again, you put him off and let me know about it. Perhaps we'll call in General Factotums to help. And don't worry about the key. They're not likely to find out who it was using the rooms if we don't help them. And there's no reason why we should. They must put a fresh lock on the door."

"If only I were a man," sighed Grace, cheered by Helen's sympathy.

"You're not, so we must find some other way. But, whatever you do, don't let him have any of your money before you see me. Promise."

"I promise, Mrs. Brown. And thank you."

Helen went back to her room. Something would have to be done about Master Gerald Kirkstall, but at the moment she was not clear what.

*　*　*　*　*

While Helen was hearing Grace's confession, Ben had finished his business, which had taken him to the other side of the river. He came across Westminster Bridge, enjoying the river scene, and then hailed a taxi.

"Chancery Lane," he commanded the taxi-man.

The taxi swung around Trafalgar Square, its fountain freshening the air, and into the Strand. London was looking clean and bright, full of colour and movement. In another month the summer would have left it dusty and worn the bright, fresh dress into the jaded material of stuffiness. June in London made Ben think of a young girl wearing grown-up clothes for the first time—a fresh, lovely girl, curiously adult, yet still gauche, with the tricks and hesitancies of the child.

In Chancery Lane Ben had the taxi stop outside the offices of Spenser and Trout.

Mr. Spenser was in and, after Ben had waited a while, he was shown into the lawyer's wide, low-ceilinged room. The dark, solid antiquity of the room pleased Ben as his eyes went quickly round before he steadied them in an examination of Mr. Spenser, whom he had never seen before. Mr. Spenser was standing behind his desk, his bony wrists and hands working together, his deeply recessed eyes watching Ben calmly.

"Sit down, Mr. Brown."

Ben sat down and was immediately hidden as he sank into the deep leather chair, by a bowl of red roses on Mr. Spenser's desk. Mr. Spenser leaned forward and moved them.

"Lovely, aren't they?" he said. "I'm very fond of roses. These are J. G. Thorntons. No scent, of course, but the colour compensates for that."

"The only rose I know by name," said Ben lightly, "is a Dorothy Perkins and even then I shouldn't be able to recognise the flower. But I'm no gardener, Mr. Spenser."

Mr. Spenser waved a thin hand as if to suggest that we couldn't all be gardeners and there was no unusual fault in Ben because roses meant nothing to him.

"I came to see you," said Ben when they had dealt with the roses, "about a Miss Victoria Logan." As he spoke he was watching Spenser closely, for Spenser was looking at him with a degree of concentration showing in his eyes that attracted Ben. He recognised in Spenser a man of power, a man who could be resolute to the exclusion of everything except that upon which he had determined.

"Miss Logan is a client of mine," said Spenser evenly. "What about her?"

"We have a client—I am not at liberty to mention his name—who is interested in Miss Logan."

"When you mention a client, you refer I take it to your business as—" Spenser glanced at Ben's card "—as General Factotums?"

"Quite. Our client is interested primarily in the Society for Progressive Rehabilitation—you know it, I imagine—and through them in Miss Logan, who is a member of the Society."

Spenser nodded gently as Ben went on with his story. Ben told how he had investigated the Society and found nothing wrong, how an odd chance had put him on to Miss Logan and how he had come to the conclusion that there was a possibility that she might have been abducted. He said nothing of the cigarette clues, but kept to a broad outline to keep his story short. He told of his visit to Hormenden and his discovery and loss of Miss Logan and his conviction that she was being held against her will, and his complete ignorance of the cause of the mystery.

Spenser listened without interruption until he had finished. Then he coughed gently and, tapping his fingertips together, said slowly:

"This is a most extraordinary story. Frankly, I find it a little fantastic. Still ... before we go into that, may I ask why you have come to me about this, Mr. Brown?"

"Because of the Burns people, obviously. I learned from the Maidstone house agents that you were acting for the Society in the sale of the house and I wondered if you could give me any information about the Burnses. I rather presumed that you would have appointed the caretakers at the Hall."

"You're quite right, Mr. Brown, in both instances. I am the agent for the Society and I did appoint the Burnses. But that appointment was made on the recommendation of the Society. Naturally, I had to allow them that right. Mr. Tomms suggested Burns, and when I saw the man I had no reason to raise any objection. I've only seen Mr. Burns that once—his wife not at all. I know nothing about them, but I do know something about Mr. Tomms. I may say quite candidly that I have a great admiration for the man. You see—"

Spenser stopped and compressed his lips. He seemed to be assessing Ben minutely, an inspection that made Ben nervously aware of his many deficiencies. The lawyer went on:

"What I am about to tell you, Mr. Brown, is confidential and would not be divulged to you unless I felt it absolutely necessary in my clients' interests. Yes, my clients—for I act for

Mr. Tomms in the house matter, of course. I do so because I do not wish you to go to the police with an unsubstantial story which might bring an entirely guiltless man into undeserved public attention. Can you be absolutely sure that you saw Miss Logan at the Hall? I'll tell you why I ask." His hand, raised quickly, killed Ben's movement to speak. "Miss Logan came to me some time ago in great distress because she had learned that Mr. Tomms had a criminal record. It was true, he had—in Canada—but he had served his sentence and in the eyes of the law was a normal citizen again. She was worried that such a man should have undisputed control of the Society's large resources. As a matter of fact, it worried me for a while. But I promised her to see Mr. Tomms about it, and I asked her to keep her information to herself until I had seen him. Well, I saw him and put the whole matter straightforwardly to him. He was most understanding. To him the Society means everything. He agreed that it would be better if the money matters were controlled by someone else as well as himself. He has agreed to bring the question before the next meeting of the Society's Finance Committee and to arrange for a panel of three to have full authority to sign cheques and other incidentia connected with the finance."

"And has this been done?"

"Not yet. You will appreciate that it had to be done naturally. He insisted upon that—for reasons which are obvious. He would not have been discreet to call a special meeting of the Committee. It is being dealt with at the next monthly Committee meeting, which takes place a week tomorrow, on the Tuesday.

He has acted entirely reasonably in this matter."

"And Miss Logan?"

"When the arrangement was made I wrote at once to her and explained everything and asked her—as I was sure she
        would—to forget Mr. Tomms's past."

"Did she reply?"

"No. But I cannot think it is because she has been abducted. In the first place, I cannot see any reason why she should be abducted. It would serve no end—not for Tomms, anyway. And, secondly, Miss Logan is an elderly spinster and a little odd in her manners. You say she is not at her house, nor has sent any forwarding address for her letters? It may well be that she does not want to be bothered with letters. It is possible that she has gone abroad somewhere or to some English resort. But if you are so convinced that something has happened to her, I will write to those places which I know she visits and ascertain whether she is at any of them. We should know in a few days. If we have no answer then I agree that we may reasonably become anxious. Don't think I am being apathetic about your convictions, Mr. Brown. I am an old man—and you are young and impetuous. You want to do the best for your client, and you say you saw Miss Logan in Kent, only for a moment or two and through a skylight —and before that you had only seen her once at a meeting. Could you be so sure that it was her?"

"I'm positive!" Ben was a little angry at the man's attitude. Spenser smiled at Ben's vociferous assertion.

"A search of the house revealed nothing. Come, Mr. Brown, admit that you might have been mistaken. I've been dealing with eccentric old people like Miss Logan all my life. Her leaving her home so abruptly does not surprise me so much as it does you."

Ben interrupted with an impatient gesture. "Then you refuse to do anything?"

Spenser's hand rose in an indulgent movement.

"I will do everything I can. Be sure of that. I will get into touch with Mr. Tomms today and have a word with him about this Burns. I cannot do more until I have failed to locate Miss Logan, and I do not anticipate failure. Good day, Mr. Brown."

171

Ben was dismissed. He stood, facing Mr. Spenser. The man was being entirely reasonable—that was the trouble. Somehow he felt that he was being too reasonable. Most men would have been inclined towards his point of view, ignoring their common sense, and have been persuaded by their instincts. He supposed Mr. Spenser had learnt to ignore his dramatic instincts. He held out his hand.

"Thank you for your patience, sir."

"That's quite all right. You did right in coming to me."

Ben turned away and as he did so his eyes rested for a moment on the ash tray which stood upon the far side of the desk. There was some ash from a pipe in it and one cigarette stub, a large, only half-smoked cigarette that was at once recognisable as hand-rolled. From the butt, as though it had been deliberately placed there to attract attention, showed a golden star and the encircled words, *Etoile d'Or*.

Spenser saw him to the door and, as it shut upon him, Ben stood still, his mind churning with thoughts and suspicions. He was in the general office of the firm. By the window a girl sat at a small switchboard. He stared at her, hardly conscious of her puzzled look at him as she spoke into her mouthpiece, delivering her words with the automatic control of one whose thoughts are far away.

"Is that Mr. Ballard's house? Mr. Dorian Ballard? Who's that? Oh! Well this is from Mr. Spenser—Spenser and Trout, yes. Would you mind giving a message to Mr. Ballard? Yes, Mr.

Spenser thanks Mr. Ballard for his letter, and he'll be glad to take dinner with him at Mr. Ballard's flat at six-thirty this Thursday. Got it? Goodbye …"

She turned to Ben at once, her eyes widening with a look which was half-alarm, half-amusement.

"Are you all right, sir?" she asked. It was not every day that good-looking young men visited Mr. Spenser and then came back into the outer office and stared at her as if she were a vision.

Her words brought Ben back to life. He smiled mechanically and made for the door.

"I was thinking about something," he said apologetically. The girl laughed pleasantly. Her friendly face brought an impulse into his mind. He stopped with his hand on the door. There was no one else in the office.

"Was that the Ballard you were phoning about then? The author?"

"That's him," said the girl. "Do you know him?"

"Only from photographs. I've just finished reading his book."

"I never have time for books," said the girl, without any tone of regret. A buzzer set her on her feet and she hurried towards Mr. Spenser's room.

Ben went, with a last nod to her, and as he walked up Chancery Lane towards Fountain Inn he was saying to himself: "Thursday night at half-past six." He repeated it like a chant.

*   *   *   *   *

"Organised villainy," said Ben, carefully parting the flesh from his *sole bonne femme*, "is seldom a complete thing. That is to say that most essays in crime are planned on the basis of chance. A chance which presents itself fortuitously to the villain or villains. That is to say—"

"Do you have to start every other sentence with that phrase?" asked Helen, sipping her *Liebfraumilch*.

"No. What I mean is this. Something happens which suddenly presents you with an opening to use it in order to bring off some criminal scheme. Until that something happens, you are not a lost soul—you're just an ordinary sort of person. But once the chance arrives and the suggestion takes root in your mind, you find that you're at heart a villain. That's why the old saying about never putting temptation in people's way is so wise. You never know that at heart you may not be a thief or a murderer."

"Where does all this get us?"

"To this. That life is never so simple that you can at any point take a pen and paper and begin to work backwards along it in a logical sequence. That is to say Sorry, mean we've reached a point in this affair when we ought to be able to sit down and reason things out and get some idea of what it's all about. But we can't. Why? Because at the bottom of it all I'll swear there's some fluky working of chance on which the whole edifice is built."

"In detective stories they always have long tables showing all the times that people arrived and the position on the window-sill of the poison bottle at every half-hour during the fatal day. But I

forgot. We haven't had our murder yet, have we?"

"Nor do we, I hope. That nice Miss Logan."

"How do you know she's nice?"

"Well, she looked nice. All women look nice when they're crocheting. Anyway, all we know is this. That there may be something fishy about the Society. That Miss Logan has disappeared and is being held by Burns, who probably is working with Tomms and or Spenser. That Spenser is a liar. That Burns must have seen him this morning and left his cigarette stub in the ash-tray. That we have a week to find out what it's all about or else Mr. Halifax calls the police in. Now what do we do?"

Ben regarded the time limit with particular regret. He had telephoned Mr. Halifax after his visit to Mr. Spenser and reported to him. He had said nothing of his suspicions of Spenser. Halifax had been adamant about the time limit—despite Ben's assurance that he was convinced that Miss Logan was being well-treated. It had taken a great deal of persuasion to stop him from insisting on informing the police at once. Only the fact that they had so little to go on made him hesitate.

Ben leaned back in his chair and looked round the restaurant. Other couples and parties chatted quietly; there was a pleasant movement of waiters and the soft noise of cutlery and china.

There was almost a devotional atmosphere about the place, a shrine consecrated to the worship of food.

"There is only one thing we can do. We must find Miss Logan. Once we get hold of her we shall know what it's all about."

"Did it occur to you that she might have been carted off because she knew that Tomms had a criminal past?"

"If that were so, why should Spenser—assuming a liaison between them—let us know that fact?"

"It's possible," Ben gazed dreamily through his tobacco smoke, "that when Miss Logan found it out, her knowledge was inconvenient to Tomms, we'll say. She was a talkative old lady, incapable of holding a secret long. But now, when we're told about Tomms, it may not matter so much, because whatever was to be done is already done and can't be spoilt by that knowledge getting abroad."

"That's speculation. The thing is to find the lady. It's no easy job to hide a woman like that. They can't keep her at Harden Hall any longer. Where is she, then? Surely we're better finders than Tomms, Burns or Spenser are hiders?"

"We are. We must watch Tomms and Spenser. You can look after Tomms and I'll see to Spenser. You'd better tell Grace as much as is good for her and get her to help. The other work will have to slide for a week. It can only be for a week, anyhow."

Helen studied Ben's face. It had that frowning, fierce cast which she associated with his moods of vigour and decision. She looked at him with affection. Love was a funny thing. When she had first met him, she had disliked him actively. She had marked him as assuming, indolent and without purpose. His dark, wellbrushed hair, his intelligent face, his general manner had all promised more than he seemed to fulfil. It was some time before she had realised that he was none of the things she had felt he was. His real character came out in an exciting contrast to her settled opinion about him, and, without alarm, she had one day found herself loving him, finding in his beliefs a sanity which she could share. Yes, love was a very funny thing indeed. She should have married quite a different type of man, someone who could give her all those things which she felt she really heeded: a man of strength who would appreciate his responsibilities towards a wife; a steady, reliable creature who would be—yes, who would be as dull and unpalatable as ditch-water. She felt annoyed with Halifax that he should have imposed a time limit upon them. It was unfair to Ben, and for a few moments she was quite unworried by any thought of Miss Logan's incarceration, unpleasant or kindly.

Ben's hand touched hers across the table and he grinned at her. "You've got quite a maternal look in your eyes, Helen. What are you thinking about?"

She left her hand with him, but said primly:

"I was thinking how tired I'd become of that tie you're wearing and then I began to think of other ties—but not silk ones."

"You talk in riddles."

"Maybe that's because I don't want you to understand me?"

Ben scoffed. "Is that another way of telling me I can't solve a riddle?"

"I know one you haven't solved—and you've only got a week left to do it in."

Chapter Twelve

Helen went back to the office alone. Ben had gone off by himself, refusing to tell her what he was going to do, and impressing upon her the necessity to keep an eye on Tomms.

As she climbed the stairs to the office, George Crane came down from Craddock and Couch's office. As he passed her, he smiled pleasantly, his broad face a genial, assuring phenomenon on the dark stairway. Helen nodded to him.

On the top landing, she met Mr. Parcross of Eastern Imports Ltd., coming out of General Factotums. He beamed at her affably and said:

"I've just returned your paste-pot, Mrs. Brown." He went down the stairs whistling merrily.

"How often does Mr. Parcross borrow our paste-pot?" Helen asked Grace.

"Fairly often, Mrs. Brown. He's just returned it. But he borrowed an india-rubber. He's always borrowing. But I think it's only because he wants to come and have a chat. He gets lonely in that office with nothing much to do. Spends most of his time at those competitions. He used to come up and talk to me when I was with Mr. Rage. I think he must have a fair amount of money."

"What makes you think that?"

"Well, his clothes. They're very good. So's his watch, and when he's talking to you he often says things that make you wonder. Besides that, he takes August and September off each year and goes abroad. All that doesn't sound like the manager of a one-man firm like Eastern Imports, Ltd."

"No, it doesn't," agreed Helen. Then, her mind reverting to a train of thought which had started on the stairs, she went on: "I passed your Mr. Crane on the stairs. You haven't talked about him much since you went to Ealing together."

"He's not my Mr. Crane!" said Grace a little sharply.

"I thought you liked him?"

"So I do. Well, you know what men are." Grace pretended to be busy with some papers.

"I do. They're gullible fish. Only the bait must be bright for them to take it." She studied Grace closely, her mind busy. She seemed to have known Grace for so long now that she had accepted her without any clear picture remaining in her mind of the girl. She was Grace—a pleasant, undistinguished creature who did her job well, who was vaguely good-hearted and sensible, but lacking in those characteristics that would make her stand out in a crowd or even attract attention in a room with a handful of men and women. Grace, Helen decided, would never be able to dominate a crowd by her looks or her personality. That was a gift given only to a few. Yet, she decided—a decision that implied that something must be done about it—Grace could be made to hold her own in a small company. Her skin was no redand-white blossom. It was neither one thing nor the other. It was just skin. Her face was thin, but, Helen was certain, it had possibilities. Its puckish quality could be developed, and the eyebrows Goodness, how unimaginative were some girls about their eyebrows.

As she talked, she was playing fairy godmother to this girl, who seemed unaware of the human convention that the female should wear the fine feathers to attract the male. No wonder George Crane took such little stock of the girl, Helen mused.

Helen went to her room and spent ten minutes telephoning. She came out to Grace afterwards, holding a slip of paper.

"Grace, I want you to put on your hat and go to these two addresses. This one first. And at each you will ask for the lady whose name I have written down and say who you are. They'll know what to do. You may find it'll take you some time, so if you are late don't bother to come back tonight."

Grace took the paper curiously. "Is it business?" she asked.

Helen smiled. "I could be pompous and say 'Yes, the great business of life'. Ben would say that. You do as I say, Grace, and you won't regret it. You want George to like you, don't you? Of course you do. Well, sometimes we have to pander to a man's semi-blindness. That's what you're going to do. Now, go on. Off with you!" She pushed Grace from the room and shut the door on her. Then she opened it again and caught Grace before she had begun to descend the stairs.

"You remember the five pounds you were going to give your brother?"

Grace nodded, her lips sealed with her bemusement.

"Well, if he turns up again, you're to let me know and I'll deal with him. But what I want you to remember this afternoon is that you might easily have not had that five pounds still. It might be gone. In fact, it is gone."

Grace did not attempt to work things out. She started for the first address. She trusted Helen and that was all there was to be said. No amount of mystery could shake her faith once it was avowed.

Helen returned to the job of watching Mr. Tomms. But Mr. Tomms did not show up. She sat in the window until her neck ached watching the courtyard. At four o'clock she was seized with a bright idea. She rang up his office on the floor below and, masking her voice, asked, when his secretary replied to her, if she might speak with Mr. Tomms. The secretary informed her that Mr. Tomms was not in, nor was he coming back that afternoon and that she, the secretary, had no knowledge of his whereabouts.

Within ten minutes Helen had left the office and got Mr. Tomms's home address from Hindle. Hindle had nearly all the private addresses of tenants in case of emergency. Mr. Tomms lived at 32 Adrian Road, Hampstead.

Helen went to Adrian Road, Hampstead. It was a long road, overshadowed by tall houses with narrow bits of garden at their feet—gardens that sloped downwards to basement windows and were morose with laurels and ferns.

Helen walked past No. 32 and was unimpressed. Its windows were heavily curtained, its brass bright, the door paint well scrubbed and the front steps newly hearthstoned. She found her way to a telephone booth and got from Enquiries the telephone number of the house. She rang the house and, when answered, asked if she might speak to Mr. Tomms. If Mr. Tomms did answer, she was prepared to become a vacuum cleaner saleslady doing some telephonic canvassing. But Mr. Tomms did not answer. A feminine voice informed her that Mr. Tomms did not appear to be in his rooms. Helen made her thanks and rang off. The word "rooms" had given her an idea. She hurried back towards No. 32, feeling very important and pleased with herself. She considered that she was showing a quite meritorious intelligence.

Her ring at the bell was answered by a pudding-faced maid, who listened to the apocrypha that she had been told by the local tobacconist—tobacconists, Helen knew, were always a mine of information about local lodging accommodation—she might be

181

able to get rooms in the house. The maid asked her in and retired, saying that she would fetch Miss Badger.

Despite her name, Miss Badger was a gentle, thin, tiny woman with a weak voice, a wrinkled throat and a timid air of wanting to please. She wore black and her pale skin and grey hair gave the impression of a mushroom miraculously moving—her fragility was fungoid and yet unrepellent. Helen was convinced that Miss Badger's lodgers bullied her. She felt friendly towards the woman at once.

Miss Badger had only one set of rooms vacant. These were at the top of the house and at the rear. They looked immediately across the line of the Hampstead Railway and then away into the blue distance of London. Helen stood by them, picking out landmarks—the red block of a furniture repository, the steely spires and domes of churches.

"It's lovely, isn't it?" said Miss Badger. Helen guessed that the woman had taken a fancy to her. "But I must warn you that if you take the rooms it'll be a little while before you get used to the sound of the trains coming by. They even make the house vibrate a little—but no one notices it after a while."

Helen felt criminal in encouraging the woman, but she had to do it. She led Miss Badger into a discussion of her house, of her lodgers and she soon learned that Mr. Tomms—"such a dear, sweet soul"—had possession of a large bed-sitting-room on the ground floor. By the time they had reached the front door, and Helen had promised to let Miss Badger know her decision about the rooms after she'd seen another one which had been recommended to her, she knew what she had come to find out. There was nowhere at No. 32 where Mr. Tomms could have brought and hidden Miss Logan.

She went—for it was now quite late—back to the flat to acquaint Ben with this news.

Grace went at once to the first address, which proved to be a gown shop near Bond Street. She entered the shop and asked for

Madame Vivier. Madame Vivier arrived, a rather plump, fullfaced woman in a black shop-gown, a pearly brooch holding it at the throat. She spoke in a husky, surprising voice.

"You are Mees Kirkstall?"

"That's right," answered Grace. "Mrs. Brown sent me along."

Madame Vivier said nothing. She stood back and looked at Grace as though she were eyeing a statue in the Louvre. She circled round her, anxious to miss none of the finer points.

"*Bien*," she said happily to Grace, and then, softly, as she turned to beckon an assistant, "*Incroyable*."

"You wear this colour stocking, always?" she pointed to Grace's stockings. Grace, mystified, agreed that she did. "And thees dress, of course, you have made yourself?" She indicated Grace's dress, which was navy blue with white piping on the sleeves.

"Yes, I did. I got the pattern from the *Girls' Forum*. It was given away one week. Do you like it?" Grace was always quick to recognise and respond to friendliness, and Madame Vivier, whatever else, was obviously friendly. For a moment she forgot her curiosity about her errand.

"I think it is very interesting," said Madame ambiguously. "And now …" She turned to a girl assistant and indulged in a long colloquy in French, during which the girl giggled three times. And then Madame turned to Grace: "You will please be good enough to follow thees young lady, Miss Kirkstall. She will see to you. You do not have to worry. Mrs. Brown has arranged everything. She is a good arranger, that woman, *n'est-ce pas?*"

Grace was flirted away into the rear of the shop and politely bullied into a dressing-cubicle.

In the next few minutes had it not been for the memory of Helen's words—and a growing awareness of their full meaning—

Grace would have lost her temper and hurried from the shop, her pride hurt. As it was she submitted, filled with a splendid faith in Helen's wisdom. Within ten minutes, she had been robbed of her rightful clothes and draped in a smart little suit and hat. She was allowed no choice. The suit and the hat were put upon her, the assistant expressed her approval, smoothed aside Grace's tentative demands for an explanation, stated that her old dress would be packed and sent to the office for her, and then Grace was out in the shop under the now approving eye of Madame Vivier.

"Ha, *ma chérie. Ça, c'est bien sûr la vraie chose*! It is perfect. No, no, mademoiselle. We do not talk of money. Mrs. Brown she is the arranger, *non*? Very well. *Maintenant, écoutez-moi, Ma'mselle*. When you want anything else new—you come to me. I will not charge dear and it is better that I choose for you. There are some people—you understand, *parfaitement*, some— for whom one must always choose. You are such, Miss Kirkstall. But do not let it worry you. You have Madame Vivier to choose for you now, and where is there such a one? *Bonjour, Ma'mselle, bonjour* ..."

Grace was in the street, dazed by the flow of Madame's words. She had walked into the shop, had her clothes taken from her, a new set put upon her and here she was in the street and still a little unsure of what it was all about.

Before she had resolved her mind she had arrived at the next address, which was not far from Madame Vivier's. It was a small door at the side of a furrier's shop.

"Miss Christopher, please?" A page-boy in a blatant yellow and red suit answered the door. He conducted Grace with a solemn strut, like a starling going down a row of peas, into a small, luxuriously furnished waiting-room.

Miss Christopher arrived. She was a young, fair-haired girl, in a white, wrap-over smock—a fresh-faced woman who would have seemed more at home in an orchard.

"You're Miss Kirkstall? Well, well. You look as though you'd been letting Helen bully you. You want to stand up to her. She's always trying to arrange people's lives. Say—" She stood back and examined Grace just as Madame Vivier had done, but her eyes never left Grace's face. "Say—I think Helen was right.

You've got something there. That's a nice suit you're wearing."

"You like it, really?"

"Sure. Well, come on. Let's get to work. It's going to be long and a little tedious for you, but you'll be all right, and if you get bored with my chatter or if I ask impertinent questions, you just ignore me. I don't mind talking to myself a bit."

And again Grace was whisked off. But this time her ordeal was far more trying and longer. But now Grace was beginning to understand. She even began to feel excited and to wonder why she had not thought of the scheme herself. She sat, thoughts turning rapidly inside her brain, and now and then some remark from Miss Christopher would set her laughing. She was alternately scared and happy. Scared when she tried to think ahead and happy when she felt her fingers on the new suit. Really, she'd heard a lot about having all these things done to your face, but well ...

In all her life Grace was never to forget the moment when she was led out of the working-cubicle, with all its shining electrical apparatus into the waiting-room and stood in front of the long mirror.

"Take a look at yourself!" Miss Christopher smiled at her in the friendliest way. And Grace took a look at herself and saw a new self. Confronting her was a young lady of poise and attraction, a girl with a slender, well-shaped face. And, looking at herself in the glass, looking at this new person, Grace miraculously began to feel like the stranger in the glass. She began to feel as though she had had a spring-clean and discovered her real self underneath the litter of the years. She felt astonishingly confident and capable, and she knew she was looking nice, so nice that she was at once seized with the desire to go quickly into the street and let other people see this new Grace and to see how they reacted.

The page-boy saw her out. He did not seem to be at all moved by the transformation, but then, no doubt, he was accustomed to the miracle. But in the street Grace knew that the miracle was lasting. She knew, without actual knowledge, that people were observing her. The feeling was strange and thrilling, and she was faintly alarmed until she got used to the smiles that slipped to the faces of men as they came towards her.

Grace was at once anxious to get back to the office and see Helen; but as she came up from the Chancery Lane Tube station she realised that she was too late. It was gone six.

She stood for a moment outside the Inn, wondering whether she would go in. A party of typists from the Granada Finance Company passed her, and she saw one of them eye her with the look that any woman will give to another whose appearance rouses interest and admiration. Grace looked at her wrist watch. It was about the time George left the office for the station. She smiled to herself and then began to walk slowly down Holborn, stopping to look in shops and frequently glancing backwards.

George Crane turned out of Fountain Inn just as the clocks began to mark half-past six. He went down Holborn, scarcely conscious of the evening traffic and crush. As he walked he could feel a letter crinkling in his breast pocket. The letter had come for him at the office by the afternoon's post. It was a letter such as would have sent most young men into the delicious vagrancy of day-dreaming. And it was not entirely without a disturbing effect on George. It made him feel happy, proud and very satisfied with himself. It offered, too, a very definite pat on the back to that very definite, very serious, thing which he referred to privately as "my future." The letter crinkled because it was expensive paper.

The paper was headed with a tiny crest and an address in neat roman capitals. George approved the design of the crest and the general layout of the printed heading. But he approved far more the content of the letter. It said, austerely, yet with a hint of congratulation that had stirred

George

"DEAR MR. CRANE,—With reference to your application for the vacant position of Assistant to the County Architect, I shall be glad if you will kindly attend at this office for interview at 2.30 p.m. on Tuesday, the 7th July. Your third-class travelling fare and subsistence expenses will be refunded to you."

Which meant, George knew, that out of the vast number of applications sent in for the job, perhaps half a dozen had been picked out and their owners requested to attend an interview. The Committee would then see each of them and make a choice, and that choice, George was determined, should fall upon him.

Next Tuesday would see him an Assistant County Architect in one of the pleasantest of the southern counties. He raised his head and smiled before him with that happy expression which seizes all of us at such moments. It is a cat's smile, a silky, slightly foolish grin that creases a cat's face as it sits and watches the fire flames after a bowl of warm milk. In that moment, London and all its millions, the streets and all their roaring, frantic traffic became very unimportant to George. It seemed to him that he was about the most wonderful, cleverest person that had ever lived. He wouldn't have told anyone that, but he believed it, and it was a healthy, encouraging belief, a belief which once lost to a man can seldom be recaptured, a belief without which ambition dies and success slips tantalisingly away.

And then George forgot about his coming interview and was aware that for some time he had been walking in the wake of a young lady about whose movements there was something strangely familiar. He was immediately aware of the external world.

The young lady was about five yards ahead of him, walking on the inside of the pavement. George studied her with a detachment that was tinged by an insistent feeling that he had some personal interest in this young lady.

She walked along the pavement, showing a pair of very neat and well-shod legs that flashed a pair of ankles that needed no excuse for rising and falling with a pert, attractive swing as though inviting attention. She wore a tiny jacket that came no lower than the waist, of a soft material that was a mixture of greens, reds and browns, and a well-shaped skirt of similar material. It was a simple little suit such as hundreds of girls were wearing that summer, and yet this suit seemed to sit upon its owner with the finality and fit of a suit which has waited long for the one person in the world who can understand and perfectly portray its piquant and unique qualities. And for hat, George was aware of a becoming arrangement which, from the back, suggested some historical lineage and yet lost no *chic* because it acknowledged the past.

The young lady walked steadily on, as though she had an objective and knew that she would reach it without need for hurry. People coming from the other direction, especially the men, George noticed, looked at her as they passed and then came down towards him, their faces brighter and somehow illuminated by the sight, their looks the not always unconscious tribute that most men pay to a pleasing woman.

Normally George would have noticed all these things and then dismissed them. There were always pretty women and always men to admire them. He held nothing against the convention and had himself been forced into admiration once or twice. But he could not dismiss so summarily this young lady. For one thing, her gait was sufficient to keep her just ahead of him and for another there definitely was something familiar about her walk, though for the life of him George could not think what it was.

George did what any man would have done to avoid the tantalisation of walking behind a mystery. He quickened his pace and in a very few steps was level with the young lady. As he drew level, he casually turned his head in her direction as though he were glancing into the shop window they were passing.

What he saw intrigued him, but it did not immediately explain the mystery. The girl was good-looking. Her skin was a pale olive colour, her lips, touched with just a hint of colour, formed a mouth that was firm and yet innocent of stubbornness, and her brown eyes were filled with a mischievous, daring light. George was no fool. He saw at once that it was a face that owed a great deal to art. The eyebrows had been plucked and given a new emphasis, and yet nothing had been done to obtrude a sense of artificiality. Every quality that could be helped had been helped and with discretion. George was admiring the judicious restraint which had proved itself by the effect he had noticed on passing men and upon himself. He turned his head and, maintaining his pace, was a couple of steps ahead when he looked round and met the girl's gaze. She was smiling and the smile betrayed her. George stopped dead, felt himself blush quickly, and the next minute was raising his hat.

"Why, Miss Kirkstall ... Well, I ... How can I have—"

Grace said nothing, enjoying his confusion. It was nice to find George confused.

Here he was blushing and stammering before her like a schoolboy. Of all the thrills of that afternoon, Grace counted that the highest.

She smiled at George and enjoyed herself. It was the first time that she had ever seen him show signs of self-consciousness.

George soon recovered himself.

"You'll excuse me for being so rude, Miss Kirkstall," he said, "but you're looking so different I did not recognise you at first."

"That's because you've never seen this suit before. Do you like it?" Here was a chance to discuss her transformation with someone.

"Ay, I do like it. But it's no the suit alone. You've got a new look altogether, Miss Kirkstall. The kind of look I should imagine people have when they come into money or hear some good news. You've had something done to your hair?"

"Why, Mr. Crane, I never knew you took such an interest in womanly things. I thought you were only interested in buildings." Her position gave Grace the chance to tease him, and she took it.

"It seems to me that there are times, Miss Kirkstall, when you imply, because I am of a different nationality to yourself, that I am curiously devoid of the ordinary emotions of all men. I like to see a good-looking woman as much as I like to see a welldesigned building, and I can take pleasure in both." George was grinning.

Grace had never known him to be so lively, and his eyes as he spoke were on her face the whole time, as though he were seeing her for the first time and finding the sight pleasant. Which was indeed the truth. George had suddenly discovered Grace and he was a little dismayed that he could have known her for so long and have been unaware of the fundamental charm and good looks that belonged to her. It was typical of his nature that he did not press her with any question to reveal the reason for her change. He accepted the emergence of the imago, content with the beauty of its flashing wings.

When they were in the train and it was nearing George's station, he turned and said to Grace quietly, "Are you interested in history, Miss Kirkstall?" He spoke quietly because there were other men in the carriage. It was these other men, too, who had brought him to the point of speaking. He could see, from the covert glances they shot at Grace over their papers, that they thought she was a smart, pleasant creature. George found himself resenting their interest.

As Helen had foreseen, George fell into the trap easily. Grace saw, too, and although she was glad, she was also—for a second or two—angry that he should have been so impressed by fine clothes and a new coiffure. Then she forgot that. After all, a woman had no right to ignore her possibilities.

"Why, what do you mean?" she asked.

"Well, I notice from the display boards that there's a film called *King of the Carribees* showing at your Bromley Cinema. It's a fine, historical film about pirates, I believe and I'm vairy interested in pirates. I have been since I was a boy. And I was wondering if you would care to accompany me there tomorrow night."

Grace knew then, and gratefully acknowledged it, the full power that lies in the hands of a woman who uses clothes and cosmetics with skill. She had caught George, made George—who had once been contemptuous in his denunciation of films and cinemas—ask her to go to a cinema with him. She knew that she ought to pretend to some hestiation, to "hum and ha" for a time just to put him into a small agony of expectancy, but Grace could not do it. She wanted to go with him, and she showed right away that she was glad to go. Before George got out, it was all arranged.

Grace's mother was as surprised as George had been at her change. But her surprise took a different line at once.

"Heavens, Grace!" There was real animation in Mrs. Kirkstall's eyes, and her cheeks were actually flushed with

colour. "You don't look like my daughter."

"Oh, Mother!"

"You look much better. Grace, dear, I never knew you had it in you. But how did it happen? Where did you get that suit, and that manicure and face treatment. They must have cost money?"

"They did, Mother. But you can do a lot for five pounds. I drew it from my Post Office Savings—and I don't regret a penny of it. Are you really surprised?"

"I should say I am."

"Then you're going to be more surprised still. Mr. Crane is taking me to the pictures tomorrow night. Yes, it's true—and I'm bringing him back here to supper afterwards."

"I can't believe it. Did you tell him Mr. Pilchard would be here. It's his night."

"Well—" Grace wrinkled her nose "—he doesn't know about the supper yet, but he'll come, and I'm sure he won't mind Mr. Pilchard. In fact, they'll probably get on very well together."

"Well, I hope so, Grace. From what you've told me about him, he seems a very determined young man."

"Oh, Mother, he is rather nice!"

Mrs. Kirkstall looked at Grace and smiled. There was a time she could remember when she had thought the same of the late Mr. Kirkstall—and perhaps she still did think the same about him. She had to admit that she was a little surprised at Grace. She would never have thought a daughter of hers would have schemed so deliberately. Well, it was useful to find that there was one member of the family who wasn't afraid to make up her mind and act. She wondered now … Ought she to decide about Mr. Pilchard?

"Coming, Grace," she called as Grace's voice came to her from the kitchen.

Chapter Thirteen

The next day, which was Tuesday, Grace learned that Miss Christopher's ministrations were to be a gift from Helen. Her bill at Madame Vivier's she could meet easily with the five pounds from her savings. When she tried to thank Helen, she was stopped at once, and the whole subject was dismissed with Helen's caution that she never wanted to see Grace looking any other than she looked that morning. That a night's sleep had not killed her magic was proven by the reaction of Ben when he entered the office and his remark after a quick stare:

"Blimey, Grace! You look like a million dollars!" Grace took as much pleasure from it as she would have done from a more gracefully turned compliment. She still felt like a million dollars.

After that they went to work. Helen told Grace about the Halifax affair and Grace, as she listened, was filled with a subtle thrill of excitement. She knew, of course, that something was "up" about the Society, but she had not before realised what the fuss was all about. When Helen informed her that she would have to share in the task of shadowing Mr. Tomms, Grace wriggled on her chair and was suddenly miles away in an Edgar Wallace land of crooks and saw herself, in dire distress, being rescued by a staunch young man, who resembled George facially and who was very openly in love with her and madly alarmed at her plight.

It was arranged that Grace should look after Mr. Tomms in the morning and Helen in the afternoon, so that there should always be someone in the office to whom a report could be telephoned.

Helen gave Grace a little lecture on the gentle art of shadowing— her own experience entirely limited to the time when she had trailed Mr. Tomms to Tower Hill—and then Grace took up her post in the window seat and waited.

And Mr. Tomms—as though he were joining in the fun— decided to go out quite early that morning.

At one o'clock Helen got a telephone call from Grace. "He's on Tower Hill, talking," reported Grace. "I'm speaking from a call-box here."

"Right you are, Grace. You go off and get your lunch and then come back here. I'll take on from Tower Hill."

And the afternoon shift was Helen's. But Mr. Tomms refused to satisfy her by doing anything suspicious or visiting any strange house where Miss Logan might be incarcerated. He finished his talking on Tower Hill and walked back to the office, stopping on the way at an A.B.C. restaurant to have a cup of coffee and two Bath buns. He was in the office half an hour and then went out again, and the last Helen saw of him that day was when he presented himself at the pay-box of the Stoll Cinema and bought a seat to see a Shirley Temple film, a choice which did not surprise Helen as much as she felt it should have done.

She arrived at the flat that evening to find that Ben had been no luckier with his investigations about Mr. Spenser.

"He lives in a small house at Hampstead. But he's got no country cottage or place like that where Miss Logan might be, and I don't see how he could keep her at Hampstead. Still, I might have to make sure of that. It's surprising, isn't it, how much you can find out about a person if you really try? I've approached Mr. Spenser's history through three people: another member of his profession, who seemed impressed only by Spenser's golf handicap, which he envied; through his tailor, who considers that he has the most awkward neck and wrists in London; and through his typist, whom I accidentally met as she was taking a stroll in Lincoln's Inn Field at lunch-time. She feels that he's hardly human and can think of only two things with any real feeling—books and roses. There are a lot of other things I learned, too, but none of them really significant. And tomorrow will be Wednesday and the end of the week draws near. Where on earth could they have put Miss Logan?"

"Was Spenser's typist good-looking?" asked Helen.

Ben gave her a look which said plainly that he was in no mood for frivolities.

"And Spenser rang up late this afternoon," Ben went on, "to say that he had telephoned Tomms about the Burnses and had been assured that they were both perfectly reliable. Burns used to run an antique dealer's shop in Oxford, but hit hard times. Still, you know how much we can trust that information."

"We do seem to be up a tree, don't we?"

"Stuck in the highest branches, and the top branches are never safe." Ben lit a cigarette and went to the window, shaking his head sadly.

*   *   *   *   *

Grace and George went to see the *King of the Carribees*. It was a swashbuckling film packed with sword-cuts and full-rigged ships, Spanish gold and dark-haired women, and Grace secretly thought that the hero was just a little like George in many ways—which is significant, if you know anything about the more delicate emotions, and very different from thinking that George was just a little like the hero in many ways. They sat in the soft darkness, close to one another and yet far away, each living in a tiny realm of thought. Grace could feel George's arm against hers as they shared the rest between the seats and, in a stirring moment of battle, his hand was on hers and she was swiftly happy to the point of staring at the film and scarcely being aware of it.

He took his hand away when the lights came up with the organ; but the gesture had been made and nothing could alter it for Grace. The organ music wrapped her in its glutinous folds and she surrendered herself to the sweet monopoly of her daydreams. Around her were hundreds of men and women, sitting like school-children, mouthing the syllabicated words of the organ's song as they were flashed on to the screen. The noise rose up to the arched vault of the palace in a series of sibilant jets, and on his altar seat the organist wriggled and squirmed, twiddled his feet and flourished his hands in the ecstasy of accomplishment, and the tails of his cream dress-suit fell in a straight fold over the back of his seat, turning him into a whitebodied, black-headed scarab beetle pushing away at the organ as though it were a ball of food. Grace was entrapped by the atmosphere. She thought how nice and friendly everything was and how pleasant it was that so many people should come together like this and, without restraint upon their mouths, sing "Red Sails in the Sunset" and forget all their little domestic worries; and she wondered however much the organist's cream dress-suit with the black piping down the legs could have cost. And George, at her side, severed now from the thrall of the adventure and colour which had held him in the *King of the Carribees*, looked round the cinema and decided that its architecture and furnishings were vulgar. The organ noises, for him, had no claim to be music, and he thought the flashed verses of the songs on the screen, with their agonised rhymes, were an insult to an adult intelligence, and he thought how typically halfhearted was the communal singing. He was a little ashamed of fellow beings and a little pleased with his own superiority. And so they sat together, both very happy and both true to their own feelings, which were so dissimilar.

It was half-past nine when they came out of the cinema. They rode on the bus to the bottom of Fisher Road and as they walked towards the house Grace said:

"I didn't say anything before, but Mother quite expects you to come in and have some supper with us. I told her you mightn't want to come in, but she was very obstinate. Do you mind?"

George was not sure about his feelings. He had no intention of being rude, so he said cheerfully: "Of course I'll come. I should like to meet your mother."

A few moments later they were in the house and everyone was happy and friendly and pretending that it was not just a few minutes since George had been a stranger to the house.

"You're an architect, eh?" said Mr. Pilchard beaming. "Can't say I know much about that. Had my shop front altered once. Cost me a lot of money and took far longer than it should have done."

"Where would you rather be," asked Mrs. Kirkstall, as she began to lay the supper, "in London or in Scotland, Mr. Crane?"

George felt the question to be a little unimaginative and very difficult to answer. "Well, that's hardly a fair question, Mrs. Kirkstall. You see, as a Scotsman I should make one answer, and as a professional architect I should make another."

"Very true. Very true," breathed Mr. Pilchard, pursing his fat lips as he eyed the table.

Grace and her mother had conspired for a long time over the supper. It was a strategic meal in many ways and Grace wanted nothing wrong. There was an enormous tongue-and-veal pie studded with half-eggs—this the present of Mr. Pilchard—a ham, a dish of cold sausages and a bowl of salad, a plain English salad;

and about the table stood a bottle of sweet pickle, mayonnaise cream and all the other touches which complete the joy of a cold supper on a summer night.

"Will you have ham or the pie, Mr. Crane?"

Mr. Crane said he would have ham, and Mr. Pilchard was asked to carve.

"Delighted," said Mr. Pilchard, and he seized the carver. "Bit of a busman's holiday for me," he grinned. "But I don't mind. Carvin's an art. It makes me squirm sometimes when I go out to dinner and see the fist some chaps make of it—and it's such a simple affair, reelly. You hold the steel so—and then run your blade upon it—so!" The knife flashed circles of blue light before their eyes and then, the sharpening done, Mr. Pilchard attacked—no, the word is too strong—approached the ham. His wrist had the flexibility and sureness of a master, the firm, imperative strokes of genius, and the ham fell in neat, even slices. "Before a man marries," he said as he carved the ham, "he should learn to carve. A good carver is an economy in the house. I wonder there ain't correspondence schools to teach young men how to carve."

"Don't you take any notice of him, Mr. Crane," said Grace.

"He likes to hear the sound of his own voice. Salad?" "Was the film good?" Mrs. Kirkstall asked as they ate.

"About pirates," said Grace nodding. "And the organ was lovely. They played that 'Red Sails in the Sunset.' "

"Pirates, eh?" said Mr. Pilchard, forgetting that his mouth still held a quantity of ham. "That would have suited you, Mrs. Kirkstall. Something with the sea in it. Seems to me there's some professions and businesses that get all the luck. They're always making films about sailors and soldiers, about diamond merchants and captains of industries. Now, if you wanted to get me into the one-and-sixpennies of an evening, all you'd have to do would be to make a film about butchers. There'd be some sense in that."

"There's no romance in butchers! You've got to have romance for the films," explained Grace.

"Anyone that says there's no romance in me can't have looked very hard," Mr. Pilchard defended himself. "I'm bustin' with romance. Why, I've got so much romance in me that it sets me dreaming of nights. All widowers, whether they're butchers or not, are stuffed full of romance."

"You may say you're full of romance, Mr. Pilchard," observed Grace, "but it doesn't seem to stop you from doing justice to your food."

Mr. Pilchard chuckled. "Ay, that's true. But I'm a sensible creature. I never let romance put me off me food. Do I, Mrs. Kirkstall?"

There was a suggestion of challenge in the question, but Mrs. Kirkstall made no answer.

"More coffee?" Grace held out her hand for George's cup, and as she took it the door-bell rang violently. "Good heavens! Who can that be at this time of night?"

She left the room and the three at the table suspended their talk, waiting as people do until the unexpected resolves itself to the familiar. They heard Grace open the door, heard a murmur of voices and then a husky tumble of sounds. Then came a snatch of song and the next moment heavy footsteps sounded on the hallway and a young man appeared in the doorway.

He stood in the doorway and smiled rather stupidly at them and then the smile changed into a leer. Over his shoulder rose the face of Grace—a worried, almost tearful face.

George eyed the young man with a frown. He wore a grey suit which was greasy and crumpled and a dark jersey with a high collar. His hair was tousled and his face carried a beard that was three days old.

Mrs. Kirkstall suddenly gasped, and then sagged into her chair. "Gerald! It's Gerald!"

The young man laughed. "Of course it's me, Ma. Blimey! What a welcome home! Seems like I've broken in on a party where I'm not wanted."

"You certainly are not wanted here!" Mr. Pilchard was on his feet. "Have you forgotten the promise you made?"

Gerald looked at Mr. Pilchard coldly, swayed a little, and then waved him aside with an exclamation of impatience "Go and play pigs with yourself, little man. What if I did make a promise. Promises were made to be broken. Weren't they, Gracie, love?" He jerked her into the room and thrust his face towards her. "Tell them the promise you made me, Gracie, my lovin' sister, to lend me five pounds and how you put the janitor on me at Fountain Inn, and then I'll tell 'em how I've spent the last few days. Whoah!" He swayed forward to the table and helped himself to a cold sausage.

"Gerald! You've been drinking!" It was the only thing Mrs. Kirkstall could think to say.

"Course I have—I've been drinking. What about it And now I've come home to rest my weary head. I've come home for good."

"You're not staying in this house!" There was venom in Grace's voice. "You're not staying here to make Mother's life a misery!" She had forgotten George, forgotten everything but her one desire to shelter her mother from the anxiety that Gerald caused her when he was at home.

"Blimey! What a spitfire!" Gerald leaned forward and twisted Grace's arm, and then, as though he had just seen George, he turned to him and laughed. "You see what kind of company you're in, mister? I suppose you're Grace's boy friend? Didn't know she was such a spitfire, did you? Well, you know now!"

George said nothing for a moment. He looked at Grace and then at her mother, and he saw at once that this was not the first time they had been hectored and bullied by this young man. Mr. Pilchard, too, seemed suddenly to have shrunk and become weak before the intemperate assumptions of Gerald.

"I don't wish to interfere in a family affair unless it's absolutely necessary," said George, speaking evenly and with a tightening of his cheek muscles.

"Why he's a dirty Jock!" cried Gerald, and, turning to Grace, he sneered: "So you picked yourself a kiltie for a lover. Well—"

"I'll thank ye not to insult me!" snapped George suddenly. "And while I'm in this room, I'll ask ye to behave yourself towards your mother and your sister."

"You do, do you? And is that all you want, MacTavish?"

George controlled himself. "No, it is not all. It seems vairy clear to me that you are unwelcome in this house. I do not know the exact reason, but a look at you is enough to convince me that the reasons are no doubt excellent. So, I'll ask you to leave at once and not come back here bothering people until you're asked."

Gerald whistled at the impudence of the ultimatum.

"Well, well," he declared in his tipsy voice. "You have picked yourself a hero, Grace."

"Gerald, please go!" Mr. Pilchard was eyeing Mrs. Kirkstall anxiously.

"I'll go when I want to and not before."

"You'll go now!" snapped George angrily. "Come on!" He stepped forward and took Gerald by his coat collar. Gerald twisted away and struck at George's face, a blow which George evaded easily.

"I'm sorry for you," he said as Gerald sparred towards him, "for I do not wish to take advantage of your intoxicated condition. But you asked for it and I'll make it short for the sake of your mother and sister."

And George stepped forward. Mr. Pilchard watched him with hope and interest. He remembered the scene all the rest of his life.

It was one of those satisfying moments when retribution overtakes the evildoer, and the virtuous may watch and for a while forget their abhorrence of the "eye for an eye" creed. Gerald swung at George and George moved his arms quickly. Mr. Pilchard had an impression of swift impact, the sound of two fierce blows and then he was watching Gerald tumbling backwards against the wall, an angry red patch on one cheek, his breath singing out of his body from the last blow, which had taken him in the solar plexus.

Grace uttered a gentle scream. Mrs. Kirkstall extricated herself from a difficult situation by fainting quietly in her chair, and George bent down and picked up Gerald like a sack of potatoes and lugged him to the front door and down the garden path. By the time he had reached the gate Gerald was recovering and sobering. George pushed him on to the dark pavement and shut the gate on him.

"In future, you keep away from this house. If you don't, then I'll deal with you—drunk or sober. Good night!"

He turned back towards the house and there was a crisp finality about his words which left Gerald in no doubt at all of his intentions. He stood for a moment, feeling his chin, and then he turned away, mumbling to himself and somehow aware that if he ever did come back to the house it would be when he was asked and not before.

Mr. Pilchard met George in the hallway.

"Grace is upstairs with her mother. We've just taken her up. She'll be all right." He took George's hand and pumped it vigorously. "I'm glad you were here tonight. You've done what I have wanted to do for years, but I could never have done it so well as you did. He's a bad lad, that Gerald—but underneath there's some good in him. You've given him a lesson tonight that'll do him good."

Grace came down.

"I'm so sorry all this happened." Her eyes were warm with tears that were close and George felt unaccountably tender towards her.

He put his arm about her shoulder protectively. "Don't let it worry you, Grace. Your brother won't trouble you any more. I'll see to that. It's getting late and I must be going." She went to the door with him.

"Good night," she said. "I think you've been so kind and understanding. I don't know what we should have done without you."

George had no answer in words. He suddenly found himself bending down and kissing her tenderly on the mouth. Then he rushed away down the garden, leaving Grace standing, happy and shocked, on the doorstep.

Things, thought George as he made for the station, had conspired with one another that night to accelerate his existence to an abnormal tempo, and he had become the victim of a conspiracy of emotion and incident. But long before he reached home he found himself pleasantly gratified by the evening's events.

After Mr. Pilchard had gone, with the admonition as he left: "Gracie, my girl—you marry that young man. He's twenty-four carat", Grace had gone up to the bedroom where her mother had retired. He had called her "Grace" and kissed her. Not even her dreams to the cinema organ had touched upon that bliss so early. She looked down at her mother, her eyes shining.

"You look happy about the whole affair," moaned Mrs. Kirkstall.

"So I am," said Grace determinedly. "I'm glad it's all settled. You won't be worried by Gerald again, and perhaps he'll have learned a lesson, too."

"I know, I know," agreed Mrs. Kirkstall. "But I do hope that Mr. Crane didn't hurt him when he hit him. Gerald was—"

"I hope that George hurt him like anything," said Grace, her lips closing upon her remark tightly. "When he picked him up and carried him out of the house I could have cheered!"

Mrs. Kirkstall raised her head from her pillow and looked at Grace. Grace scarcely saw her. And in that moment Mrs. Kirkstall understood, without any grief, that she had lost her daughter. She lay back on her pillow and found herself thinking of Mr. Pilchard.

Chapter Fourteen

On Thursday evening, at half-past six, Ben Brown was on a seat a few yards down the road from Ederley Spenser's house in Hampstead. The house—actually it was more properly a cottage—stood in a road which ran from the rise of Haverstock Hill to the lower dip of the Heath, where its ponds mark the course of the old Fleet River. The house had been built in the eighteenth century and was a charming residence, a mixture of felicitous characteristics. It had a short, gambrel-shaped roof, like the upturned bottom of a boat, two little dormers built out of its lower slope, and a plain front, partly covered with a virginia creeper, and opened with long, large-paned windows. The doorway had a scalloped fan-light, and the whole house was decorated outside with cream walls and green paintwork. The house stood in its own little garden.

At the back of the house, Ben guessed, Spenser would have his rose beds and greenhouse. The only flowers in the front were the stocks in the beds under the windows. The rest was lawn. Ben had been sitting on the seat since a quarter-past six, trying to make up his mind.

The dullness of the past hours had begun to breed a corresponding sluggishness in himself. He and Helen, with Grace, had watched Tomms and Spenser as well as they could, but neither of the men had given them any lead. Their actions were so normal that Ben almost began to disbelieve his own suspicions. According to the canon of ordered excitement, things should have happened. Tomms or Spenser should have done something to prompt Ben into action. But nothing did happen. There was this long shallow of hours where life flowed slowly, urbanely along and villainy was no part of the drift it carried downstream.

It was desperation in Ben which had brought him to Hampstead. He had recalled that Spenser had a dinner appointment that evening with Dorian Ballard and he had decided that, while the man was from his house, he would investigate the possibility of getting into the house. What exactly he hoped to find when he was in escaped him. He told himself that Miss Logan might be there, but his thoughts lacked any conviction. He told himself that he might find something which would help him, and it was this vague "something" that drew him. He felt he had to make the gesture in the dark in the hope that his hand might strike against some tangible hold. In its way it was not illogical. Men are always following phantoms and occasionally finding the solid treasure which the wraiths guard.

It was not until Ben was at Hampstead and had seen Spenser depart that the full difficulty of breaking into a house on a fine summer's evening became urgently apparent. It occurred to him, as he eyed the cream-and-green house, that there must be servants or a housekeeper left there. Helen had told him his idea was stupid and he was beginning to believe her. But he was not too eager to allow himself to respond to the cry of "stupidity." Too many schemes had been still-born because of that midwife. The old saying about fools rushing in had wisdom in it. Fools had a special lien on the gods for protection and occasionally the gods stirred themselves to discharge that duty. When they refused to stir—well, there was another disappointed fool in the world.

He was glad that he had hidden from Helen the heavy rubber jack which rested in his pocket. It was an Oxford memento—its acquisition disturbing history. He had brought it as a dim gesture towards the house-breaking profession into which he seemed to be graduating rapidly.

It was at this point that the housekeeper appeared. There were several points which decided Ben that she was a housekeeper. She wore a small black hat with a brown coat, she was tall almost to being stately, her face was firm and satisfied and she came from the back of the house, walking the path with a sureness that denoted a familiarity. She also stopped to pick off a dead stock blossom, a proprietory gesture. She came out of the garden and turned up the road, walking briskly. Ben got up and went towards the house. Spenser would have a housekeeper. He was that kind of man; she would be a sensible creature who would bully him gently and be very proud of him. There might be a maid, but more likely a woman who came in for the rough work.

Ben pushed open the gate and walked around to the back of the house. If there were a servant, he could easily adopt a professional travelling guise and talk vacuum cleaners or the *Wonders of Nature* in seven volumes for half a crown a month for a year, and from the duck-billed platypus—three illustrations in colour—he might wander to a discussion of masters and find out something about Spenser which was new to him. He might even get so far as a cup of tea around the kitchen table. You never knew—maids could be astonishingly friendly.

There were roses at the back. Four beds filled with so much colour that Ben for a moment forgot his quest and just stood looking at them. It was some moments before he realised that he was, despite the brilliance, disappointed, and his disappointment came—it was curious how the obvious evaded him for a time— from the lack of scent. So many roses should have perfumed the air and persuaded the mind to thoughts of Persia. They were modern roses and mean with their fragrance. If I grow roses, thought Ben, I shall want them to have a perfume, just as I shall want my pigs to grunt and squeal.

He pressed the bell on the green door. There was no answer. He rang three times to make sure and then—confident that the house was empty—he looked for the key. There was always the possibility that the housekeeper might be one of those people who dislike carrying a house key. There are such people. They are afraid that they may lose it and find themselves locked out. Flat-dwellers must carry their keys, but the owners of houses have the pleasure of hiding the key under the mat, under flower pots, dropping it into the roof gutter, tucking it away under the creeper, slipping it on top of the window cornice or—more subtle—leaving it in the keyhole. Ben found the key under the foot-scraper, a heavy leaden affair. It was the first place he looked, and he accepted the success as a sign that the gods had moved a weary arm, if they had not actively stirred. He opened the door, put the key back under the scraper and then—since it was a yale lock—slammed the door on himself and turned to find himself in a very neat kitchen. He had entered the house so easily that he forgot his own trepidation. He began to examine the place in an excess of pleasure at his own cleverness.

The house was furnished simply and in quiet, good taste. Only one room was unexpected and that was, Ben guessed, Spenser's bedroom. It was heavily hung with curtains and ugly with a shiny mahogany four-poster bed whose draperies were of a particularly lifeless red. It had that close, vaguely indecent front that was typical of bedrooms when the body was an indiscretion to be hid even from the mirror. Ben worked from the top of the house to the bottom. Miss Logan was not there.

Ben came downstairs and went again to the library. He had glanced in on his way through the hall. Now he decided to give it a more thorough inspection. It lay to the right of the front doorway and was a small, rather lofty room, lined with bookshelves protected by glass panels. A long, highly polished Sheraton table stood in the centre of the room and in a far corner there was a small desk. Heavy velvet curtains hung at the sides of the tall windows and about the room were placed easy chairs and a few occasional tables piled with books and magazines. It was essentially a room for books, a working and studying room making only the meagrest concessions to comfort. Its only picture was a large Hogarth reproduction from the Day and Night series half-way up the chimney breast, which was the only tract of wall free of book-shelves.

Ben went to the desk and tried its drawers. They were all locked. There were no loose papers upon the desk. He stood for a moment, reluctant to admit to himself that his house-breaking had brought no results. As he stood there he heard the front gate swing. He slipped to the window and, looking round the long curtains, saw a familiar figure coming up the path to the front door. Before he had time to move across the library and get away to the back of the house, he heard a key turn in the front door and sounds of a hurried entry into the hallway.

Ben had barely time to hide himself behind the thick window curtains before the man had entered the room. For a moment he was only able to tell the man's movements by the noise he made. He heard him stop inside the door and then move towards the fireplace. Then he heard a match strike and a little later the sound of keys. He moved cautiously, flattening against the side of the window recess and found a gap between the wall and the curtain from which he could command part of the room.

Ben saw the man's face and at once recognised it. It was a large face with thick, pouting lips. The eyebrows hung weightily over the eyes. But for all its heaviness, it was a pleasant face, a jovial, roguish face, a face fitting the tall, powerful body. It was a publicised face, fresh in Ben's memory. He was looking at Dorian Ballard.

Ballard was standing by the fireplace, his face half-turned towards it, a cigarette in his mouth and a bunch of keys in his hand. He was weighing the keys reflectively and his eyes were examining the room. There was a calculating, tense spirit in the man's manner that told Ben he was not innocently in the room, a conviction which was strengthened by his knowledge that Ballard should at this moment have been taking dinner at his flat with Spenser.

After a moment Ballard walked towards the book-shelves by the desk and, pushing up one of the glass panels, glanced along the line of books. His lips were drawn in and his face illuminated by a sweep of envy as he looked along the books. He reached up and took one down. It was a small octavo volume, bound in brown leather, and as he opened it Ben saw that the pages clung together with that old intimacy which belongs to books that have outlived their century. He sat down on the corner of an armchair and began to look through the book. Then, abruptly, as though he were suddenly aware that he was wasting time, he slipped the book back into the shelf, closed the glass panel and turned to the desk.

Ben watched as the man tried the keys and, one by one, opened each drawer. He went through them carefully, locking each one as he finished. Finally, from a top drawer of the desk, he seemed to find what he wanted.

"Here we are!" he said aloud, confident of his solitude. There was triumph in his voice.

Ben saw him pull out a slim foolscap envelope. He moved to the table with it and for a moment his back was to Ben, hiding his actual movements. But Ben saw that he was taking something from the envelope. He heard the rustle of paper and then Ballard moved back to the drawer, the keys in his hand, to lock it. On the table

Ben saw the long envelope and close to it a sheet of paper, folded to the same shape as the envelope. It was this sheet, evidently, that Ballard had come for and as he had come for it in such an odd manner Ben was curious to know its nature. It might—he could not ignore now any straw that the wind blew to his feet—have some bearing upon his own problem. Ballard had been a witness to the Colonel's will and he knew Spenser.

There are moments when a man has a compulsion to be rash, moments when the last thing he wishes to do is to consider the unpleasant consequences of an unhappy termination to his audacity. Such a moment possessed Ben. He wanted fervently and irresistibly to have that sheet of paper and he gave himself entirely to the desire. Both he and Ballard were, he was sure of it, unlawfully in the house. The keys that Ballard jangled were obviously not his own ... His thoughts slipped away into the tension of preparation as he saw Ballard turn away from the locked drawer and make for the table. Ben's hand dropped to his pocket and closed round the rubber jack. The next instant he had slipped round the curtain and, as Ballard began to move at the noise, he brought his weapon down as hard as he could hit. He struck Ballard just behind and a little above the right ear and the effect was astonishing. It was the first time Ben had ever hit a man in cold blood and he was amazed to witness the promptness with which Ballard fell forward and then slipped heavily to the floor. A glance at him told Ben that he would not long be dazed. The blow had been a glancing one and Ballard was a strong man.

Ben stopped only for a quick look at him and then he had snatched the loose paper from the table and he was out of the library. Even as he reached the front door he heard Ballard suddenly curse behind him, a curse that was broken by a low grunt of pain.

Ben slammed the door carelessly and slipped quickly down the pathway. He did not turn round, in case Ballard should have reached the window. A little later he was entering the Tube station on Haverstock Hill sure that Ballard had not seen or followed him.

Half an hour later he was at home telling Helen of his adventure.

"You see now how useful this little fellow was," he held up the jack exultantly.

"You were lucky." Helen was secretly worried at the mad risk Ben had taken and finding it hard not to be angry with him.

"I had to do something, Helen. Dash it all! I thought you'd be excited about it."

"It's the letter I can't understand. I don't see how that can help us at all. Let me see it again."

Ben handed the sheet of paper he had stolen to her. It was a large sheet of paper, its edges rough and worn thin and its creases showing thin points of daylight when it was held up. It was a dull, almost uniform yellowish colour and with the brittle, dry quality which comes with age. The sheet was covered on both sides by a letter written in ink that was faded to rust and in a hand that was not easy to read. It ran

"TO THE RIGHT HONOURABLE CHARLES JENKINSON

"SIR,—Since the conviction and condemnation of Dr. Dodd, I have had, by the intervention of a friend, some intercourse with him, and I am sure I shall lose nothing in your opinion by tenderness and commiseration. Whatever be the crime, it is not easy to have any knowledge of the delinquent, without a wish that his life may be spared; at least when no life has been taken away by him. I will, therefore, take the liberty of suggesting some reasons for which I wish this unhappy being to escape the utmost rigour of his sentence.

"He is, so far as I can recollect, the first clergyman of our church who has suffered publick execution for immorality; and I know not whether it would be more for the interests of

religion to bury such an offender in the obscurity of perpetual exile, than to expose him in a cart, and on the gallows, to all who for any reason are enemies to the clergy.

"The supreme power has, in all ages, paid some attention to the voice of the people; and that voice does not least deserve to be heard when it calls out for mercy. There is now a very general desire that Dodd's life should be spared. More is not wished; and, perhaps, this is not too much to be granted.

"If you, Sir, have any opportunity of enforcing these reasons, you may, perhaps, think them worthy of consideration; but whatever you determine, I most respectfully intreat that you will be pleased to

pardon for this intrusion, Sir,
"Your most obedient
"And most humble servant,
"SAM JOHNSON."

"Seventeen hundred and seventy-seven was a long time ago," Helen spoke softly, eyeing the date in the letter. "I suppose this Sam Johnson was none other than Dr. Johnson? It reads like him. But what—"

"Exactly!" Ben was exasperated. "What on earth has Dr. Johnson, whose shade God preserve, to do with Mr. Ballard or with Miss Logan?"

"To a collector, this letter would be valuable. It couldn't be that Ballard was stealing it from Spenser? Too crude?"

"He seemed pretty sure of himself." He dropped into an easy chair and lit himself a cigarette. "Do you know—" Ben's eyes narrowed "—I've got a feeling that Uncle Herbert would like to have a look at this letter."

"I thought he was in Palestine digging."

"No. He's back. The supply of spades or old bricks ran out."

"You can't see him tonight?"

"I know I can't. You know his habits. Bed at nine-thirty sharp. But I'll be on his doorstep tomorrow morning before breakfast." He got up and locked the letter away in his bureau.

"It is Friday tomorrow. The week's drawing to a close."

Ben said nothing for a moment. He came back and caught Helen by the arm, pulling her up to him. He looked at her soberly for a time, then he kissed her gently on the nose and said:

"Come on, let's take a turn round the block before we go to bed."

Helen tucked her arm in his and they went out.

*   *   *   *   *

"Well?" Harris, his manservant, posed the question as Ballard came into the flat.

"Well enough," said Ballard.

"You been 'it!" Harris exclaimed as Ballard turned to slip from his light coat.

"Yes, slugged. I was knocked silly for about five minutes. That was just long enough—but that doesn't matter. Has he started to move yet?" He nodded towards the lounge.

"Begun groaning just before you come in. That means he'll be sitting up and asking for a drink in a few minutes. But, guvnor, did you—"

"Don't worry," Ballard stopped him with a quick lash of words. Harris dropped away and opened the lounge door for him. "You'd better stay away," he said to Harris as he passed through. "Too many people make a man embarrassed when he comes out of a drug."

As he crossed to the window seat, Spenser struggled weakly to a sitting position and shook his head. He was conscious of Ballard's huge form standing above him. He said nothing for a little while as he waited for his brain to clear.

It was typical of the man, Ballard thought, that the first conscious action should be a glance at his wrist watch. He laughed indulgently and said:

"Yes, almost three hours. A lot can happen in three hours, Spenser."

Spenser looked up. "You drugged me. You damned scoundrel!"

"Now, now. Let's keep our tempers and acknowledge the facts." Ballard's whole tone and expression was temperate. He went to the table and poured a drink for Spenser.

"Here, take this. It'll bring you out of the subliminal and make a civilised being of you. Oh, come on. It's not tampered with like some brandies. An Augier 1875. You didn't last out long enough at dinner to enjoy it."

Spenser took the drink because he needed it. It stiffened him into vigour at once.

"Perhaps you'll explain?" he said, realising the virtue of keeping calm.

"Willingly." Ballard sat down and lit a cigarette, his dark eyes on Spenser's face. "You were drugged. Harris made the arrangements and—since you weren't able to appreciate it—I may say it went off perfectly. An excellent performance. Privately I had thought that you would reach the brandy stage and then succumb. Harris said no—and he was right. You have been unconscious nearly three hours and during that time I have been to your house in Hampstead. I took the liberty of borrowing your keys. Here they are." He handed them back to Spenser, who was listening to him intently, the only sign of emotion the drawn-in underlip as he bit on it.

"I knew I should have no trouble there. Mrs. Elison, your competent housekeeper, always goes out on a Thursday evening to the Women's League of her church—it was not hard to find that out." He paused, anxious to let Spenser miss nothing of his elation.

215

"Go on," said Spenser. "Why did you visit my house?"

"Can't you guess? There was something there I wanted." Ballard shook his great head with delight, and then, like an amateur conjurer, he drew a long envelope from his pocket and pulled from it a small slip of paper which he flourished under Spenser's face and then jerked back quickly as though he feared to let it stray too far from himself. "Do you recognise it?"

"I do. Am I to assume that the letter is also in the envelope?" There was resignation in Spenser's voice.

"That is so. You always kept them together, didn't you? Now I have them. You know how many years I have wanted to have them—and you know that you will do nothing about this."

Spenser got up and went to the fireplace, rubbing his short hair with his hand and sucking his teeth.

"I know only that we are still indebted to one another and that you can do nothing about that. You understand that!" The query was flung at Ballard with a viciousness that surprised the author and revealed that he was not the master of the thin, dried lawyer. There was threat, violence and taunt in Spenser's speech. "You understand, Ballard!"

"I do." The voice was subdued. Then he spoke again, this time with a new optimism: "But I understand also that those debts will soon be discharged, and it was because I do not intend to be made to pay three times for the same debt that I did what I did tonight. We must give and take, Spenser. You tried to drive me too hard. I think you can understand my feelings."

"Perfectly. In your place I might have done the same. It's almost like one of your little fictions, isn't it?"

"In good fiction virtue must always triumph—and life has a habit of imitating fiction in that particular." Ballard spoke lightly, his fingers feeling the back of his head where he had been struck. "I suppose you're sure—" He broke off.

"You were going to say?"

"Never mind. It was something that struck me just now. You wouldn't understand." Ballard chuckled at his joke and then rang for Harris. "Mr. Spenser is leaving, Harris. Get a taxi for him. He's still a little unsteady on the legs."

"Certainly, sir."

Harris came back to find Ballard sitting staring at the envelope.

"Harris, I've a feeling that it might be wise for us to take a holiday."

"A cruise, sir?"

"No—cruises are inconvenient at times."

"Aw, guvnor—not Ireland!"

"Yes, Ireland. But you needn't come. You can stay here. I shall be in Ireland to anyone who enquires. That's all you know. And I shall travel tonight."

An hour later he was at Victoria Station, from which there are no trains to the Irish mailboats.

Chapter Fifteen

Uncle Herbert was taking breakfast when Helen and Ben arrived the next morning. He was a lean, brown-skinned man who looked much younger than he was. His eyes had that still, watchful air as though he were waiting for some unexpected movement. He was eating kippers and reading *The Times* obituary notices.

"Too early for a formal call," he said, looking at them over his paper. "What do you want?"

"The kipper smells good," Helen wrinkled her nose.

"Shall I ask Marie to bring some more?"

"No, we'll enjoy the smell. It's almost the best part of a kipper."

"Parkinson's gone now," he said, his mind going back to the thoughts they had disturbed by their entrance. "He was with Lawrence, you know—but that was before the War sent all their good work floating away downstream to oblivion. I knew Lawrence fairly well. His tragedy as a scholar was that he hadn't any true sense of repose. It was his genius as a man."

"Do you know anything about a Dr. Dodd?" Ben asked the question quietly.

"What would he be—medicine, science, philosophy?"

"Divinity, I should say."

Uncle Herbert considered and then shook his head. "No, the name's not familiar. Why?"

Ben held out the faded letter. Uncle Herbert took it, gave it a glance and, before reading, raised his eyes questioningly to the two. Then he began to read, and there was that curious silence in the room when three people are all occupied with themselves, a silence made up of little noises, the regional movements in the house, the slow swing of the wall-clock, the purring of the cat on the window ledge in the sun and the almost tangible shuffle of thoughts.

"What about this?" said Uncle Herbert suddenly.

"That's what we want to know. What's it all about?" Ben got up and found himself a cigarette.

"You should know as well as I do. Didn't you ever do any reading at Oxford? You're like all the moderns. You read, but you don't remember. You let words and thoughts slip over your senses, tickling you for a while as a stream runs around your feet, tickling your toes, and then it's all gone."

"Tell us," Helen came round to him, pulling his ear gently. "You can lecture us afterwards."

"Well, it's a pity you don't know your Boswell. You'd have saved yourself a lot of trouble. This is a letter which was written by the Doctor—more to oblige a friend than from any real conviction, I feel—to Mr. Jenkinson, who became the second Earl of Liverpool. The line, I believe, is finished now. He wanted, as you can see, the Right Honourable to do what he could in the proper quarters to get a commutation of Dr. Dodd's sentence."

"And Dodd?"

"He was a popular preacher of the times and had begun to live beyond his means. He forged a bond in the name, I think I'm right, of Lord Chesterfield, with whom he was friendly, hoping that if it were found out the nobleman would be indulgent. But the nobleman was not indulgent and it was found out. Forgery was a capital offence in those days and Mr. Dodd was convicted."

"Did the letter have any effect?"

"It did not. It never reached Mr. Jenkinson. How it was lost was not known. Dr. Dodd paid the full penalty."

"So this letter is quite a literary curiosity and of some value?"

"True."

"You sound rather cautious." Helen had caught his tone of doubt.

"And why not, my dear. It is a literary curiosity and of some value. Dr. Johnson's letter would be a find for any collector, and if you know anything about collectors you'd know that it might sell at quite a high price if there were more than one person after it. I'm rather interested to know where you got it, but I can see that you don't want to tell me that yet. Never mind—but it might interest you to know that I'm pretty certain that this particular letter is a forgery."

"A what!" Ben almost jumped in his surprise.

Uncle Herbert smiled at him and began to marmalade his toast, spreading the conserve evenly.

"It's a forgery. I know a little about these things and I'm pretty sure it's a fake. I've spent my life amongst old manuscripts and the evidence of past work. This faded paper and the lifeless ink are easily simulated by a clever man."

"Do you mean to say that no collector would be taken in by that letter?" asked Helen.

"I don't say that. A collector who had no great experience might easily accept it, partly because he would want to believe it was genuine and partly because he would not be able to tell. But any man of experience would be suspicious." Uncle Herbert was chuckling at their amazement. "I'm sorry if I've disappointed you."

"You haven't," said Ben quickly.

"I felt somehow that I hadn't. Is this something to do with your business? Yes, I heard about that. A little uncommon, I thought, but I have no doubt that in this odd world there's a place for it. You've been a good influence on the boy." He took one of Helen's hands, and then, with a quiet air of uttering a commonplace, he said: "I also think I could tell you who made this forgery."

Neither of them said anything for a moment. Then Helen put her hands on his shoulders and shook him gently. "Uncle Herbert," she said severely, "just you forget your marmalade and tell us at once all you know of this business. Really, darling, it is tremendously important to us."

"Does she bully you like this?" Uncle Herbert looked at Ben.

"Frequently. It's no good protesting."

"Very well, I'll come across. Some of these slang phrases have a surprising virility and—what is more interesting—an authentic antiquity."

"Uncle Herbert!" Helen warned him.

"Forgive me. Well, about six years ago a man approached by letter several collectors in London who were interested in Johnsonian manuscripts with the story that he'd found, at a country sale, a bundle of letters written by the Doctor. And he sold the letters—about half a dozen—separately. But each sale was to a man who was of no great experience. Men who were just beginning a collection. You see, the man knew exactly how much examination his forgeries would bear, and he was clever. And as far as I know, he never made any personal contact with the buyers. Sounds odd, doesn't it? But you'd be surprised what collectors will do to add to their treasures. First editions and letters of value often change hands in peculiar circumstances and many—not all—collectors are prepared to shut their eyes to these peculiarities so long as they get their hands on what they want. Well, of course, once the letters were sold they were soon being shown to friends and other collectors. It wasn't long before it was found that they were forgeries. In fact, if you look up *The Times Literary Supplement* for a certain week in November five years back you'll find an article on the forgeries. Of course, by the time the forgeries were found out, the man had disappeared, leaving only a memory, unpleasant, and a name." "And the name?" Ben leaned forward.

"I was going to say, leaving a name that was useless, because it was obvious fiction—Geraint Wisden. The whole affair is dead now. He was never traced. You know, I've always had a sneaking regard for him. Some of the letters—the ones which have no record, as this one has, to check it by—are compositions so exactly in the style and thought of Dr. Johnson that they could only have been the work of a man who knew and loved his subject. Whoever Mr. Wisden was, he was cultured and a master of words." His hand went out for his toast and Helen made no move to stay him.

She looked at Ben and a common thought possessed them. "Come and tell me all about it, some day," said Uncle Herbert, reading their thoughts.

They went away, leaving him to his *Times* and coffee.

*   *   *   *   *

Grace that morning ran up the stairs to the office happily. She went in, using her key to unlock the door, and hung her coat and hat in the tiny storeroom which opened off the main room in which she worked. She caught sight of her smiling face in the tiny oblong of glass which she had hung on the wall and she stopped to admire herself, straining on to tiptoes to bring more of her body into the glass reflection.

Life, she thought, as she twisted her shoulders, was a very pleasant affair. The previous lunch-time she had slipped along to Madame Vivier's shop and got Madame to choose two dresses for her, one of which she was wearing now. She had intended it for office wear. It was a green dress, neatly waisted and falling in a wide, graceful skirt, yet not swinging so loose that it would catch on furniture as she moved about the office. The bodice and the neck were smart, with just that hint of efficiency, that suggestion of a working dress which she had wanted. She was rather sorry that Helen was not in the office to admire it. Still … George had noticed it. He had not said anything about it. She did not mind that. There were still moments of awkwardness between them, but she had seen his eyes go over her as they met and noticed the approval in them. He called her "Grace" and she called him "George," both of them using the intimacy with a reluctant yet happy hesitancy.

The telephone bell rang and she answered it, to hear Helen's voice.

"Grace? Slip through the post will you and see if there's anything important. I will ring back in about ten minutes."

Grace picked up the mail and began to open the letters. That morning she had received a letter from Gerald. It had almost made her feel sorry for him. He had apologised for his bad behaviour and said that he was sailing—it would be last night, she calculated—on the S.S. *Lorora* for America and then down the coast and goodness knows where, but, anyway, he would be away for more than a year. It looked as though George had knocked some sense into him. George … He was going to have his interview on Tuesday and if he were successful … She wondered. On Saturday afternoon they were going to Epping Forest. It was funny—all the time she had lived in London she had never been there. She and George. They were going in George's motor bicycle and sidecar. Grace had been completely surprised when George had told her that he owned such a machine. After a moment's thought, she had realised that George could sit in the saddle of a motor bicycle and still keep his dignity. She looked forward to the ride with happy anticipation.

She opened the letters dreamily and had only just finished them when Helen rang again.

"No, Mrs. Brown," she answered. "There's nothing really important. Two people want an interview, some bills and a couple of hotel enquiries and a man from Bridgwater wants to know if we can find him a bed-sitting-room overlooking the Oval during Test week."

Helen gave her a few instructions, but before she rang off, Grace enquired: "What about Mr. Tomms? Do I have to chase him?"

There was a pause at the other end. Then Helen said "Don't bother to run after him if he goes out, but you might keep an eye open in case anything curious happens. You know, if anyone odd calls to see him. You could sit in my window and knit."

Helen rang off and Grace went to the storeroom for her knitting. She was half-way across the room when there was a knock on the door and Mr. Parcross entered.

"Morning, Miss Kirkstall," he greeted her pleasantly.

"Good morning, Mr. Parcross."

"All alone?"

Grace nodded, and added, "What are you after? You're an awful scrounger, you know."

Mr. Parcross made a gentle gesture of protest. "Oh, Miss Kirkstall. Fancy your not understanding. I don't come to scrounge, really. That's just an excuse to come up and see you. I like you." He sat down and placed his veined hands on his knees. "I suppose you don't happen to have one of those little brushes for cleaning the type of typewriters, do you?"

"I do." Grace was pleasantly curt. She handed him the brush and then took him by the arm. "Now, Mr. Parcross, you must go. If I had the time I would willingly chat with you, but this morning I'm terribly busy."

Mr. Parcross went. Grace watched him trundle down the stairs. He had a light, delicate walk as though he were volatile and liable to rise in the air with each step unless he executed it gently. She was about to go back when the open door of Mr. Rage's old office across the landing caught her eye. The decorators had been working there for the last two days, but today the room was empty and silent. Through the open door Grace could see a few paint pots, some planks, and strips of old wall-paper on the floor. Although she knew she should get to her window post, she could not resist the temptation to cross to the room and look inside. The walls had been stripped and the ceiling had been freshly papered. Here and there were gaps in the wood panelling that ran at breast height around the room, and Grace guessed that the decorators had departed until the carpenter should come and make various repairs.

In one corner of the room a boxed-in ventilator shaft ran from the floor to the ceiling, a little grid near the ceiling allowing the exit of stale air from the room. All the rooms on the stairway had the same ventilation system and the shaft ran upwards from the floor level to the roof. Grace saw that the lowest facing panel of the shaft had been removed. It lay on the floor, one side of it rotted and worm-eaten. Grace stepped across the room and looked into the ventilator shaft. She was just able to get her head in and look down the dark well. A couple of feet below her she saw the grid-like rays of light escaping into the shaft from the room below, and as she looked she heard a man's voice come up the shaft clearly. It was with a sudden acceleration of her heart beats that she recognised Mr. Tomms's voice and realised that his room was directly below. He must be sitting very close to the shaft. She heard his voice begin afresh and was aware that he was dictating a letter.

"Say: 'With reference to your quotation for the printing of these pamphlets, I can confirm that we should want a first printing of five thousand and it is understood that any subsequent editions would be of not less than one thousand, so that you will appreciate the necessity of my original remarks with regard to cost. I should be glad to have your comments.' " A pause. Then, "That's all right. Get it off right away. And you might have this stuff filed."

Grace was amazed at the clarity of the sounds. She heard the shuffle of papers and the crisp, "Yes, Mr. Tomms," from his secreatry.

She stayed to hear no more, for fear of someone finding her in the room. Seated in the window with her knitting, she found her fingers nervously clumsy with the pins.

Chapter Sixteen

Helen and Ben sat on a seat overlooking the Serpentine. They had walked there from Kensington, where Uncle Herbert lived. Helen had telephoned Grace first from outside the house and the second time from a box in the Park. So far she and Ben had not exchanged a dozen words between them.

It was only now as he sat with his eyes watching the gull and duck movements about the water that Ben sighed loudly and turned to her with a look which said that it was time to talk.

"What do you think?" he asked.

"Pretty much the same as you. Only I find it a little difficult to put it all together. You know, that confusion which comes about three-parts of the way through a Sayers' story, plus a certain trembly feeling in my legs because this happens to be real and something must be done about it. There's no reading on and letting someone else do it for you."

Ben stared across the water to the spreading arcades of trees and walks. There were sculling boats on the Serpentine, men in coloured shirts pulling, there were children drawing painted toys along the walks, and a row of dirty sparrows lined along the immediate railings, considering the two of them as though they were before a jury. Not far away was the thrum of London. A boy in a ragged pair of cut-down trousers went by, his right shoulder-blade sticking from a rent shirt. He was sucking a vanilla cream cornet and Ben had a swift spasm of envy. It was just the day for ice-cream and irresponsibility. Then the masculine adult power of his pride overwhelmed him again. He had the opposition of a challenge, the taunt of dwindling time and the compelling necessity of action. He lit a cigarette, passing the case to Helen.

"I think this is where Mr. Dorian Ballard comes into the picture and alters the whole composition."

"I should imagine, too, that he comes unwillingly," said Helen.

"That's why I think I shall call and see him." Ben made up his mind suddenly. "I've a very good introduction." He patted his pocket to indicate the Johnson letter.

"I thought we were going to have a *post mortem* of the whole affair now?" Helen was a little piqued.

"It must wait until I've seen him. Maybe after that we shan't have to guess so much. Come on, we can walk together so far." He took Helen's arm and helped her to her feet.

Some time later he stood alone outside Ballard's flat. Harris answered the door to him.

"Is Mr. Ballard in?"

"He is not." The tones were uncordial.

Ben frowned. "That's a pity. I want to see him rather urgently. Could you tell me when I should catch him?"

"Mr. Ballard only sees people by appointment."

"That's all right. He'd see me."

"And Mr. Ballard is not likely to be back for some time. He's travelling in Ireland."

"Did he leave an address? I must get into touch with him."

"When the master travels in Ireland he has no address. I'm sorry." Harris's face indicated anything but sorrow, and he moved the door to close it.

"I suppose," said Ben, appreciating that Harris was more than a servant, "I suppose that Mr. Ballard's friend hasn't been here lately?"

"What friend?" Harris, not sure of Ben, was cautious and yet interested.

"The one who calls himself Geraint Wisden!" Ben watched Harris's face as he spoke the last words. Momentarily he could have sworn that the dour features moved to surprise, but the movement if it existed was almost instantly suppressed and Harris said calmly, finishing by closing the door:

"I'm afraid you're misinformed about Mr. Ballard's friends. I have never heard of anyone by that name. Good day."

Ben walked to the lift door chuckling quietly to himself. Harris was a liar. And Ballard was in Ireland. He had set out for Ireland very soon after the knock on the head he had received from Ben. Had he, Ben wondered, recognised that knock as the preliminary demand of Fate? He walked on towards home, his mind flighting in curious fancies, optimistic and satisfying.

"Well?" said Helen, "No, before you begin. Grace has just rung up from the office to say that Spenser 'phoned this morning to say that he's had three replies from various hotels about Miss Logan. They all say she has not taken rooms with them. There are two outstanding and if he doesn't receive anything from them by Monday he proposes to call and discuss the matter further with you that afternoon."

"He's a clever man, isn't he? I don't know yet what it's all about, but, whatever does happen, Mr. Spenser is going to be sitting comfortably. He's done everything that a good lawyer could do."

"What happened at Ballard's?" Helen asked.

"I didn't see him. Only his man, and he was giving nothing away, except that Ballard is travelling, with no forwarding address, in Ireland. Which means that he's probably nowhere near Ireland. But the man did seem to recognise the name

Geraint Wisden when I mentioned it."

"He did?"

"Yes." Ben followed her thought. "Geraint and Dorian are the same people. I'd stake anything on it, and it looks as though Spenser was one of the mugs who bought a forged letter."

"Only Spenser wasn't such a mug as the others, eh?" Helen walked up and down the room, rubbing the tip of her chin reflectively. "Spenser found out it was a forgery and he found out that Geraint Wisden, after a few years, had become Dorian Ballard. He's the kind of man who would hang on to the letter in the hope that it might come in useful—and it did. How?"

"I can only guess. Spenser is a lawyer and handled the Colonel's will. Ballard was a witness to that will. The only other witness is dead. A witness who was in the hands of the lawyer might find it inconvenient to be outspoken, especially if he were a man like Ballard, who now has a reason to be careful of his public reputation."

"And you think Ballard was stealing back the letter from Spenser?"

"I do most certainly."

Helen was silent for a moment, her brows curved with thought.

"Then why—" her tone was almost triumphant "—then why should he bother to steal it back after the will has been proved and the whole hanky-panky business, whatever it is, settled?"

"That worried me for a while this morning. But it's very simple, I think. Anyway, it's a postulate which sounds logical. The whole hanky-panky business isn't settled. For some reason or other, Miss Logan is being kept under cover and when we caught up with her at Hormenden they had to shift her quickly. Now, people like Spenser and Tomms can't possibly have convenient places all over

England where they could hide Miss Logan. The house in Kent was excellent, but we spoiled that, and they had to find another place quickly. They were up a tree until …"

"What?"

"Until Mr. Spenser remembered Ballard. A word from him could ruin Ballard. So he made Ballard help him again. It's a habit men have when they are in power. They make you help them once and then they come again. The habit grows. Ballard had to help hide Miss Logan for them, I feel. And he didn't like it. He disliked the whole affair, and he knew he could do nothing about it and that he would probably be called in more and more so long as Spenser held that letter. So he decided to get the letter and end the blackmail."

"But he didn't get it."

"No, that must be mystifying him. However, he probably bluffed Spenser into thinking he got it, and Spenser hasn't got the letter and—so Ballard will argue—it's almost certainly useless to whoever does hold it. That's where he's wrong,

because it's given us a lead to—"

"Miss Logan?"

"Yes. Ballard found a hiding place for her." "Where?"

"That's what I'd like to know. Pretty certainly not in his flat. That would be too dangerous. He's a man who entertains and she could never be kept under cover."

"So, actually, we are no further forward. We're still looking for Miss Logan. We can't sit down and methodically unravel the tangled skein. So we're hoping to grab at a loose end and pray that a darned good tug will put matters right."

"Encouraging, aren't you? All we have to do is to find out where Ballard had Miss Logan put, or suggested she should be put. Remember that it had to be done in a hurry. The country is the safest place and Ballard probably has a cottage in the country somewhere. All authors have country cottages. The successful ones have a Town flat and spend their weekends at the cottage, and the unsuccessful ones just have a cottage and live in it all the time. We can at least find out Ballard's country address and try

there. It's a long shot, but the only one left to make." "Long shot!" Helen waved her arms expressively.

"Why you're simply blazing away madly. There are a dozen things they may have done with Miss Logan."

"I know that. Your habit of stating the obvious is a little trying. But this country cottage slant is the only one left to us and, with time running out, I don't think we can ignore it. Men have shot at sparrows before now and brought down pelicans." Ben finished pontifically.

"What have sparrows and pelicans to do with anything?"

"Don't be obtuse, Helen Brown. We're going to find out about that cottage."

"If it is a cottage. And how do you propose to find out?"

"From his publishers or, if they don't know, from his agents." Helen picked up the telephone book and turned the pages. After awhile she said: "City 15834. Bird and Hawkridge, publishers. Go on."

Ben dialled obediently, and as he waited he said: "How did you know they were his publishers?"

Helen smiled. "Don't you read the *Observer*? They advertise regularly, a vulgar but effective display. They had a thermometer reading each week for his book showing the rise in sales—same kind of thing that churches have sometimes outside to show the increase of donations for the new organ ..." Ben waved his hand to interrupt her as the telephone call went through.

Messrs. Bird and Hawkridge were brief but expressive. They knew Mr. Ballard's Town address, but no other. Any information which Mr. Brown might want about Mr. Ballard, Mr. Brown must obtain through Mr. Ballard's agents, Messrs. Shute, More and Vessey.

"Shute, More and Vessey, Temple Bar 11054," said Helen, reading from the book.

Ben rang them and was put through to Mr. Vessey, who handled Mr. Ballard's affairs. Mr. Vessey was polite but firm.

"I'm sorry, but the only address we have for Mr. Ballard is his Town address. You can communicate with him there or through us. Yes, I think it is more than likely that he has a country address, but a man like Mr. Ballard would not make it known widely. Authors are temperamental, you know, and have no wish to be plagued by tourists when they want peace."

Ben tried hard to break down Mr. Vessey's firm front, but he was unsuccessful.

"He knows. I'm sure of that; and it sounded as though publisher and agent were expecting my question and quite ready to deny me the information."

"Ballard anticipated your move, maybe? Or perhaps he's just naturally reticent. So what now?"

"That's a damned silly and a damned irritating question, Helen—and you know it. So what? We can try *Who's Who* and the other references, but I'm not very hopeful."

They did try them, without success. And between them they waded through the back files of the popular newspapers immediately following the publication date of Ballard's book hoping to find a paragraph that might give them a lead and by the time they had finished they had decided that, although there was a great deal of publicity about the man and the book, it amounted to very little when analysed, and contained nothing about a country residence. All they knew was that Dorian Ballard had been born in Cardigan in the year 1908. There were no particulars of his education. He had worked on various American newspapers, been an air pilot, ship's steward and manager of a tanning factory. He had written one other book besides *Gold Goes Begging*, a collection of animal stories for children, and he had settled in England within the last three years. He played no games and preferred cats to dogs because cats never demanded daily exercise.

At seven o'clock that evening they gave up the search. They had telephoned to all their literary friends, bought drinks for a Fleet Street sub-editor, tried a film company's representative in London who had bought the film rights of the story and got half a dozen of the big estate agents in London to check their books for any record of a sale of property to Ballard.

Despondent, they turned into a cinema and decided to forget Ballard and the whole affair for a couple of hours.

The film did not improve their mood. It showed a detective waltzing with light-hearted unconcern through a maze of mystery and sudden deaths, picking up the faintest clues and dancing Ariel-like to a solution that left a pedestrian-witted audience mazed with wonder.

*   *   *   *   *

Grace liked Saturday mornings. The whole feeling of the day's beginning was so different from any other day in the week. There was work to be done—the familiar routine of going to the office—but with it was the hint of the afternoon's freedom. The day had an air of its own, a personality and a magic that nothing could change. If calendars and time records disappeared tomorrow and no man, woman or child could remember the day, they would have no doubt when Saturday came round. It would announce itself by that golden morning stir of expectation, the promise of afternoon joys and evening entertainments. Cricket bats, golf clubs, tennis racquets, swimming suits and rucksacks, these are the things of Saturday; spades, secateurs, paint-brush and car polish, they belong to Saturday so surely as church and roast beef with horse-radish sauce belong to Sunday and washing to Monday; there is time to stare and talk, leisure for the hundred important things of home life, the time of expansion, of fitting into the liberty of body and mind that comes from the jettisoning of office and shop. If one must die, let it be on a Monday, when all men are sad, and let the memory of sorrow live only until Friday evening, so that the Saturday may dawn fresh and beautiful and friends may rise to their pleasure without the gloom of dark memories.

Grace ran up the last flight of stairs to the office with the Saturday feeling strong in her heart. For her this Saturday was beyond all others. She was going to Epping with George. As she ran she raised one hand to her throat to still the leap of the close string of metal beads she wore. Metal beads were fashionable and Madame Vivier had advised her to wear them with the dress. It was a dark, almost black dress of a tweedy mixture and the high touches of the beads gave it life. It was lucky, thought Grace, as her fingers touched the cold metal, that she had the beads. They belonged to her mother and had been fashionable twenty years before. It was a pity the clasp was weak and occasionally came loose from her neck, but she would have that fixed.

Helen and Ben were already at the office. Saturday morning was their busiest time. There were a couple of regular commissions that had to be done on that morning in each week and it was on Saturday that they found themselves called on to meet people coming to London. Children invaded the Metropolis on Saturday morning.

"We shall both be out all morning," Helen told Grace as she put on her hat. "You hold the fort. I doubt whether we shall come back before you go, but if anything urgent turns up you can leave a note here and also 'phone a message to the flat—the porter will take it. Come on, Ben. I'm going your way."

Ben followed her sulkily. He felt it was a definite anticlimax to be hauled off to meet a couple of young boys at Paddington who had come up from Swindon where they lived with a maiden aunt, an aunt whose life they had harried until she had arranged with General Factotums to meet them and take them to the Tower of London and the Zoo. Ben was to turn them over to a family friend at lunch-time —the family friend, he gathered, knew the boys and had no desire to shepherd them to the Tower and the Zoo. Ben went on expecting the worst and wondering why he had ever supposed that playing nursemaid was a man's job. It occurred to him, as he entered the smoky vault of Paddington, that someone had once murdered two young boys in the Tower. The thought cheered him up. He recognised the boys at once from their school caps—"Magenta and yellow quarterings and a shield with a lion rampant, or." Those had been the aunt's words in her letter.

He introduced himself to them and at once knew that he was in for a harassing morning, for the taller of the two frowned and said in disappointed tones: "Gee! I made sure you'd be wearing a uniform, like Cook's man. Aunt Livia said you would."

It was a moment that made a man feel for his pipe to give his teeth something to bite on. Ben felt and found that he had left his pipe at the office. He took the boys by the arm and hurried them from the station.

*   *   *   *   *

Grace worked for an hour, answering letters that had come by that morning's post and bringing her filing up to date. It was surprising how soon she had mastered the business of the office and learned to deal with the minor enquiries which formed a large part of the work. In a way, the thought had often struck her, the office was like a neat sort of housewife that went around tidying things up for people and seeing that they got the right food and started for the office at the right time. There were days when Grace was amazed at the simplicity of the requests which came in to them. People wrote for information and help which they could have got themselves with the greatest of ease from any public library. It was interesting work and would be more interesting as the work grew. At the moment she wondered if they were really covering their expenses. If Mr. Brown made a success of this job for Mr. Halifax, it would mean a lot, and after that ... Grace began to dream a little of the future. She might not be in the office to be sent out to accompany old ladies to the theatre, or to go in every morning to somebody's flat and feed the canary while the owners were on holiday, or meet children at Paddington and see them safely across London to another station ... Some other young woman might be doing those things. She might ... It was on Tuesday that George was going for his interview. His father was a farmer in Ayrshire. He had told her that yesterday coming to the office. She would never have guessed that he was a farmer's son. He had a brother, too. He was a medical student at Guy's Hospital; and there was also a sister who worked on an Edinburgh paper. She was coming to London soon, and then there was another brother who intended to stay on the farm, but he was acquiring quite a local reputation as a preacher. That there should be so many aspects of George, other than the one she knew of the architect who travelled on the same train with her, was unsettling and exciting.

When she had finished her routine work, she took her knitting and sat in Helen's window. She was still under orders to keep an eye on Mr. Tomms. Her fingers began to busy themselves with the pins. She was knitting a pullover for George. It was to be a surprise present for his birthday, which she believed to be in August. She would be sure, she felt, long before the pullover was finished. She knitted industriously, her eyes on the courtyard of Fountain Inn, but, although she missed no movement outside, her eyes had that fixed, pleasantly unscrupulous look of a woman who is knitting a pullover for a man—a man unconscious of the destiny that the stitches pile up for him relentlessly, row upon row of one plain, one purl.

She was still knitting when she heard the clocks strike the quarter to twelve and a few minutes later she saw a familiar figure come down the far steps by the Neptune fountain and cross the lawns towards the main entrance. She recognised the man at once. When Ben had been following Mr. Spenser and after she had been taken into their confidence, she had been 'phoned for to keep an eye on Spenser while he sat in Lincoln's Inn Fields during the lunch hour. Ben had pointed him out to her and then gone off with the promise that he would relieve her in an hour. She had always suspected that Ben had gone to the lawyer's office. But she never knew. Mr. Spenser, after reading his paper for twenty minutes, had got up and gone back to Chancery Lane.

By craning her neck, she saw Spenser enter the doorway of Number One stairway. Grace flew to the door at the top of the stairs, and, half-opening it, listened. She heard footsteps come up, slowly, shuffling on the worn treads, and then she heard a knock on the door of the office of the Society for Progressive Rehabilitation. The door opened, there was a murmur of voices and then silence. Mr. Spenser had gone in to see Mr. Tomms.

For a moment Grace stood at the half-open door, wondering what she should do and as she stood there she saw the door of Mr. Rage's office. It was shut, but full of suggestion. She hesitated, her blood racing more quickly at the thoughts that swept into her mind. Then, with a determined shake of her head, she closed the door of General Factotums behind her and crossed the landing. She tried the door and it opened. Inside was still the same decorator's muddle. Grace closed the door and tiptoed across the room to the open ventilator shaft. She gently lowered herself on to her knees and half-thrust her head into the dark cavity. A voice came booming up to her from below.

Chapter Seventeen

Mr. Alastair Tomms came back from the outer door of his office holding the telegram envelope in his hand. He had not opened it. His secretary never came in on a Saturday morning and he was alone in the office. He went back to his desk and sat down and then deliberately slit the envelope with a paper-cutter.

He spread the sheet on the desk before him and read. Then he leaned back in his chair and nodded his head happily at the opposite wall. He was a picture of unfrustrated benevolence, his white hair distinguishing a broad, honest face, his pale blue eyes warm with the spirit of tolerance and goodwill. He sat for a while staring through the wall to a future that held no fears and promised an expansive happiness.

Some men, he was thinking, suffer from their conscience all their lives and die with the thought of their unexorcised evil heavy on their minds, and others, recognising the inevitable evil and good which mixes within them, work out a satisfactory compromise between the lamb and the wolf. A sinner could have a philosophy and an attitude towards his fellow men which were not altogether without charity and goodness and in a world where sin, as a mild peccadillo, was so prevalent and covertly acknowledged by even the best people, it was folly to be unduly upset by the discovery in oneself of a predilection for villainy. It had to be faced and, if possible, converted to one's advantage and comfort.

He sighed and reached for the telephone and dialled a number. When he put the receiver back he had made arrangements for a car-hiring firm to have a car sent round to the Inn for him right away.

He took up the receiver and, getting Toll Calls, asked for Hormenden 3105. He was soon speaking to Mrs. Burns. The conversation was short.

"Is that you, Clare? Good. Listen. The time has come. Today. You know what to do and where to go? No. It doesn't matter a bit how you leave things at the house. Get away today—this morning if you can fix it. Who? No. Don't worry about him.

He's one of those people who have a pathetic sort of faith in locksmiths. What's that? Well, to say the truth, I am a bit. I've grown to have a great affection for it—but we must off with the old love. Goodbye and be careful and we'll see you within a month."

He hung up. He crossed the room to his bookshelf and pulled down a gazetteer. He turned the pages for a while, searching, humming gently to himself. Then he found what he wanted and studied the page until a knock on the outer door disturbed him. He answered it and found it was the garage man reporting the car. He signed the delivery note and tipped the man. He went back to his window and looked out. The car was drawn up on the gravel, a large black saloon, powerful and impressive.

He put the gazeteer away and went back to his desk and began to go through his drawers. He transferred various papers and a small ledger into a hand-case. As he was doing this there came another knock on the door. He looked up, his face creasing into a look of bad temper. Then he slipped the case under the desk and got up to answer the door. His eyes caught the pink of the telegram sheet and he picked it up, screwing it into a ball. He dropped it into his waste-paper basket.

He opened the door to find Spenser standing outside. He held the door aside, without a word, for the lawyer to enter. They went into his office, and when Spenser was seated, Tomms said:

"I hardly expected to have this pleasure. I think you were a little unwise to come?" There was a faint, chiding note in his voice. Looking across at Spenser's thin, brittle body, he felt full of confidence and strength.

"I shouldn't have come unless I felt it was absolutely necessary." Spenser leaned forward to the desk and rested his hand on its polished surface, his fingers tapping nervously. Tomms could see that the man was strung-up, holding back his natural feelings only by a great effort of will. "Now listen to me, Tomms." There was no weakness in his voice. Spenser was speaking to a subordinate. "This affair must be brought to a conclusion—rapidly. So far everything has gone well—except for one unforeseen incident and that has been arranged satisfactorily. But there are signs now of a growing curiosity in certain quarters—I need hardly indicate them."

"You're not worried about that?"

"I am, naturally. You never know. I have risked a great deal in this, Tomms—far more than you have—and I do not mean to have anything go wrong. Anything! Do you understand me?" Spenser hit his fist against the table as he spoke the words almost viciously.

"I'm not going to quarrel about respective risks with you. But I assure you there's nothing to worry about, and, as for the conclusion, I have promised."

"Your promises are beginning to lose value with me, Tomms. You always find some reason for delay. I don't like delay. When a man in your position begins to delay it makes me suspicious."

Tomms laughed gently, as though he were discounting and refusing to hold seriously a hasty remark made by a friend.

"Come, Spenser, that's a little unfair. Have I ever given you any reason for an attitude like that? I'll admit there has been a delay. But the reason was good, as you must admit. There was the house. We have not been able to sell it. We must accept that loss, I think. And there was really no desperate hurry. That was the essence of our scheme. You, perhaps, don't appreciate my feelings towards this Society. I have been very happy here and doing a real work. You will not do me the injustice of thinking me insincere about the aims of the Society and my interest in it." He knew he was annoying Spenser by drifting from the point, and he did it deliberately.

Spenser fidgeted and sucked his teeth noisily. "I want to know when—and it must be soon!"

Tomms stretched his feet under the desk and they touched his hand-case. He smiled to himself as he felt the case and said calmly to Spenser, "Barely four months to do all I have done is evidence of industry, my dear Spenser. You are too impatient. You know how much fifty thousand pounds is, and how difficult it is to change it from old-fashioned securities and investments into bonds and actual cash that can be carted about in a single Gladstone bag. You can't make a change like that without causing comment if you do it suddenly. It takes a long time, because it is essential that the transactions shall not be traced—and you want it to be like that, don't you?" He rubbed the tips of his fingers together, as though he were settling his hands for prayer.

"You know what I want—and I want it soon. I want the day to come when you will hand me twenty-five thousand pounds in negotiable securities from your safe."

"The time will not be long. In the safe at the moment there is forty-six thousand, roughly. You have seen every bit of it put in and you know that none of it has come out. Without your key I cannot open it—nor you without mine. Would you like to have a look at it now?"

"Don't be irritating, Tomms. You know my anxiety."

"I do, only too well. You're worried because these fantastic people from upstairs have been sniffing around. Let them sniff. They'll find nothing. They were lucky to get as far as

Hormenden. And, anyway, I have good news for you."

"You have?" Spenser leaned forward, his eyes shining, and Tomms realised just how much strain the man had been under. If you wanted to avoid a strained nervous system and an impaired digestion, he thought, you had to become a rogue early in life. Spenser had begun late and was always fighting his respectability. In fact, he intended never to lose that respectability.

"I have. By Monday the last of these money matters will be cleaned up and by Monday evening I shall be gone. The Society will never recover. You will never understand the sacrifice I am making, Spenser. This Society is mine. I made it. Admittedly in the first place it was to gull old men and women and to give myself a comfortable living. But it grew beyond my villainy and became a living thing and I changed with it. Its ideas are fantastic, but no more so than the ideas of much more popular societies, and those ideas have given a great many people a fresh interest in life. I have filled the lives of hundreds with colour and dreams where before they lived dull, anxmic hours without hope or anger. I've turned them into cranks instead of uninspired bores—and the distinction is great. They are men and women with idiosyncrasies of thought now, not creatures of dullness and indigestion. I'm not over keen to leave all that work without a regret, Spenser."

"The money will salve all your regrets, Tomms." Spenser felt more comfortable now that he had received the other's assurance. He did not like Tomms, nor lately had he felt so sure of him. He had sensed a growing boldness in the other's manner and it had worried him. It was regrettable that the money had to be kept in Tomms's safe until the last moment—that had to be so to guard against the possibility, remote it was true, of enquiry from the Society into their funds. He was glad that the affair would soon be finished. He looked at Tomms, his lips moving with a flicker of contempt.

Tomms eyed Spenser, then he said quietly: "Did it ever occur to you that after your manipulation of the Colonel's will in favour of this Society I might have accepted the legacy and refused to countenance your scheme, to acknowledge that there had been any scheming? The money put the Society on a splendid financial basis and I might have decided in favour of remaining a messiah and drawing a neat income from the Society's funds for the rest of my life? There is a lot to be said for a smaller but assured return over a long period."

When Spenser spoke there was a definite touch of anger in his voice—that cold, menacing herald of a resolution which is prepared to back itself with extreme action: "It did occur to me, Tomms. Why should it not occur to me? And as a lawyer I was prepared for it. Men such as we must necessarily trust one another to some extent, but there is every reason why we should not trust one another when provision can be made. And I made provision against your deciding to stay with the Society and laying righteous claim to the money and privately repudiating me and my arrangements."

"And how?"

"You may know now. The Colonel's last and true will left everything he had to the National Playing Fields Association. That will was suppressed by me in favour of a previous will, by which your Society inherited. But the true will was never destroyed by me as you supposed. You remember that the

Colonel left me an escritoire? Well, the true will is in that, lying in a secret drawer, a drawer which I should conveniently discover if you did as you suggested and then the true will would be declared and you would lose everything. It would be so easily explained. The Colonel would have intimated to me verbally that he meant to destroy the Playing Fields will and let the previous will stand—this a few days before the stroke which carried him away. But the Colonel never did destroy the will. It would be found in the drawer with a note on it in the Colonel's handwriting that he must write to me and explain that he had decided to let it stand after all. He was an eccentric old man and there would be no difficulty in establishing the true will's validity. The forged note in his handwriting would have to be arranged, and it could be arranged with the help of a friend of mine …"

Tomms sighed. "An excellent precaution. But you will never have to employ it. I'm glad, because I feel you have already pressed your friend Ballard too much. However, by Monday evening all your troubles will be over and you may rest peacefully, knowing that you will be able to make up the various

little deficiencies in your accounts."

"How the devil—"

Tomms laughed and waved one hand airily. "Remember, I have mixed with the genteel criminal classes all my life—and an interesting lot they are largely. As I say, you will be able to arrange your accounts and still have a lot left over to buy rare editions. You need never borrow from your clients again—I hope."

Spenser ignored the thrust. Tomms had proved convenient, but he had no liking for the man. He allowed him his flippancies without comment. Tomms had been a petty thief. He had given him a chance to make money quickly, but he had no fear of him.

"And you are going as I have arranged?"

"Yes. There's a boat sailing at seven on Monday evening from Tilbury. I shall go aboard like any other passenger off on a pleasure cruise to the Northern fiords, but I shall not come back. And you don't have to worry that I shall go aboard taking your share. As you have pointed out, you have only to have the captain wirelessed and I shall be apprehended and you would then deny any connection with me beyond the suspicion raised by our dear friend Miss Logan, who is such a talkative person that we thought it wiser to confine her for a while. You really worked out everything very neatly. It's a pity you didn't start your anti-social activities earlier. You would have done great work."

"And I shouldn't advise you to try and get out of England by any of the normal routes. Customs people are very curious about people who carry a lot of money around with them, and they remember faces and dates ..."

"You are taking a lot of trouble to impress me with the obvious fact that this affair calls for trust in one another, but I suppose that is merely the legal attitude, which you cannot suppress ..."

In the room above, lying full length on the floor, her head well into the ventilator shaft, Grace had heard practically the whole of the conversation. Now and again the fall of a voice had defeated her, but she had gained enough to know that the sooner she unburdened herself to Ben and Helen the happier she would feel. She lay there, unable to break away as the men talked, fascinated by the intimacy she was holding in this scene. There was no doubt that the two men had worked together to get the Colonel's money. She found herself more shocked by Spenser's part than by Tomms's villainy. To her a lawyer had always been an impersonal figure, someone to whom confidences could be made and whose trust could be honoured. Spenser had betrayed every code that had governed his professional life. Tomms had merely acted naturally. She found herself trembling violently and wishing that she had never come into the room to eavesdrop. From below, Tomms's voice came up slow and full and the sound of it suddenly fired Grace with a vicious impulse to stop the whole beastly affair. If she telephoned the flat, Helen might be home by now. She pressed her hands against the floor to lever

247

herself up and as she did so her beads swung outwards from her neck and the clasp pulled free under the strain of their weight. They fell with a hard clash to the floor at the edge of the shaft and before Grace could snatch them away they had slipped over the edge and were dropping swiftly. They fell, rattling against the sides of the shaft and then were caught up, a few feet below, with a succession of jangles on a projection at the back of the ventilator to Tomms's room.

Grace remained tensed, like a runner on his mark, her fingers just touching the floor, her legs bent. For a time she dared not move, her heart leaping wildly, her mind filling with a swift parade of fears. Mr. Tomms might not notice the noise, or he might think it came from a piece of masonry dislodged on the roof by a bird. She made no movement, in fear that he might be listening, suspicious. There was no sound of voices from the shaft, but her head was well away from it now, and if they were speaking quietly … She tried to calm her alarm. She waited a second or two more, then she raised herself carefully and tiptoed across the room to the door … She took the handle and opened the door a little, examining the landing through the crack. There was no one in sight. With a return of confidence, Grace slipped through the door and across the landing.

She was about to push the door before her when a man spoke her name.

"Miss Kirkstall." The call was low and almost caressing. Grace half-turned and saw Tomms coming up the stairs towards her. He came, she was surprised to notice in the midst of her growing panic, with a swift, noiseless movement unusual in a big man.

"Yes." She stopped, fighting her fear and deciding to try to bluff him.

"Oh, Miss Kirkstall—" Tomms was on the landing now "—is either Mr. or Mrs. Brown in the office?"

Grace's heart leapt. It was not suspicion, but pure coincidence which had sent him up to see the Browns. "No, they're both out this—" She stopped short, her voice dying as she saw her folly, and realised that she had betrayed herself.

"That's good!" His voice changed tone a little and he looked towards Mr. Rage's door which had swung open. His eyes saw the open ventilator shaft. Slowly his head turned and he looked at Grace and she knew that he was not deceived. His eyes never left her face, as though he knew that what she thought would show there as plainly as on a cinematograph screen.

"Did you want to see—" She attempted the fiction desperately.

Tomms shook his head sadly, as though she were trying to excuse herself from some puerile transgression and he a fond uncle. He took her elbow commandingly and pushed her into General Factotums' office. He shut the door behind him with a flick of his foot. His voice when he spoke was controlled, but Grace could feel the fury behind it and her legs went weak beneath her.

"How long have you been in there?"

"Mr. Tomms, really. I don't know what you mean." Grace sought to detain her courage that was deserting her rapidly.

"Stop it!" The words were like a blow in the face. She saw Tomms's face twist into violent anger and she collapsed before him, pushed into her chair. "How long?"

"Since Mr. Spenser arrived," Grace faltered.

Tomms realised her growing fears. He patted her shoulders and spoke kindly.

"Listen, Miss Kirkstall, listen carefully. You've overheard more than is good for you, but if you do exactly as I say I'll promise you that no harm shall come to you. If you don't do as I say, or try to be silly and call for help or attract attention I shall shoot you!"

Grace looked up to see that he was holding in the palm of his hand a small black gun. Her eyes widened with panic. The sight of the gun had the effect on her that Tomms had calculated. People who know firearms only by books and the drama of stage and screen have little cognisance of the violent assault to the senses that the actual sight of an automatic can make in a lawabiding citizen. Grace eyed the gun as though it were a coiled snake, her whole body suggestive of her repulsion.

"We must understand one another, Miss Kirkstall. You can wreck my plans by shouting or screaming, but if you do I shall see that you die. That way we shall both suffer. If you do as I say, you will come to no harm. I promise that. It will be inconvenient for a day, but inconvenience is preferable to death—that's a very sound principle. What do you say?" Tomms waited for her reply, knowing what it must be. He was angry with her, but he could still appreciate her feelings and sense the turmoil of panic and common sense that were moving her.

Grace nodded her assent. She could not trust her voice. There was no choice. She did not want to die. She felt far from heroic. She wanted to be sure that no harm did come to her.

"Good! Now get your hat and bag and come along with me. If you meet anyone you know, just nod casually to them, but don't speak. Remember, I shall be by you all the time with the gun. We'll go to my office first. You'd better powder your nose and see to your eyes first."

He waited while Grace put on her hat and tidied her face. He motioned her out of the office.

"Lock the door as though you were going home. It is lunchtime, anyway."

Grace locked the door and went down the stairs with Tomms at her side. The feel of her feet on the stairs, the touch of her hands on the balustrade and the familiar panelling of the stairway were all unaccountably foreign and remote. She felt like a figure in a fantasy, lost and abandoned by the world.

"In you go!" Tomms held the door for her and Grace went in. Spenser was waiting at the window of the inner office.

He looked at Grace without speaking and she avoided his eyes. The sight of him made her uncomfortable.

"She was listening?" Spenser came forward to Tomms and took his coat lapels, shaking him nervously. Tomms pushed him off.

"Keep hold of yourself, man. Yes, she heard everything. Everything. You know what that means."

"You spying little drab!" Spenser turned on Grace and moved towards her, his thin body vigorous with a swift spasm of hatred, his eyes wide with malice and fear.

Tomms caught him by the shoulder and spun him round. "Come to your senses, Spenser. Do you want to upset the whole thing with your hysterics? Do as I say and keep your mouth shut if you want to save your skin. Keep it shut—do you hear!" Tomms stood over the man threateningly. In the face of this crisis there was no question of subordination in Tomms now. He was the master and Spenser acknowledged it.

"I'm sorry," he said quietly, and then, with rising inflexion: "But what are we to do? This—"

"Shut up and do as I say. Keep an eye on the girl. My God! She's got more dignity than you have. Give me your key to the safe. Come on. Hurry, you fool." Tomms took the proffered key and opened the safe. Grace watched him. From inside the safe he took a small black gladstone bag. She saw him snap back the catch and glance inside.

"Forty-six," he said to Spenser. "We must be content with that." He moved across the room and pulled a handcase from under the desk.

"We're going downstairs," he addressed them both. "There's a large black saloon car outside. We'll all get into it. You and the girl in the back, Spenser. I'll drive. Don't say a word to anyone. Just get in and keep your mouths shut. It's all right, Spenser." He saw the lawyer fidget with questions. "The car's mine. I've hired it for this afternoon. I was going out to see a friend at Tring."

"Where are we going?" Spenser could not keep quiet. His mouth was working spasmodically; his mind forcing him to a consideration of urgent questions. It was all right for Tomms to be so sure of himself, but with this girl knowing all … He looked across at Grace and Grace shrank away from him towards Tomms.

"You'll see," said Tomms, and he chuckled to himself as though he were enjoying a joke. "Come on. Get going, all of us, and look as though you were going out for a picnic."

He felt no fear that Grace would make any effort to escape. He guessed that she lacked the courage for that. The gun and his threat—a threat he could scarcely have upheld—had intimidated her completely.

They went out, Grace between them, and they halted a moment while Tomms locked up. "Here we go," he said reluctantly as they started down the stairs. "Goodbye to five years of happy swindling and something more than swindling. You'll never know the love that the Society woke in me,

Spenser. What a man creates, only he has the right to destroy."

Chapter Eighteen

George was sitting on his motor cycle waiting for Grace. He shifted in the saddle frequently, for he was excited and restless at the thought of the afternoon's outing, though he would have admitted his excitement to no one. He had on his thick waterproof driving-coat, a soft tweed cap and on the bars of his machine were a pair of heavy goggles. George was a serious road-user. He treated his machine with respect and gave it every care and he made no offerings to the goddess speed. Roads and machines for him were the means which enabled him to get from one place to another comfortably.

He looked down at the neat cockle-shell of a side-car and tried to imagine Grace sitting in it, smart and happy, and he grinned to himself at the picture he had formed. Then he looked at his watch and frowned. She was five minutes overdue. For all Grace's enthusiasm about it, he felt that General Factotums was not the right type of office for a girl, and from one or two hints which Grace had let slip he was certain that some of the work was most unorthodox. One day … perhaps soon … He slipped into a day-dream, the sun reflecting a dazzle into his eyes from the polished chromium of the machine.

A stir of footsteps from the stairway made him look up expectantly and he saw Grace come through the door with Mr.

Tomms on one side of her and a man whom he did not know on the other side. He smiled towards Grace and was about to swing off the saddle to go and meet her when he saw her turn away from him and move with the men towards a black saloon car that stood on the gravel drive. George was puzzled. Even if Grace had not seen him, he could not understand why she had not looked round for him. He had promised to be waiting. He saw Tomms hold the rear door open and Grace and the other man got in. The door slammed and Tomms slipped into the driving seat of the car.

For a moment George was subject to a medley of emotions. He was angry at being ignored by Grace, angry even if she did have business with the men, because she had not warned him that she might be delayed, and then swiftly and convincingly suspicious of the silent, deliberate entry into the car as though she moved under compulsion. The feeling grew and he knew that Grace could have no business with Tomms. There was nothing that … He threw his deliberations to the wind as the engine of the saloon raced and the car moved across the gravel towards the gateway.

George kicked down his starter, and as the engine fired he threw home his gear and started after the car. He swung out into Holborn in time to see the black saloon bearing away towards the West End. He spurted after it, weaving skilfully between the lunch-hour traffic and getting close enough to the car not to lose it in a jam or at the traffic lights. He slipped his goggles on and decided that he would see where the car was going, and as he followed he was slowly possessed of a mounting anxiety that there was something wrong.

The saloon went up Oxford Street and down Bayswater Road with the Park on its left, and after it went George, keeping his distance, and confident that the car had not enough speed to make it easy to leave him behind. He had been following it for fifteen minutes when he was sure that the saloon was heading west, that Tomms was leaving the City and making for the open country. An hour later George was still trailing the car, keeping a healthy distance behind. They were through Reading, but had left the Great West Road, and were heading for Wantage and Cirencester on the Gloucester road. George had stopped speculating and had settled down to the job of keeping the car in sight.

*   *   *   *   *

At one-thirty that afternoon Mr. Parcross laid down the illustrated daily paper he had been reading and, leaving his office, crossed the landing to the door of the offices of the Society for Progressive Rehabilitation. He stopped outside the door and knocked gently. There was no answer and after a second or two he tried the handle. The door was locked. The locked door decided him. His movements lost their furtive, enquiring manner and he felt confidently in his pocket and pulled out three keys. He selected one, fitted it to the lock and opened the door. He went in and shut the door behind him.

He beamed round the room as though he were commending the orderly taste of the absent occupants. It was a neat office. He moved around, opening drawers, sometimes removing a letter copy to read, but always replacing such documents as he had found them. He went into Mr. Tomms's room. He still kept well back from the window to avoid being seen from the courtyard and as he examined the room he whistled to himself gently. It was a happy, contented whistle, rather monotonous in tone, but expressive of the complete absorption which possessed him as he wandered through a forbidden territory.

He pulled open the drawers of Tomms's desk and, finding a box of steel nibs, took four of them and tucked them into his waistcoat pocket. A coloured glass paper-weight caught his eye and his hand went to it immediately. He held it for a moment, then he put it back, shaking his head. As he turned away from the desk he stopped suddenly, his attention held by a splash of colour in the waste paper basket. He bent down and picked up the crumpled red ball of the telegram sheet. He opened it out and read it. His brows contracting and remaining in an expression of puzzled enquiry. He walked out of the office holding the telegram.

He locked the door behind him and then, glancing up the stairs, hesitated a moment. He chuckled to himself and then went up the stairs.

Ten minutes later Ben came running up the stairway and entered his office to find Mr. Parcross standing by Grace's desk.

"May I ask what you are doing here?" questioned Ben.

Mr. Parcross looked at Ben as though that gentleman had committed a great breach by entering the room so unexpectedly. He stood with his knuckles resting lightly on Grace's desk, his body bent forward a little from age and from intention, looking very much like a school governor about to clear his throat before making the boys a speech on manly virtues. It was a pity that his breast pocket held a row of three brand-new HB pencils that Ben realised at once had come from Grace's stock, which she kept in her desk. Ben's eyes upon them made clear his thoughts and one of the man's hands left the desk and fluttered up to them nervously and yet a little challengingly. There was in that movement the perky, uncertain yet innocent sugestion of a pet bird caught in a table theft. Ben thought` of a jackdaw that had belonged to one of his cousins and which had never been able to resist the lure of the sugar tongs.

"Mr. Brown, I hope you're not going to be angry with me?"
"Well, I don't know." Ben hesitated. "I don't know, Mr. Parcross. I believe I'm more curious than annoyed."

Mr. Parcross's eyes widened considerably. "I'm sorry about this …" He waved his hand vaguely around the office and finished with it on the pencils, which he then pulled from his pocket and laid reluctantly on the desk.

"Then you were taking them?" Ben had almost used the word "stealing."

"I was. I'm sorry. It's a habit I can't alter. Do you understand?"

Ben shook his head frankly. He did not understand. How could he understand why Mr. Parcross of Eastern Imports, Ltd., should be caught pilfering in his office?

"No, you couldn't. But I hope you will, Mr. Brown. You see I've been at this Inn for a long time, longer than anyone else—fifty years—and I've got a reputation here which I should be sorry to lose. There's no need for me to work, of course. My wife …" He let the sentence dip to a significant silence. Then he went on. "There is plenty of money, but a man likes to feel he is the provider and my business—small, granted—does give me something to do."

"But why take my pencils?"

"I'm sorry. You're the first one who has ever caught me doing anything like this."

"Do you make a habit of it?"

"Of course. I thought you understood? I can't help it. I just have to do it. To take things, I mean. Only small things, of course, like envelopes and paper clips. I have keys and wait until people go home."

"How did you get keys?"

Mr. Parcross smiled like a child found out in a cleverness. "I've been here a long time, Mr. Brown, and seen tenants come and go from all the offices, and Hindle is careless with his keys.

Over the years I have collected a great many.".

"Then do you mind handing back the key you have of this office. Don't misunderstand me, Mr. Parcross. I'm not angry. But I feel that you must give me that key. The other people here are no concern of mine."

"Why, certainly." Mr. Parcross handed Ben a key. "I hope you do understand, Mr. Brown. I'm not trying to trade upon my age—though I am old. I don't do any harm, and I find a real pleasure in wandering through the various rooms when they're empty. I've known so many tenants. These rooms of yours, for instance. I can remember the man who had them at the beginning of this century. He was a solicitor—killed in the War. So many people, so many names, and I'm still left to remember them all. His name was Haslett and he had a place in the country where his wife bred carriage dogs, Dalmatians …"

Ben crossed the room and took Mr. Parcross's arm kindly.

"Don't worry about it, Mr. Parcross."

"You're very reasonable, very reasonable."

"Perhaps so, but you must be careful, Mr. Parcross. You mightn't always strike a reasonable person and then you'd be in the soup—and that would be bad."

Mr. Parcross moved uneasily towards the door. Ben saw a glint of pink.

"What's that you've got in your hand there?" He stepped forward and caught Mr. Parcross by the arm. "A telegram, eh? And where did you get this?"

"Mr. Brown, please!"

"Where did you get it?" Ben took the sheet from him.

"I found it in Mr. Tomms's wastepaper basket."

"You've been doing the Grand Tour this afternoon, haven't you? What did you get from the Granada Finance Corporation and from the architect's office? Really, you know, Mr. Parcross, this is a very bad habit of yours. You'll be caught, you know.

258

You can't always be lucky."

"Oh, Mr. Brown, I thought you understood …"

Ben smiled thinly. "Do me a favour, will you, Mr. Parcross? Go back to your office right away. I'm losing my mood for philanthropy. I've just spent a morning that would drive a saint to imprecations and I feel like being unreasonably violent. It's not safe for you to be here."

He held the door open and Mr. Parcross scuttled out. Ben slammed the door on him and went into his room to get his pipe. He found it, filled it and was drawing it well alight when his eye fell on the telegram he had taken from Parcross and which he had slipped on to his desk when he got his pipe from the drawer.

He picked it up. Mr. Parcross had found this in the wastepaper basket of Tomms's office that afternoon. He read the telegram and over his face came the same look of puzzled enquiry which had visited Mr. Parcross. He turned the sheet over as though there might be more on the other side, or a solution to his enquiry. He sat down and studied the message again, thick clouds of smoke indicating his intense interest. The telegram had been handed in at 9.30 that morning to a Liverpool post office. It was unsigned and addressed to Tomms at No. 1, Fountain Inn, W.C.2.

Ben studied the telegram for five minutes and then a clock striking two brought him back to earth. He picked up the sheet, put it into his pocket and hurried from the office and got a taxi.

*   *   *   *   *

It was three o'clock and they were not very far from Gloucester. Grace knew that much. Neither Tomms nor Spenser had made any attempt to keep her from seeing the road as they travelled. She was calmer now and beginning to think logically about her position. Her mother wouldn't be worrying yet, that was one good thing, and the Browns would not have missed her. But there was George. He had been waiting on his motor cycle. She had caught a glimpse of him, but she had not dared to look in his direction for fear of losing her head and shouting for help. That would have done no one any good. She had no idea where she was going, and she was pretty sure that Mr. Spenser did not know either. He sat beside her, but he never said anything. He kept biting his thumbnail nervously and lately he had been looking back through the rear window and frowning as though he did not recognise the road.

Grace said nothing to either of them, made no protest or enquiry. Tomms had promised her that nothing should happen to her and, somehow, she believed him. He was more human than Mr. Spenser. He lolled in the driving seat, his eyes on the road, and he hummed a song to himself. Once or twice he had turned and looked at them and smiled as though the sight of the lawyer, old and worried, and the girl, young and determined to be calm, had amused him.

It was as they were pulling up the long dip slope of the Cotswolds towards Birdlip that Spenser spoke. The car was running upwards powerfully along a straight stretch bordered with firs and showing glimpses of grey walls and yellow-decked gorse bushes.

"Tomms!" Spenser called his attention. "What is it?"

"I'm sure we're being followed. For the last fifty miles I've felt it."

Tomms did not answer for a moment. He leaned sideways and examined his driving mirror.

"You mean the gentleman in goggles?"

"Yes."

"I think you're right. I noticed him some time ago and I wasn't sure. There's something vaguely familiar about him. We'll soon find out."

Grace made to turn around, but Spenser's thin hand caught her arm.

"You keep looking straight ahead," he said viciously, and his fingers bit into her flesh.

Tomms accelerated and a little further up the road he swung along to the left, taking a smaller road that ran along the hill slope, rising and falling amongst the hollows, sliding into deep patches of wood and then emerging into the grey space of the open downland. The road dropped suddenly into a dark fir copse and twisted on itself. Tomms pulled up sharply, and reversed the car on to the side of the road. Grace saw that they were neatly tucked away so that anyone rounding the corner would be past them without knowing it.

"Watch the girl," said Tomms curtly, and he dropped his window and half-leaned out.

There was a terrible interval of tension. From the dark firs came the sudden insane chuckle of a jay flighting away in alarm and then back along the road swelled the noise of an engine. It grew, louder, fuller and nearer. A horn blew and at the sound Tomms's hand dropped to his pocket and rose again swiftly. Grace saw the black evilness of his automatic flash in the air and at the same time she saw his face, hard with a fixed determination. She never quite knew what she did in that moment. She threw herself forward, but Spenser caught her by the shoulders and flung her back into the seat and she saw from the tail of her eye a motor cycle and side-car round the corner swiftly. She heard the short, biting crack of the automatic, the screech of brakes, the agony of tyres across the road surface and then there was a snapping and crashing of undergrowth. She struggled up and heard Tomms say:

"My eye is still good. I got his front tyre with the first."

He turned to Grace, menacingly. "Keep quiet and behave yourself, girl. You know what I told you." Then he was gone from the car and Grace saw him cross the road and drop into the wood. In a few minutes he was back, carrying a man across his shoulders, fireman fashion. He came to the car and Spenser opened the rear door for him.

"You get in the front, Spenser. We'll put him in the back. He's taken a crack on the head, that's all. Concussion. His machine wasn't so lucky. It's smashed to hell."

"But we don't want to take him with us. We've got the girl."

"Do as I say." Tomms spoke frowningly. He lifted the man into the back seat. As he did so a voice said enquiringly from the edge of the wood where the car was stationed: "What's happened, mister? Accident?"

All three looked round to find a countryman climbing over the low fence. He was a slow, broad-faced creature, a red handkerchief at his throat, a large sack-like jacket dropping from his shoulders.

"Yes, there's been an accident," said Tomms evenly, but under cover of the car he was pointing the automatic straight at Grace.

"I thought there must 'a bin. I yeard un go smack into the wood. T'ain't the first to happen on that corner."

"He came round too quickly, I believe. We were parked here and saw it all. Luckily I'm a doctor and he's only got concussion. I'm taking him right away to Gloucester Hospital.

His machine's badly damaged. You might take charge of it until the police come, will you."

"That I will, sir." The man looked in at the rear of the car as Tomms shifted position and he shook his head. "He do look tidy messed up, I must say. That's what comes of drivin' they stinking old machines. Ha, well …" He nodded affably to Grace and then shuffled off.

Tomms grinned and got into the car and in a few moments they were back on the main road. The moment they were free of the fir copse Spenser began:

"Why didn't you leave him there? We can't cart him about with us. In heaven's name, Tomms, have you taken leave of your senses?"

Tomms ignored him. He looked back over his shoulder at Grace. Then he spoke. "Look at the girl. Doesn't that tell you what you want to know? It's her friend, her lover. I knew him from the first moment he started to follow. I didn't attempt to shake him off, otherwise he might have got on to the police when he lost us. I had to get him out here. He's only concussed. We had to bring him. When he recovered he would have put the police on to us."

Grace listened to him talking. She had George's head on her lap, her hands busy wiping the dirt and blood from his face. Just above his left eye was a dark wound, bruised and seeping blood that she did her best to staunch.

"Don't worry. Here, use this." Tomms tossed her a large handkerchief. "He's all right. I know concussion when I see it. I didn't fire at him."

Grace took the handkerchief and spoke for the first time, addressing herself to the two men.

"If anything happens to George because of this," she said, her voice low and vibrant with hatred of them, a flickering sword cut that threatened them, "I'll kill you both. I'll see that you both suffer for it. You won't escape. Even if I can't stop you, you won't escape. Men like you never escape. The whole world's against you. You filthy beasts!"

Tomms shook his head and started to hum his song again and Spenser began to gnaw again at his thumb-nail. His eyes were on the road ahead, but his thoughts were searching a hundred avenues of possibilities. He was holding back a hundred questions that he wanted to ask. The time had not come, but the time was coming, and when it did he meant to be heard. For the moment this blundering Tomms had his way. It was the only way. Those two in the back, this girl and her young man, they were in his way now. In his way as Miss Logan had never been …

Chapter Nineteen

Ben banged into the flat like a whirlwind.

"Helen! Helen!"

He swung into the room and found her watering her window box of mignonette.

"It's about time you learnt to enter a room like a gentleman," she said.

"Stop watering those flowers and come here. Look what I've found—or, rather, what Mr. Parcross found in Mr. Tomms's wastepaper basket this afternoon."

Helen carefully finished her watering and then came over to him. "What is it?" She wasn't going to be stampeded into enthusiasm by Ben.

Ben held out the telegram and she took it. She read

WEST LONG FOUR FIFTY NORTH LAT FIFTY TWO FIVE. SUNDAY EIGHT A.M.

"How did you get this?" Helen asked.

"From Mr. Parcross. I caught him snooping." Ben explained how the telegram had come into his hands.

"I wonder what it means? Is it code, do you think?"

"To my simple mind it looks like a latitude and longitude position and a time. We can soon see whether it makes sense.

Where's our atlas?"

Ben went to the bookshelf and found the atlas.

"Here we are," he said, coming back and opening the book to the Northern Hemisphere. "Now then, let's work it out." For a moment they were silent as Ben used the edge of a magazine for ruler and with his pencil marked out the position.

"There!" He screwed the point of his pencil into the page and indicated the position.

"And what about it? It seems silly to me," said Helen. The point fell in the sea off the coast of Wales, not far from St. David's Head. "You must have worked it out wrong or else it isn't just a nautical reading. Let me do it." Helen worked out the position for herself, but it was the same as Ben had found.

Ben sighed. "I thought we had something. It must be code and I'm quite sure I could never work it out. Codes are beyond me. Even a simple anagram is beyond me."

"But why should it be beyond us? It can't be code. No one normally would see the telegram—if it contains important news— and Tomms must have felt happy about it because he just tossed it into his basket. If it were code, he would have destroyed it, just in case—"

"And if it were a plain message, why shouldn't he have destroyed it as well?"

"Because he never dreamt anyone would find it before Sunday at eight and by that time—I wonder what?"

"So do I. And I'm sure there's a flaw in your reasoning. Why should anyone indicate a spot off the coast of Cardigan and give a time?"

As Ben finished speaking, Helen snapped her fingers and cried ecstatically, "I've got it! I've got it!" She danced around the room for a moment. Then she came back to Ben and spoke more soberly. "At least, I hope I've got it. Cardigan—don't you see? The position is in Cardigan Bay, not so far off Cardigan itself."

"It's nearer Fishguard by the look of it."

"That doesn't matter. It's Cardigan that counts. Don't you remember from yesterday? Cardigan is where Dorian Ballard was born. Now do you get it? Dorian Ballard and then a telegram to Tomms, which seems to indicate a place off the Cardiganshire coast, a spot that could easily be reached from somewhere on the Cardigan mainland by boat."

"Go on," said Ben coldly, deliberately repressing any enthusiasm he might feel.

"Well, if Burns and Tomms are going to make a getaway together what more likely than that they should arrange to slip off from the place where they've got Miss Logan."

"And where is Miss Logan?"

"In Wales, I'm sure of it. You see, Ballard is from Cardigan. What more natural than that he should have a country place in his old home parts when he comes into money. The Welsh, you know, are tremendously patriotic."

"Supposing that were so? How are we to find out where he lives?"

"You're dull, Ben Brown—dull and undeserving of me. Where would anyone find out? Ring up the Editor of the local Cardigan paper. Local editors know everything, and if Ballard lives anywhere around they'll be on to it. You can get it from him. Pretend you're a London journalist who wants to come down and write up an article on Welsh authors. That'll draw any local Welsh Editor."

"But I don't know any Welsh authors."

"That doesn't matter. The moment you mention Welsh authors, the Editor will do the rest. You can ring up the information bureau of one of the daily papers. They'll give you the name of the local Cardigan paper and the telephone number. It'll be quicker than going down to the office for the *Press Guide*. Now, go on. I'm going out for a moment." Helen pushed Ben commandingly towards the telephone. She saw him pick up the receiver and then she left him. She slipped out into the street and almost ran up the quiet roadway.

Fifteen minutes later she entered the flat to find Ben still on the telephone. He was smiling childishly, a grin all over his face and he was nodding his head and breathing into the mouthpiece

at intervals, "Yes, yes, quite. Thank you. Of course." Helen waited and finally Ben freed himself.

"Well?" she asked.

"I've got it," said Ben triumphantly. "It worked like magic. *The Cardigan Recorder*. Couldn't get the Editor. He was out. But someone in authority spoke to me and the moment I mentioned Ballard and Welsh authors I got all the information I wanted right away, and a lot more I didn't want about Welsh authors."

"And what did you get?"

"Everything, Helen. I really think we're on to it at last. And about time too. Ballard lives in Wales all right. He bought a little island off the coast some years ago—I wish we had a map of the district."

"We have. I followed my hunch and went out for one. Here it is." Helen opened out on the table the Ordnance Survey map of St. David's and Cardigan. "Did you get the name of the place?"

"I did. It's called Cerig Gallant, and it's a small island off the coast between Cardigan and Fishguard. Let's have a look." They bent over the map.

"There we are." Ben stabbed his finger down. Cerig Gallant was a small island, roughly shaped like a right-angled triangle, lying about a mile off the coast and a few miles down from the wide estuary mouth that led up to Cardigan itself.

Helen grabbed the magazine and Pencil and working from the divisions at the edges of the map, plotted the longitude and latitude positions. The point fell about two miles due west of the island.

"What does that look like to you?" She turned her face up to Ben. Ben smiled, kissed her quickly on the forehead and said sharply, "It looks like we're going to go to Cerig Gallant today—this afternoon. It may turn out a wild-goose chase, but it's our last chance."

He went to the drawer of his desk and took out a small black automatic. "This time," he announced seriously, "I'm not going to have any monkey business from the Burns family or anyone else."

Ben came back and studied the map. The nearest point to Cerig Gallant on the coast was a small inlet, named Ceibwr Bay, into which ran a small stream that came down, kept company by a narrow road, from the inland village of Moylgrove. Within fifteen minutes they were heading westwards, impatient of the Saturday traffic.

* * * * *

Sleep claimed Grace against her will. For hours the car had raced westwards through the afternoon. They passed Gloucester and were soon over the Welsh border and climbing into the hills. For an hour after they had taken George into the car she had no thoughts for anything beyond his welfare. But there seemed nothing she could do for him. He lay stretched on the wide back seat, his muddy and bloody head couched in her lap. His eyes were closed, his breathing quiet, broken occasionally by a restless movement, as though deep down in the limbo he were struggling against the oblivion that claimed him. Grace wiped his face with Tomms's handkerchief and cleaned the cut on his forehead. After a while the blood congealed.

"There's nothing you can do," said Tomms once, looking back at her. "Concussion is a curious thing. He may be under for an hour or ten hours. But he'll come out. He's young and healthy."

Grace did not answer. After a time she found herself watching the road. She had never been into Wales before, and its July beauty, despite her anxieties, set her admiring. She had glimpses of long, mountain slopes, reaching away to the wind-blue sky, of stretches of dark oak forest and of deep defiles where rivers moved in disturbed silver streams. Sometimes the road ran alongside the rivers through woods that were mossy and cool, and sometimes they came out on to wide stretches of moorland, where sheep moved in dull patches across the young grass and stonechats played over the crozier tops of the new bracken. Gorse bushes were ablaze with bloom, and here and there against the grey boldness of a crag-side she saw the delicate silver and green of a birch. Now and again they swept through a small village or town, but after a time the scenery held Grace no longer. The day was wearing on and the continual roar of the high-powered engine, the swing and dip over the roads as they travelled at speed, worked their influence on her and she began to feel tired. She fell asleep, and Tomms, glancing back, smiled. He was sorry that he had been forced to drag the two into trouble, but he had been given no alternative. Privately, he decided that he would see they were all right. But he was troubled about Spenser.

The lawyer had sat for the last two hours without a word, his eyes on the road ahead, his thoughts turning and churning over one problem. Tomms did not have to be a mind-reader to know what it was that worried Spenser. And yet even Spenser had to defer his queries until they were free of the car; Spenser had to do as he told him and later ... Tomms began to whistle gently between his teeth.

Grace was awakened by the jolting of the car. It was dark and for a moment, until she remembered where she was, she had a swift spasm of panic. Then she saw that it was just gone ten by the car's dashlight clock. There was a faint slip of moon and she made out that they were bumping over a rough road that ran along a steep valley. To her right she could hear the sound of a stream. Suddenly the car dipped downwards, swung about and before them was the dark surface of the sea. They had pulled up on a flat piece of ground above a sharp slope of sand in a small bay. On the far side of the ground stood a small black building.

Tomms ran the car across to the building and parked it in the shadows. He turned to Grace.

"Get out. We'll leave your friend here for a moment." Grace found herself following Spenser and Tomms to the front of the building, which faced the sea. A narrow concrete slipway ran down to the water.

"We're lucky the tide's in," said Tomms, "otherwise we should have to drag the thing over a few yards of sand, and that's not so easy."

He opened the door and they went inside. By the light of his torch, Grace saw that there were two boats inside and a winch for hauling them up the slipway. One was a light motor boat, and the other a heavier, engineless boat.

"Come on, lend a hand!" Spenser snapped at her irritably as the men got hold of the motor boat and began to haul it towards the door.

"I'll do nothing of the kind!" Grace was defiant.

Tomms chuckled. "You don't know how to handle women," he told Spenser. The lawyer muttered something to himself.

In a few moments the boat was down the slipway and riding easily in the water at the side of the concrete run. Tomms tied the boat to the side and motioned Grace to get in. Then he moved away with Spenser.

Grace looked around. The bay was very small, enclosed by tall cliffs. A few gulls, disturbed by the car, cried noisily out towards the open sea. The only other sound was the wash of water against the runway and its seething back-drag over the sands. It was a lonely spot.

Tomms and Spenser returned, carrying George between them. They dropped him into the boat and Tomms went to the engine. He put his two hand-grips behind him, patting the little gladstone bag as he did so. "We mustn't leave this behind, eh, Spenser?" he joked.

The engine started after a little persuasion, and very soon they were outside the little bay and rolling on a gentle swell that came swinging down from the north-east, the wave crests breaking into foam occasionally as a following wind cut them into spume. They swung around the protecting curve of the bay and headed for the open sea, due west, and Grace saw, a fair way out, low down in the water, the dark shape of an island.

"What's that?" she asked, surprised into the query.

"That?" Tomms looked towards the island. "That's Cerig Gallant. Cerig, I believe, is Welsh for an island. I'm not sure. But that is Cerig Gallant, which is an island. Mr. Spenser knows
all about it. A friend of his owns it."

"Shut up, Tomms!" Spenser flared up.

Tomms was about to make some further provocation when a loud groan from George took their attention. George groaned heavily, twisted on to his side and began to struggle to sit up, his eyes half-opening.

"Tie his hands and feet at once!" Tomms took command again, snapping his order to Spenser. "He's coming to. We don't want any trouble with him." He tossed Spenser a couple of lashings from the boat's locker, and Spenser knelt down and tied George's hands and feet.

There was nothing Grace could do. She watched George's face and once his eyes opened and looked at her and she felt that he recognised her.

It was cold on the water. The wind chilled her through her thin coat and tossed her hair about wildly, and wet spray came over the bows and dewed her hands and face. Tomms steered for the upper end of the island, and Grace saw that it ran out into a small promontory. They headed for this point and presently they rounded it and swung sharply into a narrow cove that faced north-west and was protected by an outcrop of rocks that stretched across its mouth, blocking it except for an opening about thirty feet wide. Then they were in a narrow waterway, running towards a stone quay, from which a flight of wooden steps ran up the steep cliff-side to a squat house that topped the cliff, a grey, crouching building, looking cold and menacing in the dim moonlight. Tied alongside the quay was a short, clumsylooking cabin-cruiser.

There was no room at the quay for two boats. Tomms ran the motor boat alongside the cruiser and made it fast. As he did so a man came down the steps from the house to meet them. He was a strongly-built man, his hair crisp and fair and his face a mass of cheerful wrinkles—a cheerfulness which died for a moment as he surveyed the boat-load.

"What's this, a Sunday school outing?" he asked brusquely.

Tomms waved a hand impatiently. "Don't start asking questions yet, Burns. Give us a hand with this fellow."

They carried George up to the house and Grace went with them. They went into a wide, comfortable living-room with windows on either side. Tomms motioned her to follow Burns, who was carrying George over his shoulder as though he were a sack of meal.

Grace followed and a door opened suddenly and she found herself in a small back room in which there was a table, a few chairs, a bed and a sofa. A fire burnt low in the grate and a woman was sitting in an easy chair by it, a book held before her, reading glasses perched on the end of her nose to give her rather a myopic, owlish look.

Burns dropped George on to the sofa, and before Grace could move he was out of the room and she heard the lock snap over. There was a moment's silence. Then the woman rose and came over to Grace curiously. Grace recognised her as she recognised Grace.

"It's Miss Logan."

"And you're the girl from Fountain Inn! And that's your young man."

"That's right, said a masculine voice suddenly and angrily,

"and somebody's going to know about all this from me." George suddenly sat up and shook his head.

"George," Grace sprang to him. George put an arm around her, comforting. "George, are you all right now?"

"I'm all right, Grace," he said slowly. "I have been for a while, but I thought it was better to lie quiet and see what was happening. What in the name of Saint George is it all about?"

"I can probably tell you that," said Miss Logan. "We're in the hands of scoundrels, and the first thing is to let them see that you aren't afraid of them and that you insist upon being treated decently. I have, and I must say that so far I have been treated with respect. It's all Mr. Tomms's fault. That's why I was abducted. He must have found out what I knew about him and thought I would tell people and insist upon the money of his society being placed in other hands. So I would have done. It's a good thing I did go to my lawyer about it. They're bound to miss me sooner or later and when they begin to search—" Miss Logan breathed deeply, a breath of splendid retribution "—Mr. Spenser will deal with Mr. Tomms."

Grace looked at her. Her adversity seemed to have brought a firm spirit from her. It was a pity to destroy her hope, but Grace felt she had to do it.

"Your Mr. Spenser won't be able to help you much, Miss Logan. He's one of them. He and Mr. Tomms."

Miss Logan frowned at Grace for a moment. "What did you say?"

Grace repeated her remark.

"I don't believe it!" Miss Logan was almost indignant.

"It's true," said George. "He's here now, on the island. He came down with us from London today."

For a moment Miss Logan stood, looking at George, her eyes wide with amazement. Then she dropped suddenly into her chair, her body and spirit collapsed, and she was just a frightened old lady. Grace went to her and put her arm around her shoulder.

"Cheer up, Miss Logan. It's going to be all right. Mr. Tomms has promised me that. They'll get away with the money, perhaps, but they'll not touch us. Will they, George?"

"But the Society!" Miss Logan almost wailed. "It'll be ruined, and it meant so much to so many people."

George, who could not bear the sight of a woman crying, went to the door and rattled the handle fiercely. "If I am kept here so that I canna make my appointment on Tuesday," he announced solemnly. "Then I'll not hold myself responsible for my subsequent actions. It's all vairy irregular."

Chapter Twenty

The yellow-and-black AA sign—Moylgrove—came up in the glare of Ben's headlamps, a welcome sight. The car dipped to a stone bridge over a rushing stream and as they swung into the village Ben had a glimpse of a squat church and a dark yew guarding its yard. He drew the car up and pulled out the road map. At his side Helen stirred and then came awake, yawning and stretching her arms. "Are we still travelling?" she asked with slight irritation.

"We are, my love. This is Moylgrove, and if you'll stop waving your arms about I can keep my torchlight on the map long enough to find the road to the coast."

"Let's find an inn here and go to bed. You can turn the whole affair over to the police. I'm so tired."

"You'll wake up when you get out of the car. And, anyway, there's no accommodation here. Cheer up. We'll be at sea very soon."

"What time is it now?" Helen asked as Ben drove on and swung to the left out of the village.

"Twenty minutes past midnight and there's a lot of cloud coming over the moon. It's been quite misty in some of the hollows the last few miles."

"Can you manage a boat—if there is a boat?"

"There'll be a boat somewhere. If not we'll go into Fishguard or Cardigan and hire one. Of course I can handle a boat. I had a holiday on the Broads once. There's a lot of the sea in my blood."

"As long as you keep it in your blood and out of the boat, I shan't squabble with you. Getting on for one o'clock and here we are nowhere in Wales, chasing a phantom."

"You've no stamina!" The car was bumping down a narrow valley now. "You started all this business. It was your idea, but you lack the vitality to complete your plans. In a way, that's why we make an excellent man and wife. What you begin I can finish, and what I begin you can finish, and what we both begin—"

"It's too late for that kind of reasoning. And, anyway, I began this little sleep I was having and I want to finish it. Call me when we reach wherever it is."

Helen dropped quickly to sleep. Ten minutes later Ben pulled the car up at the head of the little bay, Ceibwr.

Ben got out and looked around. The tide was just beginning to ebb out of the steep walled bay and the roar of the water was like the sound of a great wind. Over the top of the cliffs moved a faintly luminous trail of mist that sometimes veiled the slip of moon. Helen was standing at his side suddenly. "Is this it?"

"This, from the map, seems the nearest jumping off point. The Editor, too, mentioned something about Ceibwr. It's lonely enough."

Helen took his arm and pointed to the black block of the boathouse. They walked across.

"Look, there's a car there!" she whispered.

Ben froze, holding her back. For a moment he was afraid that there might be someone in the car. There was no sound or movement, and after an interval they went forward carefully and were soon standing at the side of the saloon car.

"Radiator's still warm," said Ben, and he flashed his torch into the car, at the same time trying the door handle. "It's locked."

"A hired car, too," Helen pointed out as the torch showed up the garage plate on the dashboard. "And Good Lord, Ben" Look at that!" She snatched the torch from his hand and flicked it on to the rear seat. Ben saw a woman's hat, a small hat of distinctive shape.

"What is it?"

"It's Grace Kirkstall's hat. I'm sure of it. She was wearing it this morning." Helen turned to Ben, her eyes finding his and for a moment they looked at one another, their minds filling with disturbing conjectures.

"Are you sure?" asked Ben after a while.

"I'm almost certain. Remember—the telegram said Sunday at eight. That's only a few hours off now. That's why this car is here. Maybe … Heaven knows what's happened, but the sooner we get on to the island, the better. I can't even see any island out there."

"It's probably masked by the corner of the bay." Ben spoke hurriedly as he turned away from the car and went round the boathouse. He flashed his torch inside and found the boat.

"Come on, my girl! Get your back into this. Another halfhour and there would have been no hope of getting it down.

There's just enough water at the bottom of the slipway."

Helen took one side of the heavy boat and Ben the other. For a time they struggled. Getting the boat to the top of the run was a herculean effort. Once there it slipped easily down to the water.

Some minutes later they were rowing clumsily out of the bay, each on an oar, and Helen trying not to think of the damage she was doing to her hands with the great sweep. At the mouth of the bay they were rewarded by a sight of the island, far off and hazy through a light mist that moved and twisted quickly in the breeze.

"There we are," said Ben cheerfully and he held up his handkerchief to the wind. "And a nice north-easterly wind to give us a good slant over to the island."

"You're going to hoist a sail?" Helen was incredulous.

"Of course." Ben went forward and stepped a small mast that lay in the bottom boards and very soon he had hoisted a coarse brown sail, shaped like a leg of mutton, an enlarged dinghy sail.

"How's that?" he asked as the wind filled the sail, and, taking over the tiller, he headed the boat for the lower end of the island. The wind running between the mainland and the island allowed them to make a great slant, direct for the lower end of Cerig Gallant.

"I didn't know you were such a good sailor," said Helen proudly.

"I'm not. A good sailor wouldn't go smack out into unknown water like this in such a tub. It's dangerous. Only a rash sailor would do it. But we have to be rash, and it's lucky there's a fair wind and we can see—at times—where we're going."

"Why don't you steer for the top end of the island?"

"Because that's where the map shows a house to be. We'll get off lower down and work our way up to see how the land lies." Half an hour later they were on the plateau of the island. Ben had run the boat ashore on a steeply shelving beach of shingle at the end of the island, and then they had been faced with a climb up the cliffs. Helen had more than once during that climb been filled with the panic which comes to poor climbers when they find themselves poised on a thin ridge of rock unable to move up or down. She wished that she had stayed behind at the boat, as Ben had wanted her to do. Only Ben's commanding voice and his arm had saved her from the tears and weakness she felt so close. They went up through a tangle of thick briars and evilsmelling ivy that coasted the broken rocks, over loose scree and finally reached the top, where Helen dropped to the turf, exhausted.

It was then that they both noticed that the mist had thickened as they had climbed until now it was impossible to see more than a few yards ahead of them. It was a strange, white mist, white from the moon behind it, and heavy with moisture that very soon had coated them with dampness and touched each grass blade with a pearl and hung each sprig of gorse and heather with jewels that were pale and ghostly.

Ben took Helen's hand and they set off, stepping warily. Once they heard sheep cropping away to the left, a hard, insistent noise, thrown back to them by the mist, and occasionally from the sea on their right there would float in the sudden clamour of sea-birds, rising and wailing through the mist.

*   *   *   *   *

Burns half sat on the table, facing the fire. The red light of the dying logs threw strong shadows across his face. The only other light came from a pair of candles at the side of the room. He was cleaning a single barrel sporting rifle as he sat, working the cleaning rod rhythmically. He looked like a comfortable farmer, filling his evening with the pleasant task of looking after a favourite gun.

Only the clock on the mantelshelf, pointing to four o'clock, and the strained expression on Spenser's face spoilt the fiction. Burns went on cleaning his gun, occasionally his eyes moving gently towards Tomms, who stood at the side of the fire filling his pipe and watching Spenser. The three had been like that for the last hour, uncommunicative except for desultory, unreal scraps of conversation. Before that, Tomms had insisted that they should eat and have no discussion, and eat they had, Burns and Tomms with great appetite and Spenser scarcely touching his food.

"I wasn't bored here," said Burns, addressing no one in particular. "The old lady behaved herself. I got quite to like her. We had quite a few long chats. And then there was this rifle, of course. I guess Mr. Ballard must have used it for just the same thing I did."

"Seal?" Tomms jerked the question out as he bent for a light at the fire.

"Yes, seal—and the sea-birds. It's a nice gun. If it wouldn't be a breach of hospitality, I'd like to take it. When you hit a seal—

plunk—" he smacked his fist into his palm "—he goes under for a second, then bobs up with a tremendous wallow of water and then goes under for good. At least I never saw any of them again. I liked snap-shooting at the puffins and razor-bills best. Never touched them sitting. That was too easy. But they fly erratically and you have to be smart. Ever do any shooting, Mr. Spenser?"

Spenser seemed hardly aware of the question. He sat, one thin hand rubbing his chin, his eyes staring before him with a fixity that was hard to imagine human.

"What did you tell her?" he asked suddenly, and then loudly. "What did you tell her?"

"Tell who? Miss Logan?" Burns chuckled.

Spenser twisted his head towards Burns and glared at him, his eyes full of hate.

Tomms said quietly, "Why don't you accept the inevitable, Spenser?"

It was the remark they had been waiting for, the licence to the thoughts that had been broiling in Spenser's mind, the lead for which Burns had waited.

"What is the inevitable?" Burns turned to Tomms.

"He can't go back to London. He's finished there."

"I'm not! I tell you, I'm not. It's impossible!" Spenser sprang to his feet and fronted Tomms. Tomms put his hands on his shoulders and pressed the man back into his chair.

"Sit down and be sensible," he ordered, and there was an impressive note in his voice. In that room he was master; his influence was heavy over everything. "Things haven't gone right. It's nobody's fault, but you can't alter them now. If it had only been Miss Logan, then the whole scheme could have gone off nicely and she could have been discovered after we had left and you would still be sitting in your office, a respectable lawyer. But now there's the girl and the young man. The girl knows all about us. Miss Logan knows all about you by now, Spenser. Are you a fool, man, to think that you can still go back to London? You've got to come with us. It's your only way out."

"It's the way you want me to come, too, isn't it?" Spenser spoke quietly, cunningly. "You'd like me to do that, wouldn't you, so you could double-cross me at your leisure somewhere abroad? Do you think I'm a fool, Tomms?" His voice rose with his anger. "Do you think I'm blind, that I haven't seen that this chasing away to the island has fitted in with some plan you've already got for double-crossing me? It was convenient that you had a hired car waiting outside; and there was nothing unusual, I suppose, in the fact that Burns was obviously expecting you. I won't come with you, I tell you, and, what's more, I'll see you never leave here until you agree to my plan." He stood up, his breath coming and going rapidly, his eyes wild with the torment of his position. They had nothing to lose, these two. They could go off and begin another life with their money. But he had a position in London, a business that could be salved still, and a house and possessions that meant so much to him. How could he move away from a life that he had made and appreciated to the cold, shifting unsettled existence of a hotel-dweller on the Continent. His sacrifice was greater than theirs—and not necessary. There was the other way.

"Tell him!" said Burns harshly, putting down the gun and beginning to play with a few loose shells from the box which stood on the table. "Tell him, for Pete's sake, and get it over. I hate a whiner!"

Tomms smiled and shook his head sadly, as though he deprecated equally Spenser's lack of control and Burns' fierce irritability.

"Why shouldn't I tell you, Spenser? You were clever, weren't you, when you thought of this scheme and you got us to help—and also planned various little ways of preventing us from double-crossing you. But you stopped up the seams of the barrel and forgot about the corking of the bung-hole. We meant to double-cross you, Spenser, from the start. Why shouldn't we? We disliked you. We disliked your lack of trust in us. It's true that I was coming to Cerig Gallant, anyway, and it's true that in a few hours' time I had arranged with Burns here to go out a couple of miles to the westward of the island and be picked up by a cargo steamer which is captained by a friend of Burns, a friend who is in the arms trade and doing quite well in the Mediterranean these days. He doesn't object to our type of passenger. We were double-crossing you, all right, Spenser, and you deserved it. But at least you would have been left as a decent lawyer in the eyes of the world. We weren't going to spoil that pretence for you. But now it's different. You're in a fix. You can't go back to London. And that makes us sorry for you. So sorry that we're prepared to forget the past and take you with us."

"That's right, Spenser. Can't you believe the truth when you hear it? We're not so low that we'd leave you in the hole you are. You've got to come with us."

"And still be cheated later on? You've admitted you were going to cheat me. Do you think that makes me any more willing to come? No." Spenser faced them, his back to the fire, his thin body animated by his passion. "You must do it my way. Why shouldn't you, if you really do feel for my position?"

"What you want is impossible—and not a safe solution." Tomms drew at his pipe and walked restlessly up and down the room. "We can't calmly murder those three people, and get rid of their bodies effectively, so that you can go back to London and disclaim any knowledge of the affair. It's fantastic!"

"And, anyway, I'm not mixing myself up with murder!" snapped Burns definitely. "That's one thing you can forget right away. I like Miss Logan, and anyone that tries to harm her gets it from me."

"They've got to be killed!" Spenser's words were vicious.

"It's the one way for me to go back to London safely." "You're mad!" Burns made an impatient gesture.

"I shall be if you fools don't see reason. What do they matter? What do their lives matter against mine? I'm the one you've got to think about, and you've got to help me. You've got to help me ..."

Burns began to roll himself a cigarette, his eyes covering Spenser's face. Every line of that face, every motion of the lips and cheeks showed the strain the man was under, and Burns was slightly disgusted. It was always the same with men like Spenser. They played for high stakes, but they could never take a loss. They played only to win, which was an incomplete philosophy of gambling. There were always losses.

"There's going to be no killing," Burns said firmly.

"I don't want to alarm anyone and I absolutely insist that you go on talking as though nothing has happened," said Tomms casually, "but I've an idea that I saw someone look in through the window just then."

The words were uttered so smoothly that it was a few moments before the others realised that any warning had been given to them.

Burns held himself back, but Spenser almost jumped forward. "You what?" he cried anxiously.

"Keep calm," said Tomms. "It may have been a trick of the mist outside, or the candlelight in here, but it looked like a face. Don't look towards the window. I'll watch, but if I give the word, Burns, you head for the launch. We must see that no one interferes with that. I'll go out after whoever it is and you can stay here, Spenser. You're in no condition to go chasing into the night."

"How could anyone be on the island?" Spenser spoke thickly, fighting to keep down his panic.

"How do we know?" snapped Burns fiercely. "What questions! Why did we ever get tangled up with you?"

"You can well ask yourself that question, and if it comes—" "There it is!" Tomms's voice cut across their bickering. "Quickly now!"

He jumped towards the door and flung it open. They stood, listening, and through the swirling banks of mist came the unmistakable sound of someone moving rapidly away from the house. Tomms pulled out his automatic, and spoke over his shoulder to Burns: "Get to the launch and blow the hooter if everything's all right down there." He jumped forward into the mist and Burns followed him. Spenser was left at the door. For a second or two he stared into the white movement of vapour and then he darted back into the house and reappeared holding the rifle, his hands busy filling the chamber with shells.

If there were someone else on the island, they must not be allowed to escape; and when they had been dealt with he would settle with Tomms and Burns and then the others. He had almost forgotten the power a rifle gave to a man. He laughed suddenly, a long, pleasant laugh of a man enjoying a private joke. Then he was stumbling into the mist.

He had not gone five yards before a figure came out of the mist at his side. Spenser threw up his rifle to fire. A hand caught his arm and it was Tomms speaking to him fiercely:

"Be careful, you fool! What do you think you're doing?"

"Let me go!" Spenser shook himself free. "I'm going to find them."

He darted forward into the mist and as he went Tomms halfraised his gun and then dropped it again. He turned back to the house. It was not wise to leave it unguarded with all the money there and, anyway, this mist made any attempt to find who had looked in through the window an impossibility. He had not realised that it had come down so thickly. He was half-inclined to treat the face as an apparition born of the fog and his desire to stop the conversation. Spenser had been getting worked up.

*　　*　　*　　*　　*

Ben lay now two hundred yards from the house, crouched in the angle made by a furze bush against an outcropping boulder. Three feet away, and just visible, was the naked edge of the cliff and three hundred feet below the sea, its lapping coming up to him strangely muted by the mist. Ben dared not go further, because he might lose his bearings in the mist and never find his way back to Helen. He was anxious to return at once. He had seen enough through the window to give him a plan of action.

He and Helen had reached the top end of the island after a difficult scramble through the mist and had found the steps down to the harbour before they had realised they were so close to the house. In the harbour they had discovered the cabin cruiser and the motor boat and he had left Helen on the cruiser while he had gone back up the steps to explore the possibilities of the house. Tomms's sortie had cut him off from the steps and he had been forced to slip away into the mist to the right of the house.

Suddenly from behind came a quick succession of shots. Five shots, one after another, that filled the mist with whickering echoes and at the same time Ben heard a loud shout, and the earth trembled with the vibration of feet. He lay still, waiting.

There was silence for a moment, and then nearer there came another cry, an incoherent yell, and then a shot. Ben heard the bullet whine through the air above him and he crouched against the boulder, his hand fingering his gun. Then unexpectedly from behind him the mist was filled with the clamour of a man's voice, the snap of a shot and the wild, stampeding bleat of sheep. The next moment a sheep leaped by him, followed by the others. They streamed by, their eyes large with panic, their heavy quarters dewed with fog, rising and falling as they raced away from their pursuer and Ben saw them head straight for the cliff's edge. He saw the leader baulk and try to swerve, but from behind the others pressed on, and in a mad, bleating confusion the animals slipped and tumbled over the edge until one or two swerved away from the danger and turned the flock. Ben heard the unfortunate sheep bleat and cry as they fell and then the mist swallowed their noises and the rest of the flock were gone along the cliffside.

From the mist a man stumbled towards the cliff edge. Ben raised his head slightly and looked at him. He stood there, holding his rifle tightly, his head tensed forward listening, his eyes roving with a queer eagerness. His clothes were wet where he had stumbled and his mouth worked quickly as he talked to himself. Ben recognised Spenser, and recognised, too, that the man was excited and almost out of control.

Away to the left something moved. Immediately Spenser threw up his gun and fired blindly into the mist. A sheep sprang away into the darkness, calling in pain, and Spenser laughed, shouting after it:

"Don't try to hide with the sheep. I'll get you. I'll kill you. I'll kill the others. I'll get the others ..." He turned away from the direction the sheep had taken and came towards Ben slowly, his eyes staring straight ahead of him. Ben held his breath and gripped his gun ready. But Spenser went by him, murmuring to himself, "I'll get the others."

He stumbled back towards the house, following the line of the cliff, and as he walked his hands filled the rifle magazine from the shells in his pocket. He had taken a good supply. They would be necessary. There was no one on the island, no one out there but sheep. It had been a trick of Tomms's to get him out of the house. Yes, that was what it had been. They were afraid of him. He had killed some of the sheep. He knew he had. He'd seen one of them lying on the turf, its long white skull broken, large eyes staring, and blood pouring from its nostrils. The sight of the dead sheep had filled him with a kind of ecstasy that made his hands tremble and move on the rifle stock and barrel.

The house came up out of the mist. It would be morning soon, he thought. He saw Tomms standing by the open doorway, a broad figure against the pale light of the candle-lit room.

"Is that you, Spenser?" Tomms called into the mist. Spenser chuckled and raised his rifle, calling gently as he did so, "Yes, it's me, Tomms. Is Burns back yet?"

"No. Where the devil are you, man?"

"Here," called Spenser and as he spoke he squeezed the trigger. The bullet struck the cross piece of the door above Tomms's head and Tomms ducked back into the house, the door slamming after him.

Spenser swore to himself and raced across the turf to the head of the steps that led down to the launch. He drew back a few yards along the cliff top so that he could cover the steps. Burns was down at the launch and Tomms was in the house and neither of them could move unless he allowed them to.

A window opened in the house and Tomms's voice came through the mist. "Spenser! Where are you? Don't be a fool. You can't get anywhere acting as you are. Put down your gun and come over here and we'll settle this thing sensibly."

For answer Spenser sent a shot towards the house at random, calling after it, "That's my reply, Tomms. I'm master now and you'll do as I say, or you'll not leave this island in time to meet that steamer. You know what I want done!"

From the dark gulf of the little harbour, two hundred feet below the house, there suddenly rose the raucous note of the cruiser's horn. It bellowed and sung through the mist.

Spenser heard it and sent a shot downwards, defiantly. Burns would do nothing without Tomms. And Tomms heard it and was thankful that their line of retreat was secured. If he could get down to the boat now with his gladstone, he would be without any compunction as to Spenser's fate. As for the three locked up in the house … He sucked his lips angrily. Damn it, if he left them with Spenser free he might have murder on his hands. Spenser was beyond all reasoning now. He discovered that he could not leave the house and the three to be helpless against Spenser … He moved quickly to the candles and put them out.

The three in the back room heard the hooter, as they had heard the confusion of shooting and calls. George had his arm around Grace. He had made the women stand aside from the window and doors, in case any shots came that way. Fear and hope raced through their minds.

And Ben heard the hooter with definite alarm, for he had left Helen with the understanding that if anything went wrong with her she was to blow the hooter. The sound of the hooter meant that someone had gone to the launch. He was suddenly anxious to return to her. He moved cautiously back to the house. It was in darkness now. He waited for a moment, lying full length on the turf, straining his eyes through the mist so that he could just make out the front door of the house and the top of the steps.

Something moved by the door and a shot snapped across the mist and he heard Spenser's voice call from a point on the cliffside: "Don't try the steps, Tomms. They're dangerous." The man ended with a laugh that echoed eerily through the mist and Ben guessed that Spenser had broken with Tomms. He saw, too, that anyone wanting to go down the steps to the harbour had to reckon with Spenser. There was no other way down the sheer cliff drop.

He wriggled back from the house and began to circle. In ten minutes, moving with infinite caution, he was on the far side of the cliff edge from Spenser and moving forward taking advantage of the outcropping boulders which characterised the cliff crest.

The grass was short and slippery with mist, and the cliff edge fell away in dangerous slopes to the final drop. In a few minutes Ben saw Spenser. He had come round behind the man. The mist was lightening now as the morning approached. There was that brightness growing in the east which foretold the coming of the sun. Now and again a stirring wind tore the mist veils aside to give a swift, unimpeded view. It was down such a lane that Ben saw Spenser. The man was lying close to the cliff edge, at the top of a short, steep slope, his rifle trained towards the steps, his whole attention on the house.

Ben edged nearer. He decided not to use his revolver. He still had to reach Helen and he did not want to give Tomms or Burns his position. Hampered with a long rifle Spenser would find it difficult to turn and fire quickly. He was within six feet of Spenser, tensed, ready to fling himself forward when he realised that the man knew he was behind him. He saw Spenser's body stiffen, the fingers move stiffly around the rifle. Spenser must have heard him breathing or have acted upon the uncanny sense which tells a man that he is not alone. Ben flung himself forward as Spenser twisted over and tried to bring his rifle round. The rifle was thrown clear by the shock of Ben's spring and the two men rolled together over the grass, Spenser's hands at Ben's throat, Ben fighting to hold his hands away.

They tossed and struggled, silent save for their great breaths and the dull beat of their legs and bodies against the wet grass. Spenser was mad with anger and his strength equalled Ben's. He fought, his body twisting and squirming, his hands and nails scoring at Ben's neck. Ben rolled to throw the man from him. But Spenser clung to him and the roll carried them from the level piece of turf to the grassy slope away to the cliff edge. Spenser was unconscious of their danger, his thoughts held only by the desire to strangle and crush this new assailant. Ben, as he felt himself rolling, knew what was happening. They went down the wet slope, crashing through the small tufts of gorse and the clumps of sea pinks. Ben dug in his heels to hold himself. They slipped on. He felt himself flung against a low outcrop of stone and the jerk freed him from Spenser's grip. Spenser slithered away from him. They dropped together, Ben fighting to save himself on the wet slope, grasping at grass and earth in his frenzy to stop his momentum. A low thorn bush saved him. He grasped its thin stem and held it, but he could do nothing for Spenser. The limp body rolled once or twice then slithered with growing speed down the slope that narrowed into the steep chute of a miniature overhanging valley and then it disappeared over the edge with a momentary upflinging of arms and head as the body jerked forward.

Ben shut his eyes from the horror of the sight. To his ears, a long while afterwards it seemed, there rose the dreadful thump of an inert body against rocks and then a splash that waked a hundred echoes in the harbour, echoes that clamoured in the mist for a while and then subsided into the murmur of sea sounds, of waves and gulls moving around the rocks.

Ben turned gingerly, digging his toes into the slope, and began to work himself upwards. It was no easy task. The soft earth slipped from his foot-holds and his hands were slimy with the wet mould into which he dug with his nails for a grip. He reached the patch of turf where Spenser had been lying, his breath loud with his exertions, and as his head came level with the top a hand reached down and pulled him to safety. Ben lay, oblivious of any desire for the moment except to get his breath, and as he lay there Tomms quietly deprived him of his revolver, so that when Ben sat up he found himself facing a smiling Tomms and the black mouth of an automatic.

"I saw it all," said Tomms quietly. "I intended to do the same as you. I thank you for saving me an unpleasant task. I might even have lost my life, since I doubt whether I should have retained my presence of mind as you did. No one could survive that fall. He's dead."

Ben nodded. "Poor devil."

"There was nothing you could do. And, anyway, his life was broken. He had not enough mental resilience to be a villain. Get up!" This last was an order enforced by a jerk of the automatic.

"What's happening?" Ben stood up, his mind working quickly.

Tomms read his thoughts. "Don't try anything, Mr. Brown. We know one another well, don't we? Go down to the launch. If your admirable wife is there, my friend Burns will be looking after her. Your other friends are quite safe, and will remain so as long as you behave yourself. Go on!"

Ben said nothing. He moved forwards and Tomms followed him, holding his gun and a small black gladstone bag. They went down the steep, wooden steps, zigzagging their way to the harbour.

They reached the quay and Tomms whistled sharply. At once there was a movement on the launch and in the half-light Ben saw the man Burns appear from the interior of the launch.

"What's happened?" Burns asked. "I found a woman on the launch."

"Spenser's gone. Dead," said Tomms curtly. "He fell over the cliff. Turn the woman out on to the quay. We're going. The sun will be up in a while."

Burns went below and a little later Helen appeared, her hands tied behind her back, her mouth stopped with a white handkerchief. Burns helped her ashore and Tomms motioned Burns to remove her gag.

"Start her up," he ordered Burns and handed him the gladstone bag. "Keep this safe."

Burns went back to the launch.

Tomms turned to Ben and Helen, backing to the launch as he covered them with his revolver. "I'm sorry to have to take advantage of you like this, but it is one of the rules of the game, and you will understand. However—" He shrugged his shoulders.

"Is he getting away with the money?" Helen looked at Ben. Tomms answered her.

"I am, Mrs. Brown. I shall need it all. You'll find your friends safe at the house. I presume you came in some kind of boat—the other boat in the house at Ceibwr? Well, that won't help you much. It'll be hours before you can get anyone to help you from the mainland and by then—" He smiled and stepped on to the boat as its engine started, the water bubbling under the stern.

"Why do you wear a wig?" asked Ben suddenly.

"Because," said Tomms, not at all surprised at the question, "because a white-haired prophet is more likely to be believed. I started a paying Society on the strength of it. There is also the point that a man who lives as I do must be ready for a quick change occasionally. He may have to wait five years before it comes in useful. But the time comes. Goodbye!"

Burns had cast off and taken the wheel. The cabin cruiser began to move away from the quay leaving Ben and Helen standing there. Ben saw that the motor boat was being towed out as well. That, he thought fiercely, would be turned adrift somewhere. And they only had a clumsy sailing boat left to them. Tomms was right. They had no chance of getting after him for the next three hours at least.

He watched the cruiser slide into the growing morning light, and the last he saw of Tomms was a small figure at the wheel, one arm waving gaily back to him. Then the mist took up the boat and they were alone on the quayside.

*   *   *   *   *

Two hours later the steamship *Ben Hur* moved slowly down upon a cabin cruiser that rode lightly to a gentle swell some miles to the west of Cerig Gallant. The island had long been lost in the morning distance.

A telegraph bell rang sharply. There was a quick word of command on deck. The Ben Hur back-watered with a violent white rush of foam under her counter and a rope ladder dropped from the rail. A fat man, sucking an empty pipe, his face babysmooth and round, looked down at the launch.

"If it isn't the New Messiah and his privit Archangel come to pay us a call now," he roared in a raw brogue. "Come abroad, you scuts."

Tomms and Burns climbed the ladder, Tomms holding the gladstone bag carefully.

"Is it in there it is?" questioned the Captain, pointing to the bag.

"It is," said Tomms. "Fifty thousand."

"And all by way of selling tracts and inventin' queer exercises! Tes aisy money against sellin' the sinews of war. What about the cruiser?"

"Leave it," said Tomms crossing the deck without another look towards the boat. "It belongs to quite a decent fellow and he might like to have it back."

A few minutes later the *Ben Hur* drew away from the launch and it was not long before she was hull down on the horizon.

Four hours later the Captain, Tomms and Burns sat round the Captain's table, drinking whiskey. Tomms had ust finished his story.

"Ay, it went fine and dandy for you," said the Captain. "Ye're lucky swabs. I've never set eyes on so much money in me life. Would you please an old friend by allowin' him the pleasure of running his peepers over so much wealth in one place?"

Tomms chuckled and reached for his bag on the bunk behind him. He snapped back the catch and laid the open bag before the man.

The Captain looked, first at the bag and then at Tomms. "Faith, now," he said uneasily. "You have a curious sense o' fun."

Tomms looked—and found that the bag was full of paper, the loose sheets torn from an old catalogue of an Olympia Motor Car Show.

Chapter Twenty-one

Dorian Ballard tamped the loose ash of his pipe down with his thumb and shook his head slowly at Ben.

"You have had some interesting experiences, haven't you, Mr. Brown?"

"I thought you would find them so," said Ben smiling and approving of the calmness which had so far marked his interview with Ballard.

"And, of course, I can appreciate why you should think I might be interested. After all, I knew the Colonel and I knew poor Spenser. You know, of course, that the Colonel made about fifty wills in his lifetime and that I witnessed a good many of them? So many that it was difficult to remember them all. I never dreamt that Spenser had suppressed the last will. I had it from him that the Colonel had destroyed it. The fact that it has been discovered in his house surprises me. And as for the fact that my island residence was used—" He laughed easily. "Spenser was taking a liberty with my property when he invited his fellow villains to use it."

"I'm glad you feel like that," said Ben. "For a while I held the most unworthy feeling that you had suppressed your suspicions about the will which was proved and that you had allowed the use of Cerig Gallant out of ... Well, as I said, it was a silly idea of mine and quite unworthy."

"Quite," said Ballard rising. "And now, Mr. Brown, I am a busy man."

Ben took the hint and rose.

"It's a pity your mission was not quite a complete success and that this Society scoundrel got away with the money," said Ballard as they moved towards the door.

Ben felt in his breast pocket and turning to Ballard said quietly, "Oh, but they didn't. I was going to mention that point. You see, the young man, George Crane, when he was left alone in the car while they went for the boat, was already recovered from unconsciousness and he guessed there was money in the bag and he took the opportunity to take it out and hide it under the car seat. He stuffed the case full of pages from a Motor Show catalogue that happened to be in the car pocket. It never occurred to Tomms to look in the bag while on the island."

"How ingenious!" He looked at the envelope Ben was holding out to him. "Why, what is this?"

"It's a literary curiosity which you might like to keep, Mr. Ballard."

Ballard hesitated for a moment, then his face wrinkled into an appreciative grin. "Not a Johnsonian relic, Mr. Brown?"

"How did you guess?" Ben's eyes were laughing, but his face was serious.

Ballard took the envelope. "Goodbye, Mr. Brown—and thank you." There was a sudden, unexpected sincerity and gratitude in his last words and Ben went out feeling that Mr. Ballard was in no danger from the police or—and more important—from the old Ballard.

He got back to the office at half-past four. Helen was writing at her desk.

"You'd never believe the amount of expenses we've got to charge Mr. Halifax with," she said.

"People always reckon to make a bit on the scandal sheet.

Where's Grace?"

"She's gone off to Paddington."

"To Paddington?"

"Yes. Have you forgotten that this is Tuesday? She had a telegram from George at three o'clock. As far as I can remember it ran: I HAVE BEEN APPOINTED. WILL YOU MARRY ME. MEET ME PADDINGTON FOUR-THIRTY."

"From that I should deduce that he was very excited when he began the telegram—too excited to think of saving his pence— and only got his native caution back towards the end."

"You should have seen Grace. I could hardly hold her." Helen came across to Ben and put her arm in his. "We shall have to have another typist when she goes, which will be soon. We can almost afford it with comfort now."

Ben smiled down at her and kissed her on the nose quickly; as his eyes came up he saw old Hindle moving across the courtyard of the Inn, a flurry of sparrows rising from the grass to the shelter of the limes as the old man disturbed them.

"Heigh-ho!" he stretched his arms wide. "What next, I wonder?"

Also Available

When George, the eldest son of Matthew Silverman, announces he won't follow his father's footsteps as editor of the family-owned local newspaper, the family finds itself on a course for change. The newspaper has been going for nearly 100 years.

With younger brother Alexander and sisters Loraine and Alison growing up fast too, and gradual progress in the world around them, can Matthew do what's best for them all?

The Uncertain Future of the Silvermans
by Victor Canning

Also Available

Mr Edgar Finchley, unmarried clerk, aged 45, is told to take a holiday for the first time in his life. He decides to go to the seaside. But Fate has other plans in store…

From his abduction by a cheerful crook, to his smuggling escapade off the south coast, the timid but plucky Mr Finchley is plunged into a series of the most astonishing and extraordinary adventures.

His rural adventure takes him gradually westward through the English countryside and back, via a smuggling yacht, to London.

Mr Finchley, Book 1

OUT NOW

About the Early Works of Victor Canning

Victor Canning had a runaway success with his first book, *Mr Finchley Discovers his England*, published in 1934, and lost no time in writing more. Up to the start of the Second World War he wrote seven such life-affirming novels.

Following the war, Canning went on to write over fifty more novels along with an abundance of short stories, plays and TV and radio scripts, gaining sophistication and later a darker note – but perhaps losing the exuberance that is the hallmark of his early work.

Early novels by Victor Canning –

Mr Finchley Discovers His England

Mr Finchley Goes to Paris

Mr Finchley Takes the Road

Polycarp's Progress

Fly Away Paul

Matthew Silverman

Fountain Inn

About the Author

Victor Canning was a prolific writer throughout his career, which began young: he had sold several short stories by the age of nineteen and his first novel, *Mr Finchley Discovers His England* (1934) was published when he was twenty-three. It proved to be a runaway bestseller. Canning also wrote for children: his trilogy The Runaways was adapted for US children's television. Canning's later thrillers were darker and more complex than his earlier work and received further critical acclaim.

Note from the Publisher

To receive background material and updates on further titles by Victor Canning, sign up at farragobooks.com/canning-signup

Printed in Great Britain
by Amazon